Inherent Strain

A.M.NIXON

Copyright © 2016 Adam Nixon

All rights reserved.

ISBN: **9781973349488**

CHAPTER 1

The room began to shake for the fourth time that night. She kept her eyes closed tight, tried to concentrate, but it was no use. Alex Forster grasped the edge of her quilt and threw back the stifling covers with much more force than was really necessary. She waited for the familiar low rumble to grow to its inevitable crescendo, and then fade once more as yet another freight train rumbled along the railway tracks a few hundred metres from her small box bedroom. Alex shuddered and opened her sore, tired eyes. She lay there catatonic, her clammy body stuck fast to her thin cotton sheet, her mind again busy with the same thoughts. How long could she keep it up for? How many more sleepless nights could her exhausted body take before it finally gave in?

Alex didn't know how much time had passed before she found the motivation to move again. To her everything that had happened recently had all seemed one big blur. Still, things had to continue, she had to carry on. She eased herself up and swung her sticky bare legs out of bed. Another minute or so seemed to pass as she sat motionless on the edge of her single bed, until at last with sleepy effort, she stood up and meandered over to the window.

Alex reached out her unsteady arms and pulled open one side of her pale lilac curtains. Her breath misted up the cold glass as she gazed down on the street far below from the vantage point of her tenth floor flat. The view seemed strange, eerily peaceful almost serene, a stark contrast from the hustle and bustle of the day. Only a few brief movements in the shadows of the alleyway across the street broke the stillness.

The muffled sound of a car door slamming at the far end of the road drew Alex's attention. Beneath the dingy orange glow of an old fashioned street lamp she could just make out the figure of a woman in an immorally short skirt and bright red high heels. She seemed to be having a heated argument with a taxi driver whose arms were pointing and waving in her direction. Alex watched in a sleepy daze as two suited men emerged from the alleyway and began to make their way towards the disturbance, only to make a hasty retreat as the siren and flashing lights of a passing police car prematurely interrupted their unspoken plans.

Alex's tired mind didn't realise, after all how could it? She couldn't have known how important those seemingly innocuous events that her blurred eye's had just witnessed would turn out to be. How things would change in her life, indeed in everyone's life, from this point on.

This would be the day that put into motion events that could very well alter the course of human history and in the process put the fate of human kind very literally in Alex's hands. Although she didn't notice, for her, today was the day it started...

With little left to distract her attention in the now quiet street, Alex's heavy eyes started to drift. The sky was still dark and the silent rain was whipping against the double glazing. She stood there for a while all but entranced by a small lonely raindrop as it slowly eased its way down the pane of glass in front of her. Her eyes followed its haphazard lazy path until it accelerated almost with enthusiasm as it merged with another of its like minded companions. With a long audible sigh she wrestled herself away from the cold window and retreated back to the warmth of her waiting covers. She closed her tired eyes and tried to will herself back to sleep. She hated living so close to the railway but at least it was a roof over their heads.

When morning actually arrived, Alex lay there still unsettled in the type of restless daze that insomnia could bring. Every so often her head would rise to glance up at the clock on her bedside table, until with a great frantic cacophony the incessant ringing of her wakeup alarm began. With a wry smile she thought it ironic that she needed an alarm to wake her up when she couldn't get to sleep. For a fleeting moment the idea struck her to hit the snooze button but it would only make things worse. No matter how much she wished that time would stop, at least for another ten minutes, she had to get up. She couldn't afford to be late for work again.

The convenience store job in the city centre paid minimum wage and the wretched manager would only give her twenty hours per week, far less than she needed. It wasn't too bad to begin with, there were lots of new things to learn to keep her interested, but recently it seemed she'd been stuck on checkout duty forever. It was tedious, menial work. It was like she was being punished, day after day. listening to that annoying beep, enduring its jarring sound every time she had to scan an item for a customer. If she closed her eyes now she could still hear that wretched beep, beep, beep at the back of her mind. If there was any real alternative she would have quit in a heartbeat, but jobs seemed to be few and far between these days and she needed the money, now more than ever. Things will change, she thought, someday things have got to get better than this.

After wrapping her soft dressing gown tightly around her waist Alex walked over to the wall. She reached out her hand towards the off white radiator hoping in vain for a little warmth, recoiling immediately with a wince as she felt the cold chill of the metal draw what little heat she had out through her thin skin. The gas meter hadn't had any credit put on it for over a week and Alex was starting to worry about the coming winter. Heating hadn't been a priority during the summer but now it was late October and they'd already had an early frost. It would be extra money she'd need to find, another thing to stress about.

Alex cringed as she looked over to the pile of unwelcome letters on the shelf. The bills were beginning to back up. Each new one she received seemed to shout louder and louder for attention. Even with the little bit extra from her mother's disability payments, her measly wage no longer stretched far enough. No matter how much she tried, there simply wasn't enough left to cover her mounting responsibilities.

Alex opened her bedroom door and walked through dragging her feet as she went. She tried to ignore her rumbling stomach. She knew there was precious little in the cupboards. There wasn't enough money left this month to buy more food. She had to make what they had last. Life had become so complicated for her over the last couple of years. Alex closed her eyes, let out a loud drawn out sigh and tried to pull herself together. Even though she knew deep down that she was losing the battle she had to keep going, she had to struggle on for both their sakes.

The two bedroom council apartment where she lived with and cared for her mother was the only option they had. The flat itself came moderately appointed but it was badly in need of renovation. It still had the original dated fixtures, made from what looked like chipboard coated in a thin veneer of plastic. A large angular analogue television set sat quiet in the corner of the living room. Apart from a few video tapes that they watched now and again, the obsolete appliance wasn't much use any more. It had remained silent ever since the terrestrial analogue signal had been turned off in favour of the new digital one.

Alex eyes widened as she cast her gaze over to the dark brown coffee table in the middle of the room. Her mother's empty mug still sat where she'd left it last night next to an untidy pile of her faded lifestyle magazines. A few more lay scattered on the carpet. Alex didn't feel herself breathe again until they were stacked in a neat pile once more. Still cringing she made her way into the next bedroom to wake her mother.

Alex was used to the symptoms now, she knew what to expect. She needed to help her mother get cleaned up and dressed, a routine she did every morning. Margaret was her usual self, unsure of where she was and a little unsteady on her feet, but before long and with a bit of coaxing Alex led her to the living room and served her a simple breakfast of porridge with a couple of slices of wholemeal toast and a cup of tea. Alex spooned a small amount of honey into the porridge and gave it a swirl just how her mother had done for her when she was a child.

Alex didn't eat breakfast herself, it only made her hungry. She'd got used to the empty feeling now and at any rate making sure her mother had enough to eat was more important to her. She couldn't bear the thought of telling her the food was running out over and over again.

"I've made you some sandwiches for lunch

mum," Alex said. "I've left them in the fridge for you all labelled up."

It was one of Alex's tasks to leave notes around the flat for her mother, strategically placed so she'd see them when she wandered around. Short memos reminding her of a few everyday necessities, like what to do at certain times, where she could find things she might want and probably most important of all, reminding her mother where she was and that she is safe.

Once back in her bedroom Alex fished out a clean white blouse from her wardrobe and picked up the tacky name tag from the bed side table. The left corner of her top lip curled into a sneer as she pulled on her black work trousers. They felt looser than she remembered and with numb acceptance she pulled her black belt in another notch, the last one. Stooping down she rummaged under her bed for the comfy flat black shoes she kicked off yesterday. They didn't look very attractive but at least her feet didn't hurt on top of everything else.

"I'd better hurry up and get going," Alex said glancing down at her wrist watch. "I'm leaving for work Mum. I'll be back later on."

"I'm sorry," her mother said reaching up to affectionately stroke Alex's hair.

"Don't be silly mum, for what?" Alex asked.

"For everything. For this, for me. You know I

love you don't you honey? Don't ever forget that."

"I love you too Mum. Listen I need to hurry, I'll be back after work." Alex kissed her mother on the cheek and smiled.
"You don't need to worry about anything, OK?"

Alex took one last look at her mother, grabbed her bag and waterproof jacket and made her way out of the flat.

"I'm sorry things are like this," Margaret's voice wavered. "Did I tell you I loved you?"

"Yes mother," Alex shouted as she closed the front door behind her. She placed her hands on the door frame for support, allowed her eyes to close and took a few deep breaths.
"I know mum," she whispered. "You tell me every day."

Margaret hadn't been well for a couple of years, she was suffering from early onset Alzheimer's disease and couldn't cope living on her own any more. Alex tried hard to keep her mother as happy and as healthy as possible. She didn't mind looking after her, it wasn't a chore, she didn't even question it, but it wasn't easy, especially on the days when she seemed to forget her.

Her mother was the sole family member she had left. Her only two grandparents had died a long time ago in a car accident when she was a small child. If she tried hard, Alex could just about recall a few hazy memories of them when they were alive. It was a different time then and she was a different Alex. So full of wonder and amazement for the world. Everything was perfect and she was safe. It had broken her heart the day her mother had taken her aside and told her something bad had happened to her grandparents. It was the first time she'd experienced the cruel reality of the world. That was when the first little piece of her innocence was lost.

Alex had never known her father. All she knew about him was he'd left her mother just before she'd found out she was pregnant. Her mother had never told her why. Alex wished she'd made the effort and asked her more about him while she still had the chance. She often wondered what he was like and what happened to him, but now she'd never be able find out. Her mother couldn't remember that part of her life any longer, no matter how often she asked.

The only keepsake Alex had that even hinted at the man she'd never had the chance to meet was a tattered old photograph. She'd found it amongst her mother's belongings when she was packing them up ready to move her into her flat. It was a time she didn't like to think about, a time spent watching her mother slowly deteriorate from a strong willed successful business woman to an individual that now found it hard to understand what time of day it was.

Margaret was still her mother, she looked exactly the same, but her mind was slipping away. The disease was cruel, slowly eroding her mother's personality, taking away the person who Alex knew and loved. Alex was prepared though. The doctors had told her that in reality there really was nothing they could do to stop the degradation. They could only slow it down and hopefully prolong the time Alex still had left with her.

Margaret was a sweet proud woman even now, she always liked to be dressed and made up well. Just in case visitors came, but people seldom did. Alex thought it strange how her mother's friends had drifted away since the disease had taken hold. They weren't interested now that her mother's money and status had gone. Why couldn't people just like you for who you were, not pretending to care when it suited them? Hoping that by being acquainted to you it would somehow add to their wealth and social standing. Real friends wouldn't act like that, but how do you know who they are and where would you find them? In a world full of people Alex felt alone, just one of the many passersby.

Alex still remembered the moment when she'd found the aged photograph of the stranger with a protective arm wrapped around her young mother. She was initially surprised. She wasn't expecting to find anything unusual. She'd come across it when she'd attempted to remove a sentimental baby portrait of herself from the wall in her mother's bedroom. The six by nine inch matt image just happened to flutter to the ground from the safety of its hiding place.

On later inspection Alex had found a small thin slot had been carved out of the hard wooden frame. The groove was just large enough to loosely hold the photograph in position. It was definitely odd, why would her mother go to the effort of hiding such an innocuous image?

Alex had since treasured this single photograph. She kept it in the top draw of her bedside cabinet. She longed for it to be an image of her father, but she'd no proof and there was no longer anyone she could ask. The image appeared to have been taken at the seaside on a lovely sunny day. Alex recognised the location. In fact she'd been taken there herself as a child. It was just down the road from a caravan site where she'd spent a happy summer vacation.

Her mother looked young, possibly even younger than Alex did now, maybe twenty or twenty-one. She looked attractive, her face free of make-up just with the fresh complexion of youth. She had long blonde hair that flowed down her neck and came to a rest on an ankle length thin flowery summer dress. The male figure looked slightly older, perhaps in his late twenties. He was handsome with rugged well-defined features. He had a strong athletic physique with very broad muscular shoulders.

The couple in the photograph looked happy, what had gone wrong? If he really was her father why had he left so suddenly? It didn't make sense. As she'd admired her potential father she'd had the distinct impression he must have been quite dashing in his youth. She wondered how many other young ladies lost their hearts to him.

Alex took one last deep breath then turned to make her way down the communal corridor that separated the two halves of the tower block. The automatic overhead lights didn't quite give off enough light and their flickering only enhanced the claustrophobic nature of the narrow passage. Her gaze drifted towards the small patch of daylight in the solitary window right at the far end but it did little to brighten the gloom.

Angry shouting was emanating from a badly damaged door a little way in front and as she passed she heard a sickening guttural thud followed by some quiet whimpering. Poor dog she thought. Probably hasn't even done anything wrong. Alex lowered her head and kept walking but with a subtle increase in pace.

At the end of the corridor Alex made the same choice she did every day. She took the stairs. She'd learned soon after moving into the tower-block that the lifts hardly ever arrived, no matter how often you pressed the call button.

The stairs were a challenge in themselves, it was a long way down and you never knew who or what you'd come across on your way. Alex skipped down the stairs sometimes two or three at a time, sometimes even leaping down whole staircases in one go using the hand rails for support. Almost like a gymnast on the parallel bars, a skill she enjoyed trying to master.

Overnight a large new graffiti mural had appeared on the wall in the entrance way. Alex took a moment to look it over. She didn't mind most of the graffiti. She thought it livened up the drab walls, added a bit of colour to the otherwise lifeless décor. This one in particular looked like a piece of art. It had obviously taken some real skill. If only the person responsible could turn their hand to a piece of conventional art. Then maybe they could make some money and they wouldn't have to live here in this place of all places.

Alex pushed her way through the heavy front door and made her way into the outside world. It felt like escaping from a prison, breaking out from the depressing confines of the tower block and into the freedom of the fresh air. Alex inhaled deeply, clearing the dank stale air from her lungs. It certainly felt good to be outside again.

The street was full of people scurrying about making their way to work, if that was indeed where they were going. Most of them could just as easily have been making their way to the job centre to collect their benefits cheque. Alex knew since the recession had started scores of people in the area had resorted to state handouts after being made redundant.

Alex's rambling thoughts led to a pang of guilt, things were bad for her but not that bad. At least she still had her job, no matter how much she hated it. Alex mentally shook herself, they all weren't deserving of her pity. The cruel jibes she suffered on a daily basis emanated from such a group of people. A number of her old school acquaintances seemed to relish in trying to make Alex's life as hard as possible. It wasn't easy for her always being the butt of their jokes. She'd hoped they'd have grown out of it by now, but the morons still seemed as immature as ever.

Catherine 'Cat' Poole was one of her tormentors, a local bully that had plagued many of the children at Alex's high-school during their time together. Mocking them, beating them and all in all making their lives a misery. From there Cat had graduated to an undistinguished life of petty crime, usually being the mule for more dominant criminals. On occasion resorting to mugging the odd passerby in the hope of getting something to sell to feed her habits.

Cat was of average height but slightly stocky and knew how to carry herself. She could be quite intimidating if she wanted to be. The half shaven haircut and the strange tattoos on her neck helped. Alex thought she'd have been quite pretty, but the makeup was over the top and the mass of elaborate silver jewellery was too much. Alex preferred a more modest look. She favoured things that didn't attract attention. She didn't like people staring at her. She didn't feel comfortable with it.

Alex might have got on with Cat if she didn't keep picking on her. She didn't have many friends and after all she'd known her for well over ten years. It was a shame. Instead Alex preferred to avoid her now, to keep her as far away as possible.

As she looked out through the throng of passers by Alex caught sight of Cat hanging out with a couple of her pals on the steps outside the tower-block on the opposite side of the road. Alex kept her head down as best she could and tried to disappear into the bustling crowd.

Sometimes it worked. Occasionally she managed to avoid the intimidating encounter.

Cat had never actually tried to mug or even hurt Alex physically. She didn't seem to think it was worth it. Instead she seemed to take great pleasure in just tormenting her with that exact fact. Rubbing it in about how broke she always was, picking fun at her appearance and the clothes that she wore. Generally pointing out how much better Cat looked compared to her. Alex longed for the torments to stop so she wouldn't have to pretend it didn't affect her. She tried to hide it, especially from her Mother. She couldn't let her get worried about such trivial matters.

Maybe one day she'd get her own back and turn the tables on the bully. But that took guts and today, well today Alex really didn't feel like she had any to give. For now she just kept moving, submissively letting the stream of the crowd guide her as she made her way to the bus stop. Alex felt herself shudder when the mocking shout rang out above the din of the background noise. She tried hard to ignore the provocation and carry on.

CHAPTER 2

Alex kept her determined pace as she marched along the footpath, every now and then glancing down at her wrist watch. She was cutting it close. Hopefully the bus hadn't already left. As she rounded the final bend she heard a much more welcome voice shout her name. It was coming from behind her, from the alley she'd just passed.

"Alex."

Her name rang out again, echoing between the tower block walls. It was soon joined by the clattering of running shoes on cobbles. She stopped and turned around as the noise grew closer.

Suddenly in a blur of swinging arms and legs her best friend burst out from the hidden alley and ran straight into her. With a thud they both crumpled to the floor one on top of the other.

"Ah... sorry," Bob said. Wincing as he pulled himself to his feet. "I couldn't stop."

Alex glared at him as she grabbed his outstretched hand resulting in another sincere apology.

"Come on we're going to miss the bus." His voice was tense. His face looked even more anxious.

Alex followed his gaze into the distance towards the unmistakable outline of the bright red number nine bus. It was weaving its way through the traffic towards them on its way to the city centre. In a fair bit of pain the pair dusted themselves off and made their way towards the bus stop at the end of the road.

"I'm sorry," Bob said yet again. "I slept in. I forgot to put the alarm on."

Alex huffed.

"I've just got dressed in less than five minutes and ran straight out of the house." Bob's face was flustered. A line of individual sweat beads was forming just below his hairline.

"It's all right for some people," Alex said, still a little unsettled from the encounter. "At least you can get to sleep."

"Another rough night, can't you take something to help you sleep?" Bob asked. His eyebrows narrowing into a frown. "Why don't you have a talk to your Doctor? Maybe he can prescribe something for you, to help you relax I mean."

Alex shook her head. "I don't know how you do it? How do you manage to sleep with the stupid railway so close?" She let out loud sigh. "It's driving me crazy."

"You know me, I sleep like a log," Bob said grinning "nothing can disturb me once I've dropped off."

Alex first met Bob at junior school. He was in the same year as her. They didn't immediately become good friends. That happened later, after a rather slow start.

It was out of a sort of mutual loneliness that the pair eventually found their friendship. They were the odd kids at school. The ones that stood on their own in the corner not joining in with the others. The ones that got chosen last for sports teams. The ones that the popular kids didn't like.

Bob now lived in a flat just three blocks away so it was easy for them to keep in touch. The two friends also had to take the same bus to work most mornings, giving them ample time to exchange day to day gossip.

Bob was slightly taller than Alex but carried barely any extra weight. He had the pale complexion and non-athletic emaciated looking physique of a person who spent as much time indoors glued to his computer screen as possible. Not that it bothered him too much. He was never popular in real life, but on the computer he could be and do anything that his heart desired. It was something he found hard to drag himself away from.

His day job too was based around computers. Even there he spent most of the day either staring at a computer screen or inside it's innards attempting to bring it to life. He was a technician for a small computer shop that sold custom made PC's from an outlet in the main shopping arcade.

"You look a bit off colour this morning. Anything I should know about?" Bob asked as they waited at the bus stop.

"No, not really. No more than usual anyway."

Bob continued to stare at his friend until she carried on.

"I think I'm just worn out," Alex conceded. "Not being able to sleep on top of all the other things I've got to stress about. It's starting to wear me down."

"Yeah I can imagine. I know things must be hard for you at the moment, but try to keep your chin up. You're doing the best you can. No one could ask any more of you."

"To tell you the truth, I'm not sure if it's going to be enough," Alex's voice was heavy and laboured. "I don't know how much longer I can keep it up."

"Tell you what. I know how to cheer you up. How about I come around again tonight and cook something nice for you and your mother?" Bob exaggerated his smile.

The beginnings of a smile started to form on Alex's face.

"Yes... that would be lovely. If it's not too much trouble that is?"

"Don't be silly, of course it's not. You know I like cooking and it'll give you a rest. Your mother enjoyed it last time too. I'll be round at seven thirty. Dinner will be ready at eight."

"Thank you," Alex replied, her voice a little lighter.

"Hey, can you get a few ingredients from work for me? I won't have time to get them later. Here take some money." Bob withdrew a twenty pound note from his wallet and thrust it in to Alex's hand. "I'll make some spaghetti bolognese. I've never had any complaints with that. Well there was that one time with the Italian student," Bob's voice trailed off. "I'll need some spaghetti, some beef mince, a few onions and a couple of tins of tomatoes. I'll bring the rest with me."

"OK, no problem," Alex said looking down at her hand. "You've given me too much money again though you know?"

"Ah, don't worry about it. I'm sure it will come in handy," he smiled again.

The bus soon arrived and the pair stepped on along with the other weary looking commuters. Alex and Bob flopped down into their usual seats near the back as it began to move. Alex shuffled up close to the window and stared out into the street without really concentrating on the passing scenery.

"So how are things really? How's your mother doing?" Bob asked in an attempt to start up a conversation.

"Hmm..." Alex murmured turning her attention back to him. "Well things have definitely been better. I think Mum's doing OK. I suppose some days are better than others. The doctors told me what to expect," she said with a week smile.

Bob remained silent but nodded along.

"Do you know what the worst part is?"

Bob shook his head.

"She forgets what's wrong with her. It's one of the more inhumane aspects of the condition. Can you imagine what it must be like to hear the bad news for the first over and over again? It's heartbreaking for me let-alone my mother."

"Oh dear," Bob said "that must be awful. Is there anything I can do to help?"

Alex took her time to respond, she was looking down at the floor. "You're coming around later, that'll cheer Mum up. Don't worry we'll be OK."

The bus pulled into their stop a few minutes later and the pair eventually made their way to the front and down onto the pavement.

"Well then, see you later, don't forget the ingredients," Bob said waving his farewell as the friends parted company.

The automatic sliding doors parted as Alex arrived to start her only long shift of the week at the supermarket. The store manager Stan was already waiting next to Alex's usual checkout. He was leaning over chatting to Lorraine, the young seventeen year old girl fresh out of college. He was probably talking in that smarmy, slimy way he had with women, Alex grimaced at the thought. As she approached Stan looked up at her.

"What time do you call this?" he said with a sneer.

"I'm sorry Sir the bus was late, honestly, I couldn't help it," Alex replied.

"Well you'd better be here all the earlier tomorrow to make up for it hadn't you? Remember what I told you, last chance, three strokes and you're out."

"I'm sorry Sir it won't happen again," Alex replied, her voice was quiet this time.

She couldn't have been all that late Alex thought, five minutes at most. She checked her wrist watch, it said seven fifty five. She was on time.

"Wait a minute," Alex said, her voice raised. "I'm on time, I'm not late."

Stan remained silent leering at her for a second before breaking out into a smile. "I'm watching you Alex, last chance." He stood up straight and walked off towards the store room, head held high.

"God I hate him," Alex said to Lorraine. "He's always got it in for me."

"Oh he's not that bad." Lorraine said smiling without looking at her. "I think he'd be quite cute really if he wasn't so clingy." She turned to face Alex. "He's just given me another six hours work."

Alex's head dropped as she turned back to her till. "Great, that's just what I needed to hear," she whispered under her breath. "Welcome to hell."

Alex reluctantly stomped off to the staff cloakroom, stuffed her bag and coat into her locker and slammed it closed. She stood for a moment steadying herself against its hard cold metal. She inhaled deeply and held her breath for a second before releasing it with a slow sigh. After a few more controlled breaths she spun round and marched back over to her checkout. It was going to be another long grind.

Lunchtime break arrived four long, long hours later and as usual the energetic Lorraine was first to stand up.

"Do you want to come for a stroll around town? I feel like stretching my legs. I'll grab some lunch from the deli round the corner on the way."

"Sorry, not today," Alex replied. "I don't really feel up to it. I think I'm just going to get myself a banana or something and go sit in the square for a while."

"Ah OK, well then see you in a bit then," Lorraine said before making her way out the front doors.

Alex went to her locker and reached in for her bag. She rummaged through its contents and withdrew the meagre lunch she'd brought with her. An overly ripe banana and pair of sorry looking thin salmon paste sandwiches. Then made her way through the store room towards the rear staff entrance, walked out onto the access road and headed for the sanctuary of the secluded courtyard garden.

It was hidden between the maze of office

blocks and businesses not far from where she worked. Not many people went there, not many people knew about it. Alex preferred it like that. It was like her own private retreat.

Nestled beneath an old gnarled apple tree was a Victorian style cast iron bench. It was her favourite spot. She liked how the dappled light passed through the apples fading autumnal leaves and made them glow with a beautiful golden hue.

Alex enjoyed her lunch more than she'd expected and helped herself to a couple of the ripe apples that still clung to the overhead branches. A gift for her mother. After twenty minutes of peace she strolled back to work in a much better mood than when she left.

The last four hours of Alex's shift seemed to pass quicker than usual. She was looking forward to Bob coming around and cooking for them again. It was something he'd done many times and they always enjoyed his company. It would also give her a chance to take a well earned rest. Being able to relax wasn't a luxury that she could afford herself very often.

Alex got to her feet as her shift came to an end and took a moment to stretch before heading off to clock out. Lorraine did the same and followed her.

"Well that's another day done. We seemed busier than usual this afternoon," she said to

Alex. "Same time tomorrow?"

"Yeah," Alex replied. "I'm always on earlies. Stan's never changed my shifts or hours. I've asked him plenty of times for more but he just turns me down flat," she added with a grimace. "It's really annoying. I've been here for nearly two years."

"I guess I'm just lucky," Lorraine chuckled.

"Yeah, I suppose," Alex sighed. "Mondays are all right for me, he's got me on eight till four. But the rest of the week is awful, he's only got me on half shifts, just eight till noon. He won't give me anything at all on Friday, Saturday or Sunday."

"That sucks," Lorraine replied. "I'm on eight till four from tomorrow and I've only been here just over a month."

Alex took a deep breath and exhaled slowly again. "You must be doing something right," she said trying to make an effort to smile. "Anyway, I'll see you in the morning. I've got to pick up a few things for dinner tonight. Have a nice evening."

The two parted company and Alex made her way to the grocery isle. She'd soon found and picked out the freshest looking produce from its hiding place at the back, at least working there had some benefits. Whilst she was at it, since she could put Bob's extra change to good use, she also grabbed a couple of store cupboard staples to keep her and her mother going for a few more days.

Alex paid the bill, placed the groceries in her bag and began the lengthy walk home. She preferred to walk back whenever she could. She enjoyed the fresh air and there was no rush, she could take her time. The three kilometre walk always gave Alex a chance to think things over and anyway, the exercise was good for her. She took the same route almost every day. She liked to stroll through the park on the way home. Being surrounded by greenery even for a short time made her spirits lift, it was her escape.

Just as Alex exited the park something unusual caught her eye. A brightly coloured sign had appeared in the window of the local Foodbank. In large bold writing it read 'Volunteers badly needed please help enquire within.' As she was feeling in a much better mood than she had done recently, she decided to find out more. After all, she could spare an hour or two on her way home a couple of days a week.

With a bit of trepidation Alex opened the glass door and entered into the foyer. An elderly lady was busy knitting behind her desk. She was wearing a very thick handmade purple woollen jumper and had a matching purple rinse, nice colour Alex thought. The sound of the door shutting behind Alex jogged the lady from her thoughts. She looked up, noticing her for the first time.

"Oh, hello there, can I help you dear?" She said in a surprised voice.

"Hi..." Alex managed a shy smile. "I've just come in to ask about volunteering. I saw the sign on the window as I was passing."

"Oh I am glad. Hardly a soul has come in to help all week." The elderly lady beamed at her. "There's always plenty of needy people come through the door. But very few come and offer to help out. Here have a look at this. It'll give you all the details."

Alex accepted the leaflet and smiled.
"The people here are all very friendly. It's a nice place to spend an afternoon."

Alex thanked the lady and leaflet in hand walked back out into the sunlight. She quickly scanned it then found a safe place for it in her bag. She'd have a serious think about it later. She did like helping people, it was good Karma. The thought brought a smile to her face. Maybe someday it would come back around.

Alex reached her block of flats an hour after setting off and plodded up the many staircases to get to her apartment. She knocked like always before letting herself in. As she opened the front door she called out in a loud voice to let her mother know who it was. She didn't like startling her. There was always so much confusion before she realised who it was.

"Hi mum, it's only me.... Alex, I'm back from work." There was a short moment of silence before a quiet sleepy reply came back from around the corner.

"Oh hello dear, I'd forgotten you were coming. I must have dozed off."

Alex heard her mother chuckle as she pulled herself out of her chair and made her way to greet her.

"What time is it dear? Do I have to take my medication?" A look of confusion was starting to creep across her mother's face.

"It's just coming up to five o'clock," Alex said. "Did you take the tablets I left you with your lunch?"

"I'm not sure. I erm... I think so," her mother replied. "Well lets go take a look shall we?" Alex put her arm around her mother's shoulders and led her towards the kitchen. "Don't worry mum, your memory isn't as good when you've just woken up. It'll get easier in a couple of minutes."

"I... I..."

"Hey, I've got some good news for you," Alex said trying to change the subject. "Bob is coming around again tonight. He's going to cook up a nice meal for us. That's something to look forward to isn't it? He'll be here about half past seven."

"Bob?" Margaret said, her voice sounded guarded. "Have I met him, I can't recall?"

"Yes mum, once or twice," Alex grinned. "Shall we get freshened up and get the place looking nice for our guest?"

Alex took the opportunity to clear away some of the clutter that had accumulated over the last couple of days. She never let the house get really untidy but there were some areas that needed attention.

A knock at the door just after seven thirty sounded his arrival and Alex and her mother went to great him. Bob was standing in the hallway smiling with his hands behind his back. He looked quite spruced up, wearing a new pair of jeans and his favourite black t-shirt. The one with the strange Morse code motif on the front that he'd assured Alex contained a humorous message. Bob brought his hands around to the front to reveal what he'd been hiding. A bottle of red wine and a bunch of fresh flowers. He handed the wine to Alex and the flowers to her mother.

"I know you like flowers Mrs Forster, so I picked these up for you on the way over."

Alex's mum beamed. "Oh, they're beautiful, thank you very much. I'll go pop these in a vase right away," she said before disappearing into the kitchen.

"That was thoughtful," Alex said realising she'd been watching her mother. She turned her attention back to Bob who was still waiting in the hallway. "Sorry, come in, come in. We can't leave you standing out there all evening now can we?"

"Ah can't forget these," Bob said reaching down to retrieve the backpack concealed to the side of the front door. "I'll go get started in the kitchen, I bet you two are starving, I know I am."

"OK and I'll put this to good use," Alex replied raising the bottle.

Full of confidence Bob paced off into the kitchen. Along with some herbs and spices, he pulled out his chef's apron and a few choice utensils from his backpack. Alex followed, reached up to open the cabinet above her, removed three large glasses and poured everyone a drink. Meanwhile her mother had been making herself busy arranging the cut flowers in a large elaborate vase. When she was satisfied with her work she walked back into the living room and placed the vase onto the coffee table.

"See, they brighten the place up a bit don't they?" She said in a loud voice to no one in particular.

Alex popped her head around the corner to have a look, then picked up two glasses and strolled over to her mother.

"Here you go mum," Alex said as she handed her mother her drink. "They look lovely."

Half an hour later with the inviting aroma wafting in from the kitchen Bob announced that the food was ready. The hungry friends were soon tucking in with enthusiasm.

"This is delicious, it's so tasty," Alex said as she devoured her portion.

"I'm glad you like it," Bob laughed. "It's a real easy one. I always make sure I get a lot flavour into the sauce to begin with. That way I know it's going to taste nice at the end. What do you think Mrs Forster?"

Alex's mother paused for a couple of seconds in thought.

"It's great, really nice. You'll have to write the recipe down for me."

"No problem, I'll do it for you before I leave," Bob replied.

After the meal Alex and Bob cleared away the dishes and washed up.

"I'm glad you came around," Alex said. "It was very nice of you cooking for us. I do feel a lot better now."

Before Bob could reply Alex's mother walked into the kitchen looking worried.

"I don't feel very well, my head feels funny."

"Maybe you're just getting tired," Alex said to try and calm down her agitated mother. "Don't worry too much, you'll feel better in a minute or two. Go and have a sit down and I'll bring you a nice cup of tea." Alex turned to Bob again. The smile was gone from her face. "Oh well, perhaps you'd better go. It looks like Mum's going to have another bad spell. I'll see you in the morning."

Bob nodded his agreement and tried his best not to make too much noise as he closed the door behind him.

Alex made her mother the tea and went to sit down with her on the settee. After a while the colour on her mother's face started to return.

"Well that was nice dear," Margaret said. "What was that nice young man's name again?"

"Oh, Bob," Alex replied.

"Have I met him before, I can't quite recall?" Her mother's voice still sounded unsteady.

"Yes Mum... He's been around a couple of times. He likes to cook." Alex replied hoping that it would suffice. She was starting to feel tired herself.

"Are you two, well you known, an item?"

"Oh," Alex giggled. "No, it's nothing like

that, we're just good friends. I've known him since school."

"Well I just thought... well you know, you've been single for a while now and he seemed like a nice guy. I'd like some grand kids at some point."

Alex watched as a mischievous grin came over her mother's face. "Oh mum," she whined. "I thought you were being serious. You got me again."

Alex and her mother laughed together for a while before retiring to bed.

CHAPTER 3

Alex sat bolt upright. The annoying sound of the alarm clock was ringing in her ears. She reached across to the bedside table fumbling with the contraption until she finally found the right button to make the infernal thing silent. She sat still, dazed for a moment, looking around her bedroom. Was it morning already? It felt like she'd only just gone to bed. Had she really managed to sleep right through the night? Alex reached up towards the ceiling with both arms and stretched, damn it felt good.

Alex's mother was still fast asleep when she crept into her bedroom.

"Time to wake up sleepy head," Alex said in a soft voice. Her mother let out a quiet groan before rolling away from her.

"Mum it's time to get up," she said again, a little louder this time.

Alex's mother opened her eyes and looked up at her.

"Oh hello dear," she said blinking a couple of times. "I wasn't expecting you... I must have fallen asleep." She looked around the room and back at her. "It's nice of you to come and visit."

"Come on Mum, I need to get you up and dressed," Alex said frowning. "I've got to go to work soon."

Her mother eased herself up out of bed continuing to gaze at her with that confused expression Alex had seen many times.

"I don't feel too good dear," her mother said with a little difficulty. "My head feels funny. I think I've got a headache coming."

"Don't worry Mum," Alex replied. "Your memory will come back in a couple of minutes. It's always the same after you've been to sleep." She put a comforting arm around her mother. "Come on let's get you dressed and get some breakfast inside you."

Alex rushed around the kitchen making the usual breakfast and left her mother's lunch in the fridge. Remembering what her manager had told her the day before, she glanced down at her watch. She'd just enough time left to check the memos dotted around the apartment.

"Are there any headache tablets in the cupboard dear?" Her mother asked with a wince. "My head's still hurting."

"Yes there should be. I'm sure there's a couple left in the cupboard." Alex dashed over to get them along with some water. "I'll pick some more up while I'm out," she added before grabbing her things and hurrying out of the apartment.

By the time Alex had reached the ground floor a large storm front had moved in. Great that's just what I need, she thought. Rain would make the trek to work even more depressing. As she opened the door to the outside world she heard the rumble of distant thunder. The sky above looked oppressive, its darkness still made it feel as though it was the middle of the night. She tightened the pull cord on the hood of her coat and shivered before walking out into the gloom.

Alex didn't like rain at the best of times. Her slender malnourished frame made it hard for her to body to retain heat. She raised an arm in a futile effort to shield herself from the painful onslaught as the wind and rain lashed at her exposed face. Her skin stung, she could feel sleet in the air. It won't be long before this will be snow, she thought shuddering again. Alex felt herself beginning to yearn for the bright extended days of summer. She knew her perpetual state of tiredness would only increase as the nights grew longer and longer throughout the winter season.

Alex was surprised to see Bob leaning against the tower block wall as she rounded the corner. He was already waiting for her, sheltering under a simple black umbrella.

"Finally," he said with a big grin. "I thought you weren't coming. I was beginning to think you'd tricked them into giving you the day off again," Bob added laughing.

"Oh no, I wouldn't miss it for the world," Alex replied starting to chuckle herself. "It's what gets me out of bed in the morning."

As she walked past, Bob pushed himself off from the wall and joined her on her way to the bus stop.

"So... how are you liking the weather?" Bob asked cringing as a bolt of lightning lit up the sky.

"It's lovely isn't it? It makes everywhere look so nice and colourful," Alex huffed. "Thanks for cooking last night. It was really nice of you."

"No worries, I'm glad you liked it," Bob

replied.

"Hey... I even managed to get a decent night's sleep." Alex's voice lifted. "I didn't wake up once."

Alex was soon at work. This time sure that she was on time. Lorraine was already in the cloakroom when Alex walked in after clocking on.

"Hi there," Lorraine said without looking up. "I'd stay away from Stan today. He's in a bad mood. I don't know what's up with him. He was really crabby with me a minute ago."

Alex stuffed her things into her locker before replying.

"It's going to be another fun day then. Thanks for the heads up." She wasn't particularly struck by the news. She only had to work until lunch. She could handle one of Stan's moods till then.

Alex followed Lorraine over to the checkouts and started to settle herself into the mundane tasks. A few early customers came in to purchase their lunches or something quick for breakfast before heading off to their places of work. Then the lull hit.

Alex's unchallenged mind started to drift. She couldn't shake the feeling that somehow the atmosphere was wrong. The rest of the staff seemed on edge and she was beginning to get the distinct impression that Stan was lingering. He kept coming back to check the same stock in the isles closest to her, every now and then making a fleeting glance in her direction.

"Do you know what's going on?" Alex asked Lorraine in a hushed whisper.

"I have no idea. Something has definitely happened though," Lorraine replied.

Three hours into her shift Alex's wandering thoughts were interrupted as an unseen hand tapped her on her left shoulder. She turned to see Stan standing behind her with a troubled expression on his face.

"Can I have a quiet word with you in my office after your shift finishes?" Stan asked. His voice sounded subdued. "There's something we need to discuss."

Not knowing what to say, Alex just nodded. Stan hurried away without another word.

"What was all that about?" Alex said to Lorraine. "I haven't done anything wrong today."

"I honestly have no idea... sorry," Lorraine replied shaking her head. "Perhaps you're getting promoted."

Almost fifteen minutes after her shift officially finished Alex plucked up the courage to go to Stan's office. Dragging her feet she walked over to the door and knocked.

"Yes, come in," a stern voice boomed.

Alex eased the door open to reveal herself.

"Ah yes, Alex come in, take a seat," Stan said leaning back in his seat.

Alex walked over to the oversized desk and sat down on the waiting office chair. Stan remained silent for a moment.

"I'm sorry to tell you this, but I'm afraid I've got some bad news for you."

Alex took a sharp intake of breath.

"We had a visit from the owner early this morning. He'd been going over our finances," Stan said. His face looked troubled. "I'm sure you're aware that trade has been down since the recession started."

Alex nodded.

"The truth is it's killing us. The business is losing way too much money. The owner wants us to make cutbacks wherever possible. Unfortunately that means the staff budget needs to be cut."

Alex felt a thudding against her ribs.

"I've been giving people the bad news all day."

Alex opened her mouth ready to speak but no words came.

"I can't do anything about it. It's out of my control. I'm afraid we've got to let you go."

Alex gasped for air. She hadn't noticed she'd been holding her breath.

"Now we just need to go over a few things, to put your mind a little more at ease," Stan said noting something down.

"But... but I need this job Sir," Alex stuttered.

"I'll write you up a favourable reference letter, you don't have to worry about that."

"But I need the money to look after my mother," Alex pleaded.

"You've worked well here, for nearly two years isn't it?" Stan kept his head down but his eyes looked up.

Alex nodded.

"I'm sorry, I really am," Stan said putting his pen down.

"But... but... I."

"I can't help you this time I'm afraid," Stan interrupted holding up both hands.

Alex shoulders sagged.

"You should be all right for money for a while," Stan added. "Your two week notice will start from Monday and you're entitled to one month redundancy pay for every year you've worked here."

Alex closed her eyes and sighed.

"I'll bump it up to the full two years for you. You also had to work a month in advance when you started here, so you'll get another month's pay on top of that."

What little colour there was drained from Alex's face. She didn't feel like talking any more, there wasn't any point. Being polite under the circumstances, she excused herself and left the office. Keeping her head low, she exited the building. She didn't stop to tell Lorraine what the news was.

Alex didn't know what to do. She didn't know what to think. What was she going to do now without a job? How were they going to cope? Alex's mind was awash with a multitude of agonizing thoughts all at the same time.

It had stopped raining now and the day was bright, but Alex hadn't noticed, she was walking in a daze not concentrating on where she was going. She pushed her way through the throngs of people in front of her, trying to get as far away as possible.

Through her random wandering she ended up at the town square, an expanse of concrete dotted with strange statues and monuments. Alex walked up to one of the vacant cold concrete benches and sat down exhausted. She needed to think, to clear her head. She sat there motionless with her head in her hands for what seemed like an eternity.

A group of feral pigeons gathered around her ankles hoping for some crumbs, but Alex wasn't there to eat. She just wanted to be somewhere outside, somewhere in the open air. After a few fruitless minutes the pigeons gave up and flew off to a different bench. The noisy disturbance of their flapping wings broke Alex's train of thought. She tilted her head to look up at the clear sky. Something was going to turn up. She would find another job. Everything was going to be OK, she told herself again and again.

Twenty minutes had gone past before Alex had gathered up enough strength to stand again. Mentally she shook herself before starting the long walk home. She could do this. She'd managed before. She could manage now!

It took Alex much longer than usual to stroll home, her feet felt heavy and her legs didn't want to move. She was still worrying when she entered the towering block of flats. How was she going to break the news to her mother and how she would react? The thoughts kept running through her mind over and over.

Absent-minded she made her way towards the lift and pressed the call button. A creaking sound came from somewhere above in the shaft, but it made no effort to come down to the ground floor. In a huff she traipsed off to start the long assent of the stairs.

Lost in her thoughts again, Alex made her way up one flight of stairs after another. She didn't notice the warning signs at first. She paid no attention to the noisy commotion. At last Alex's troubled mind made the connection, but it was too late. She'd walked right into the middle of it.

She started to feel sick as the mistake she'd made dawned on her. She raised her head. She was surrounded by people that she recognised. People she wanted to avoid.

Cat was the first to start.

"Well, well, look what we've got here?" She said blocking Alex's path.

Alex tried to turn but a couple of Cat's stern looking male friends stopped her.

"You want to get passed lady, you've got to pay the fare," the younger looking thug said with contempt.

"Don't be stupid Daz, she hasn't got any money," Cat said with a cruel laugh. "I mean look at her, she's poorer than you."

Alex's heart was beginning to race.

"Hey, what you staring at? You fancy me or something?" Daz said with a sneer.

"I wasn't staring and no I don't fancy you," Alex replied with rather more force than she'd intended.

"Why, are you a dyke or something? You sure look like one," Daz added looking her up and down. "Hey I bet she fancies you Cat."

"What her fancy me? Don't be daft. I've known her for ages. She's not a dyke, she's just weird."

Alex became aware of the laughter, her heart sank.

"You look a bit rough around the edges hun," Cat said as she turned her attention back to Alex. "If you're short of cash you could always come and work for me again. The offers still open you know."

"I'll think about it." Alex tried to smile. "I might have to take you up on that."

"What, her come work for us?" Daz was now the one to look shocked. "What's she going to do, bore people to death?"

"I'm sure I can think of something," Cat said with a one-sided smile.

Alex didn't catch the gesture. She was busy trying to calm herself down.

"Go on, get out of here," Cat winked at Alex. "Before my dogs start getting nasty."

Maybe she was going to get out of this without any trouble after all. Alex took the hint and hurried passed up the stairs. She felt a sting of pain as someone slapped her backside. She didn't look back she just kept going.

"See you tomorrow darling," a rough voice sounded from below as she vanished from view.

Alex banged on the front door with her left hand as her other fumbled in her bag for her keys.

"Mum it's me, Alex, let me in," she called. At last her fingers grasped the right key. She forced it into the lock and wrenched it around.

Alex shoved the door open, rushed in and closed it firmly behind her again. She rested there with both hands pressed on the closed door taking deep breaths. It was over. For now at least.

Out of the corner of her eye Alex noticed her mother walking towards her.

"What's the matter? I heard a noise."

"Nothing Mum. It's nothing," Alex sighed. "I just had a long day that's all," Alex added as she pried herself away from the door.

"What time is it dear? I'm getting hungry it must be nearly lunch time."

"It's just gone passed two." Alex's eyebrows narrowed. "Haven't you had your lunch yet?" Her voice was harsh. Her mother always remembered to eat lunch. She'd never had to remind her before.

Her mother stared at her. She looked unsteady on her feet.

"Are you feeling OK Mum? How's your headache?"

Her mother frowned. "I er... I'm not sure."

Alex went to the cupboard to check if her mother had taken her tablets, they were still there.

"Mum... you forgot to take your tablets again."

"Oh, Have I? I'm sorry. I thought I'd already had them."

"Don't worry about it. You can have them now. No harm done. I'll get your lunch out of the fridge for you."

Alex didn't hear the muttering as her mother sat down at the table.

"There you go, take these."

Alex went to retrieve the sandwiches she'd prepared earlier that morning and sat them down beside her mother. She wasn't feeling hungry herself. The news at work and the encounter with Cat had unsettled her too much. Instead she made them both a cup of tea then sat with her mother in silence while she ate.

"Do you want to go to the park and get some fresh air? Alex asked. "I don't feel like staying in? You could take your pencils and draw something."

"Yes OK dear," Alex's mother replied after a short pause. "I feel like getting some fresh air as well. It might clear my head." She stood up and disappeared into her bedroom.

After a few minutes Alex's mother reappeared, canvas in hand.

"Have you got everything Mum?"

"I think so."

"Put your waterproof coat on as well, it might rain again later."

Alex dropped an extra banana into her bag, just in case. Then led her mother out of the apartment and the pair made their way down the corridor towards the stairs.

"Shall we try the lift today?" Alex asked in a strained voice. "I feel like I've been running up and down these stairs all day."

"It's up to you, we can try if you want," her mother replied frowning.

"I don't mind waiting, I'm feeling lucky," Alex lied.

The lift doors creaked open a couple of minutes later and they both stepped in.

"See, what did I tell you?" Alex said as the doors slid shut, relieved to be in relative safety for a change.

It took almost three minutes for the lift to come to a jerky halt. Alex helped the struggling doors slide apart and the pair set off towards the park at a sedate pace. Alex wanted to take the time to enjoy their journey.

The afternoon was pleasant enough for her mother to indulge in her hobby. The sun was bright and provided a little warmth. The wind had finally died down and the dark rain clouds of the morning were now just a distant memory. Alex's mother enjoyed to sketch and Alex tried to encourage her. It seemed to focus her attention, stopped the worrying, for a little while anyhow. As long as she was being artistic her mother felt like she could still do something by herself. She was being creative and she felt useful.

As they neared the park the pair passed by

the Foodbank.

"I'm thinking of doing some volunteering there after work." Alex cringed as the words came out of her mouth. She couldn't tell her mother now, it wasn't the right time. She wanted her to be enjoying her art work so she'd take the news better.

"That's nice dear," her mother said with a broad smile. "You like helping people don't you? You're nice like that."

Alex tried to hurry the pace, to distract her mother from the building. Her mother looked like she was about to say something but Alex cut in.

"There are lots of people in the park today. I hope our spot is free."

With a little reluctance her mother turned towards the park and caught up.

The wrought iron gates at the entrance were still wide open and the pair followed the long sweeping footpath through the large communal lawn area. Many of the other locals had gathered on the lush grass, making use of possibly the last autumnal sun. Most were students from the university, lounging about on blankets reading or chatting to their friends. Some of the more energetic people were running around chasing a football. Alex even saw one chase a Frisbee.

Alex and her mother continued on, making their way deeper into the park towards the less populated area. Few people lingered in this part, they just passed through to look at the beautifully scenery. The pair found their favourite place, a bench nestled between three rhododendron bushes overlooking the ornamental lake with its Japanese Style Bridge and pagoda. Alex smiled. It was a tranquil spot to spend a few hours.

Alex sat captivated, watching her mother's experienced hands flow over the darkening canvas with ease. The confusion she so often saw in her mother's face was gone. She looked happy. Alex made a loud audible sigh. How long would it be before the disease robbed her mother and herself of this last bastion of hope?

She reached into her bag, her hand searching for the book she'd picked up from the library. Alex read, she read a lot. It passed the time at night. Insomnia could be a real bugbear. This week she'd chosen a factual piece of work concerning the dark ages in Britain. It made a change from the mythological thrillers she usually picked up. It didn't have the tension and romance they usually had, but it was interesting none the less.

Her fingers wrapped around the book, it felt strange, the cover felt different. Alex turned it over in her hand. The flier from the Foodbank was staring up at her.

"Mum," she said sighing again. "I had some bad news today at work."

Her mother's hand froze on the canvas. She turned her head to look at her. "Why, what happened?"

Alex took a deep breath. "They're making me redundant. The shop has lost a lot of money since the recession started and they can't afford to keep as many staff on any more."

"Oh dear," Alex's mother said placing the pencil down.

"Most of the temporary staff got laid off today, all that is except the managers new favourite," Alex grimaced. She put a comforting hand on her mother's leg. "But don't worry Mum, I'll sort something out. I'll find another job, everything will be OK I promise."

After the awkward conversation the rest of the afternoon passed in relative silence. Neither of them felt much like talking. Alex's head had been stuck in her book while her mother had been busy finishing a rough sketch and making a good start on a final piece.

With a loud crack Alex's mother slammed her pencil down. Alex looked up startled. Her mother was wincing with pain clutching her head.

"What's up?"

"Can we go back now please? I've had enough and my head is killing me, I need some more pain killers."

"If you're sure, I don't mind," Alex said. "I'll tell the doctor about your headaches the next time we see him, you're getting them too often."

Her mother nodded.

"Come on then, let's get you back to the flat."

As soon as they were back inside, Alex got her mother a couple more painkillers and a drink.

"I'm going to go have a lie down." Her mother winced again. "It might make my head a bit easier."

"OK Mum. Do you want me to come wake you up in a couple of hours?"

"No it's all right dear, I feel tired. I think I'm going to have an early night." She kissed Alex on her cheek before disappearing into her bedroom.

Alex was getting even more worried about her mother, she was getting worse. I'm going to ring the doctors up tomorrow, she thought. Maybe I can make an earlier appointment.

CHAPTER 4

Alex grew weary from reading. She couldn't concentrate. She kept losing her place as her mind wandered. After a couple of hours of barely making any headway, the book snapped shut. She tossed it onto her bedside table and reached over to turn out the night light.

Alex lay back and gazed up at the ceiling, waiting for the faint patterns to emerge as her eyes became accustomed to the darkness. Out of the gloom the shapes of more and more glowing stars began to appear. She watched as they began to join up to reveal the familiar star chart of the night sky.

There was something about looking up at the sky that calmed Alex down. It helped her mind to unwind. The small act of attaching those innocuous 'glow in the dark' stars had allowed Alex's mind to escape the confines of the tower block. At least she could imagine being somewhere else, somewhere free of this prison.

A loud thud in the living room made Alex jump, wrenching her from her thoughts. She looked up at the bright halo of light surrounding her bedroom door. Oh not again, Alex thought shaking her head. It was probably just her mother trying to find her way to the bathroom. Alex threw back the covers and swung her legs out of bed. She should at least check that she was all right.

The bedroom door creaked on its dry hinges as Alex pulled it open. Her dishevelled mother stood shivering in the centre of the living room.

"What's wrong mum?" Alex said trying to keep the tone of her voice calm. "Are you feeling OK?"

Her mother's head snapped around. Alex cringed, the whites of her mother's wild eyes shone out as she focused intently on her. Her face looked grey, the colour all but gone, drained out.

"I thought you'd all left me on my own. I... I didn't know where everyone had gone. Did they tell you where they were going?" Her mother's voice quivered as she tried to get the words out.

"I think I'm supposed to meet them somewhere but I don't know where, I can't remember."

"Mum calm down. Don't worry. You haven't got to meet anyone it's all right. Come on let's get you back to bed."

"I... I don't want to go back to bed. I want to know where they've gone. Hey don't touch me, leave me alone." Alex's mother stumbled about on her unsteady feet before collapsing into the armchair.

Alex crouched down next to her. She could tell her mother was crying. She brushed her mother's hair away from her face and stroked it a few times.

"You're OK, really you are. You're at home with me. I'm your daughter. Nobody else lives here. You must have been dreaming and got yourself confused again."

Her mother's shoulders rose up and down as she continued to weep.

"Let's get you cleaned up a bit and back off to sleep. I promise you'll feel better in the morning."

"But I don't know, I don't remember," her mother whimpered. "I can't think straight, nothing is making sense."

"Mum listen to me, I'm telling you the truth. You don't have anything to worry about. You don't have to be anywhere. Look you've got a problem with your memory. It gets worse when you're tired. That's what the doctor gave you the tablets for."

"Oh... I'm sorry dear, I'm tired. I don't... I don't understand anymore." Her mother sobbed. "I don't know what's happening. I'm scared."

"I know mum, don't worry. I know for the both of us," Alex said trying to remain calm herself. "We'll be OK. Somehow," she whispered under her breath. "Now let's get you back to bed or neither of us will be much use in the morning."

Alex didn't get any sleep again that night. Her mind was awash with troubling thoughts and ideas. Instead she just lay awake on her bed, her body still but her mind in turmoil. Even the occasional annoyance caused by an odd passing freight train did little to interrupt her from the restless thoughts. At five o'clock the next morning she gave up the idea of trying to get to sleep, maybe she could do something useful instead.

Alex got herself changed into her work clothes before going over to the window and opening the curtains. She looked out into the darkness trying to decide what the weather would be like later on. The sky looked heavy. She was going to need her big coat again. Alex sighed with the thought of more rain to look forward to.

It was as her eyes dropped down towards the

street below that she became aware of someone staring straight up in her direction. The same taxi she'd seen a few nights earlier was parked opposite her tower block behind a black sedan. Two suited gentlemen were standing next to the driver's side window, apparently talking to the occupant. Alex's eyes met the gaze of taller of the two. A slight feeling of dread began to rise from the pit of her stomach. She shuddered and turned away from the window.

What was that about, she thought still a little agitated? As realisation dawned on her tired mind Alex told herself to settle down, to stop being so jumpy. Oh, I'm probably the only person in this block crazy enough to be up and about at this time. My light was on. He must have seen me open the curtains. She needed some sleep. She needed to rest, to get away from the hassle in her life. Bleary eyed she wandered into the kitchen to make a cup of coffee, she couldn't see a way out but maybe the caffeine would help for a while.

As the kettle rumbled away in the background Alex made up her lunch to take to work, packing it away in her bag as the kettle came to the boil. The supplies she'd picked up from the store the other day were coming in useful. Coffee in hand she set about sorting out the things her mother would need for the rest of the day.

Half an hour later Alex's brief spark of energy had waned and she found herself sitting on the settee scanning through one of her mother's magazines. She didn't really find anything worth reading but a pull out article with a few simple designs for things to make to decorate the house caught her eye. Maybe they could have a go together sometime. Alex placed the article on the top of the magazines before straightening the pile up again. Finishing the last of her now cold coffee Alex set about cleaning the flat until absent minded fell back into her normal routine.

Alex's sleep deprived mind was still in a foggy daze when she met up with Bob on the way to work.

"Good morning trouble," Bob said with what Alex thought was too much enthusiasm. "Hey what did you get up to last night? You look like death warmed up!"

"Ah, sorry..." Alex replied realising she was obviously frowning. "I didn't sleep at all again last night. My mother had another bad turn, she got really upset."

Bob opened his mouth to reply but Alex cut him off.

"I don't feel too much like talking about it at the moment. I feel completely knackered," she sighed. "I'll be glad when today is over."

"Are things getting worse? With your mum I

mean," Bob replied ignoring her objection. "Isn't there anything the doctors can do for her? Can't they give her some different pills, something to ease the symptoms?"

Alex began frowning again as Bob continued to talk.

"I don't really know much about her condition other than it slowly makes people forgetful."

"No, not really," Alex replied after a few seconds. "The doctors change her medication now and again. It works for a while but her condition keeps deteriorating." Alex's expression dropped. "It's not fair, I hate seeing her like this. She's too young. Why did it have to happen to her, to us? Why now on top of everything else?" Alex sighed deeply again. "She's all I have left. What am I going to do without her?" Her voice trailed off. "It's too soon." She fell silent once more.

Bob put his arm around his friend, "You're doing the best you can for her. Don't be too hard on yourself. Your mother would be proud of you. Come on try to cheer up a bit, I'll still be here for you no matter what happens."

"Thanks," Alex whispered, a bit chocked up. "Oh no!" she added stopping in her tracks. "I'd meant to give the doctors a ring about my mother before I left. I wanted to try and make an appointment for her," Alex said rolling her eyes.

"She's been getting really bad headaches recently." Alex cursed at herself under her breath. "I won't get a chance to ring until I get home now."

Bob fished into his pocket and retrieved his mobile phone.

"Here, borrow this, give them a ring."

"Are you sure?" Alex smiled. "Thank you." She dialled the well rehearsed number and waited for the connection. Her enthusiasm didn't last long though as the engaged tone greeted her again and again. "It's no use I can't get through."

"Maybe they aren't open yet," Bob offered.

"No, they should be. It's just busy like usual," Alex said shaking her head as she handed the phone back to her friend.

"Don't worry about it. Give it back to me later." Bob smiled. "I'm sure I can survive without a phone for a few hours."

"You sure?" Alex smiled back. "You're too nice to me."

Alex tried calling the doctors a few more times when she got to work but with time running out she gave up and made her way in to begin her shift. It was the same every time she tried to make an appointment for her mother. Always an engaged tone and when eventually she did get to speak to someone, the doctor couldn't see her for days. Why couldn't something be easy for a change? The whole world seemed to be conspiring against her recently. It was just another of life's annoyances to add to the list.

"So tell me how you got on then?" Lorraine said to Alex as she sat down in the adjacent checkout.

Alex looked at her puzzled

"Yesterday, I mean silly. When Stan called you into his office. I saw you rush off afterwards. Come on the curiosity is killing me"

"Oh, that," Alex sighed. "It was bad news I'm afraid, he's making me redundant. Apparently he's doing the same with all of the temporary and part time staff. You must be one of the lucky ones." Alex smiled slightly out of the corner of her mouth.

"Oh, oh dear," Lorraine replied. "That's not what I thought, not at all. That's terrible. No wonder he looked troubled yesterday."

The rest of the shift dragged but as usual came to an end at last. Alex tried the doctor's number once more and surprisingly managed to get through. The surgery was as expected very busy. The earliest the doctor could fit her mother in was next Tuesday afternoon, almost a full week away. Still at least she'd managed to sort it out, one less thing she had to worry about. Lorraine caught up with Alex as she was shutting her locker.

"Hey Alex what are you doing for lunch? I remembered to bring some sandwiches today, I was thinking of going into town to find somewhere to eat them? Do you fancy coming?"

Alex thought about the offer for a moment. "Tell you what, how about I show you a really nice place instead? It's not far from here, only about five minutes walk." Alex sighed as a wave of melancholy washed over her. "I doubt I'll get chance to go back there very often after I leave here."

Lorraine shrugged "Sure why not, lead the way. Just remember I've got to be back here after lunch for the afternoon shift."

Alex headed out the rear door, Lorraine in tow, as the pair made their way towards her retreat.

"It's a bit hard to find, probably why not many people know about it, but it's worth the effort, you'll see," Alex said glancing back at her companion.

Alex guided Lorraine through the back streets of the city centre and down a few narrow pathways nestled between crowded office blocks. As they rounded the final bend of the concrete jungle the beautiful vista of the secluded courtyard garden opened up before them.

"Wow, I never knew this was here!" Lorraine said. "No wonder hardly anyone knows about this place, there's no sign of it from the main road. It's completely hidden."

Alex smiled to herself as the pair walked through the opening.

"It's really peaceful isn't it?" Lorraine spoke again. "Hey thanks for bringing me here, it's lovely."

"Yeah, I like it. I come here quite often at lunch time, it helps me unwind," Alex replied. "I found it about a year ago, by accident really. It was marked on a map in the library. It was the only green area anywhere near to work, so I thought I'd have a look to see what it was."

"It's like walking into your own little oasis cut off from the world," Lorraine added as she twirled around.

Alex motioned towards her usual bench. The pair made their way over and settled down to eat.

"It's a shame you got made redundant, I was just getting to know you," Lorraine said before taking another bite of her sandwich. "Have you got any idea what you're going to do for work now?"

"No not really," Alex replied. "I haven't had much time to think about it. I'll be all right for a while but I do need to find something as soon as possible."

"I think it's going to be hard for you." Lorraine grimaced. "There doesn't seem to be much work going at the moment. Lots of people seem to have lost their jobs recently. You should see the amount of them on our estate."

"Actually I think I'm going to go sign up to do some volunteering in the mean time," Alex replied. "It'll look good on my CV and in any case hopefully something good might come from it."

Lorraine glanced at her watch after finishing her lunch.

"Well it's time for me to head back. Do you need to come back for anything?" Lorraine asked. "It's OK if you want to stay here. I can find my way back, I think," Lorraine giggled.

"I'm going to stay here, if you don't mind," Alex replied. "I'm worn out. I don't feel up to moving just yet. Are you sure you can find your way back all right?"

"Yeah I'll be fine, see you tomorrow," Lorraine waved as she made her way out of the garden.

Alex sat motionless on the bench listening to the birds and enjoying the tranquillity. She didn't notice when her eye lids started to close as the tiredness caught up with her.

A few cold drops of rain landing on her cheek woke Alex from her slumber. She looked down at her watch. It was nearly three in the afternoon. Alex rubbed her tired eyes with her finger tips and yawned. She did feel a bit better. The couple of hours sleep in the open air seemed to have done her good.

Alex heard the patter of a few more rain drops landing on her coat. I'd better make a move before the rain starts to really come down, she thought. She gathered up her things and put everything back into her bag. As she checked her pockets one last time her hand landed on bob's mobile phone. It was nice of him to lend it to her, she thought. I bet he's lost without it. Maybe I should drop it off on the way home. But... She cringed at the thought. She'd have to walk passed all those shops.

Alex threw her bag over her shoulder and started on her way back across town. The shopping centre where Bob worked wasn't that for away but it took her longer to get there than really necessary. Since the money had started getting tight she'd tried to avoid the temptation of going to those kinds of places. It took a lot of willpower for her to pass by the shops in the town centre. Alex cringed at the thought of all those window displays invitingly dressed with fancy new clothes and jewellery, trying to lure her in, seducing her in to spend hard earned money. The thought of all those things she couldn't afford made her feel worse. It made her heart ache again.

INHERENT STRAIN

Alex entered the shopping arcade at pace. A few people glanced up from their coffee mugs curious as to why this stranger seemed to be in such a hurry. Alex just kept her head down and tried her best to get through the experience as fast as possible. She was walking as fast as she dared without breaking into a jog. Running in public just didn't seem to be the done thing. The only people who did around here were almost always up to no good. Alex carried on through the brightly lit corridors. Passed shop after shop, trying not to look at the flashing neon signs, ignoring the massive red sale signs with their buy me now enticements. A few minutes later she arrived at the escalators and went down to the lower floor.

The store where bob worked was down there amongst the other less fashionable outlets, the ones that couldn't compete with the huge advertising budgets of the big boys. Still this area of the arcade was busy enough for them to get by. It attracted its own kind of clientele, the kind of people that perhaps weren't so main stream, those that seemed to have their own agendas.

Alex was surprised to see Bob behind the help desk as she walked into his store. His peripheral vision caught the movement breaking his concentration from his computer. He smiled with recognition as his eyes refocused on his friend.

"Hi," Bob's face lit up. "I wasn't expecting to see you here. What's up?"

"I thought I'd drop your phone off on my way home. I didn't want you getting withdrawal symptoms," Alex chuckled.

"Don't worry about it, what are friends for?" Bob replied.

"Thanks for lending it to me. I managed to sort it out. I got her an appointment for Tuesday next week. Maybe the doctors will be able to give her something stronger."

"Oh, well done," Bob smiled. "Thanks for bringing it me back. I probably would have overslept tomorrow. I use it for my alarm." Bob placed the phone back in his pocket. "Hey! I just remembered. It's your birthday on Saturday isn't it?"

The unexpected remark caused Alex a moment of panic as she racked her brain for the right reply.

"Er, is it?" She stalled. "I'd completely forgotten." Alex sighed as she took the news in. "I've got too many things to worry about at the moment," she replied and went silent. Another year gone and I'm still living like this, what am I going to do? She thought, trying not to let her expression give away to Bob what she was actually thinking.

"Have you got anything planned? I could throw you a surprise party, invite all our friends, things could get pretty wild," Bob chuckled.

Alex just stood there frowning.

"Come on let's do something, it's your birthday after all. Let's go out for a drink at least. It'll help you forget about things for a bit."

"You know what?" Alex sighed. "I could do with a drink, but not somewhere expensive this time, you know I can't afford it."

"Oh it's all right it's your birthday. I'll pay. My treat."

Before Alex could reply another potential customer entered the store stealing Bob's attention.

"I suppose I'd better get back to work. I need to finish installing some software before the client turns up." Bob's hands returned to his keyboard. "Thanks again for dropping my phone off. We can sort things out on Saturday. I'll come round in the day to make arrangements and drop your present off."

Alex said her goodbyes and, a little bewildered, headed off back through the perils of the arcade. By the time she exited back onto the street her mood had lifted. She actually had something to look forward to at the weekend. She made herself a mental note to remind her mother about her birthday. It upset her when she forgot about it.

Still feeling energetic after her nap and in a positive mood for a change, Alex decided to call into the Foodbank on the way home and offer to volunteer. If she put it off any longer she knew she'd never get around to it. The good intentions were always there but until she'd actually signed up she knew that's all they'd be.

The glass door complained as Alex pushed it open and stepped in. The foyer was small, set out as a simple waiting area. Cheap looking plastic chairs lined the side walls where a man and child sat waiting. Alex smiled a greeting as the man looked up at her, then made her way over to the desk where she'd met the elderly lady a few days earlier. This time she was greeted by a pleasant middle aged woman.

"Hi there, can I help with anything?"

"Hi, er... I came in a couple of days ago and spoke to an elderly lady about doing some voluntary work. I've decided I'd like to give it a go if I can," Alex replied.

"Oh good, I am glad. We need some fresh blood, so to speak," the lady grinned. "I'm sure we can find something to keep you busy. I'm Stacy by the way. I'm the manager." She held out a hand for Alex to shake. "I look after the running of this place."

"Oh... hi, nice to meet you, my name's Alex."

"Have you been told much about what we do here?" Stacy asked.

"Not really, I was given a leaflet that I've had a look through," Alex replied bracing herself for the sales pitch.

"Basically we're a Trust that was set up to provide a service for people suffering through hardship. We try to provide support and emergency food for people struggling to feed themselves and their family in a crisis. It's a short term solution to a big problem at the moment."

"I bet the recession has affected a lot of people around here just lately," Alex added. "That's why I want to help out if I can."

Stacy smiled. "Yes, it's hit a lot of families in the area but unfortunately we don't have enough resources to help everyone that walks through our front door."

"What do you mean?"

"The people we help here have been referred to us by other agencies that deal with poverty. Usually Social Services or the Citizens Advice Bureaux, sometimes the police or schools. They have to bring an authorised voucher in to us filled in with their personal details and signed by the agency that gave it to them." Stacy reached under the desk to retrieve a blank example and showed it to Alex. "If they don't have one, we can't give them any food."

Alex accepted the voucher and scanned it as Stacy continued talking.

"Our volunteers generally take the people through to the canteen and have a chat with them over a hot drink, and if we're able a meal, while we get their food ready," Stacy added.

"Oh, I didn't realise there was a canteen here," Alex said looking up from the voucher.

"Yes it's very useful. Some people we see haven't had a hot meal in days. They really seem to appreciate it."

Alex smiled again and passed the voucher back to Stacy.

"But there's a limit to what we can do here. We try to point people in the right direction to where they can get further help. Hopefully to find a more long term solution to their problems."

"Yeah I understand," Alex nodded.

"As for volunteering, we need help in a lot of areas. You could help us out front talking to people. You could work out back organising the food. You could even help out by collecting donations. What do you think you're good at?"

"Well I work in a supermarket, for the moment at least," Alex replied. "I'm used to sorting food out."

"Well that'll come in very useful here,"

Stacy beamed. "How much time do you think you'll be able to spare?"

"Hmm, I can manage a few hours most afternoons," Alex replied. "I just have to fit it around work and looking after my mother."

"Great, we need all the help we can get. Now if I could just get you to fill out your details on one of our forms, it will make it all nice and official." Stacy passed Alex a printed form and a pen. "It's just to make sure you're covered by our insurance, keeps things all above board."

Alex sat down and began to read through the form.

"When would you like to start? Stacy asked.

"Any time really." Alex shrugged her shoulders. "When do you need me?"

"If you can come back tomorrow that would be super," Stacy replied. "I just need to make sure there's someone here who can show you around. I'm very short staffed today I'm afraid."

"Yeah that's fine," Alex smiled as she handed the completed form back to Stacy. "I'll pop in again after work."

CHAPTER 5

The rain had started sometime during the night, the drawn out perpetual autumnal type, the seemingly never ending saturating drizzle that sucks the very life from the world. Alex greeted the monochromatic view from her window with distinct loathing. Her mind and body both wilting in unison. This is going to be a long day she thought as she let out a long audible sigh. Still at least the night had been uneventful for a change. Her mother hadn't been restless and Alex had at last managed to get some sleep. The soothing repetitive sound of the rain had helped muffle the irritating noises of the neighbourhood and calmed Alex's tired mind allowing her to slip into welcome unconsciousness.

Work had come and gone. The day seemed to have dragged more than usual. People spent the day going about their business absorbed in their own thoughts, the heavy sombre atmosphere affecting one and all. After work remembering her rather rash promise the day before, Alex made her way across town to the Foodbank.

Her hand hesitated on the cold door handle a few moments before depressing it. She took a deep breath then made the effort to push the front door open. She still felt unsure that what she was doing was the right thing, but she urged herself forwards. The prospect of saving some of that good karma up for herself kept her moving. After all she'd used up her fair share as a teenager hadn't she, she shuddered. Alex raised her eyes towards the front desk expecting to meet the gaze of the lady from yesterday... Stacy... was it? She tried to remember. Instead Alex was stopped dead in her tracks, taken aback by the unexpected greeting.

"Hello there, can I help you?" A pleasant deep manly voice said.

Alex stood motionless with one foot in the door, her hand still grasping the handle, transfixed by the stranger she saw before her.

"Come in, please, I won't bite." The stranger

smiled beckoning her inside. "Besides it's cold out there, you're letting all the heat out."

Alex could feel her heart thudding inside her chest, hear the blood gushing in her ears, it was a curious sensation. It took her a while to realise she wasn't breathing. The sensation started to ease as reality came flooding back. She snapped her open mouth shut, tried to smile and turned to close the door behind her.

"Sorry," Alex exclaimed. "I... I thought I'd got the wrong building." Alex lowered her head again.

It wasn't a great excuse but it was the best she could come up with on the spot and besides she wasn't about to admit the truth. She could feel her legs shaking as she made her way across the empty waiting room and over to the desk.

"Hi, I'm Alex," she blurted out. "Did Stacy tell you I was coming in today, to start volunteering? She was going to show me around."

Alex started to feel the unmistakable warmth of blood making its way through the capillaries in her face as her cheeks began to flush.

"Nice to meet you, I'm Stephen with a 'ph'." He started to chuckle, obviously aware of the affect he was having on this young lady. "Yes I was expecting you. Stacy told me you'd be calling in today. She's just been called out, you've got me for the rest of the day I'm afraid."

"Oh, OK er... good, I think," Alex muttered. She stood still, exposed, self-conscious. Sure her face was glowing like a beacon.

"Let me just call one of the others in to cover and we can get started."

The confident, rugged, handsome man rose from his seat and walked over towards the door at the back of the room. Alex took the opportunity to run her eyes up and down his heavily muscled physic as his back was turned. Who was this stranger that stood before her? Why was she so drawn towards him? She didn't know but she was aching to find out.

She followed Stephen through into the back room and guided the door shut behind her, not wanting to let it bang on her first day. Alex felt her anxiety beginning to play up, she was starting to hyperventilate. It was more pronounced than in most people. Being in uncertain environments with people she didn't know generally made her panic. Over the years she'd learned to gain some control over it. She took a brief moment to close her eyes, took another deep breath and composed herself before turning back towards Stephen.

The pair made their way along the small empty corridor that allowed access to many rooms in the building. Stephen pointed out the door to the staff room, toilets and side access to the canteen as they went. He came to a stop in front of the staff room door and eased it open just enough to pop his head around the corner.

"Boo..." Stephen shouted and began to laugh.

Alex heard the muffled sound of a chair squeaking followed by a coughing fit.

"James," Stephen said as the coughing calmed down. "Can you do me a favour and take over at the front desk? The new girl has arrived and I need to show her around."

Alex heard a surprised reply. "Oh... yeah, er... no problems mate." A few more coughs ensued. "I'll just get my things."

Stephen stepped back and Alex watched as the corpulent figure hobbled out through the door towards her.

"This is James." Stephen motioned towards the man in front of her.

"Nice to meet you, I'm Alex" she smiled and held out a hand.

"Same to you," the flustered voice replied as James struggled to adjust his cup of tea and biscuit into a single hand.

James soon disappeared out through the door towards the entrance after the brief handshake.

"He's a nice chap," Stephen said with a broad smile. "Makes me laugh. You can almost always find him in there. He's always sneaking out, blames it on his blood sugar levels." He chuckled to himself. "Nobody minds though, it's a friendly place, people do what they can to help out. Come on I'll show you the storage room," he motioned for Alex to follow. "Stacy mentioned you thought you could help out back?"

Alex caught herself staring for too long into Stephen's deep blue eyes and realised he was waiting for a reply.

"Yeah, sorry," she shook her head slightly to clear her thoughts. "I work, well for the moment at least, in a small supermarket. Have done for a couple of years now. So I think I should be able to help with organising and packing the food parcels."

"Good," Stephen said "we need all the help we can get. Over the last couple of months we've been getting inundated with increasing numbers of needy people. It's all we can do to keep up."

Stephen led the way through and out the main door at the end of the corridor. Alex followed eager not to be left behind. The space opened up into a cavernous store room lined from floor to ceiling with rows of metal shelves stacked high with tins and packets of food.

A loud deafening bang rang out behind Alex that seemed to echo for an age around the room. Three or was it four people stopped what they were doing and turned around to see who it was. Alex closed her eyes, her face flushing bright red as she realised she'd let the door slam.

"Yeah, you have to watch out for that one," Stephen said, still his jubilant self. "I should have warned you."

"Sorry I... er... got distracted," Alex replied.

"Don't worry about it, no harm done. You needed to meet everyone in any case." He chuckled. "You've just got their undivided attention. Why not introduce yourself to them all at once?" Stephen was still laughing when he patted Alex on her shoulder.

"Sorry," Alex repeated, her hands covering her glowing face.

"You apologise a lot don't you? There's no need to worry," Stephen teased. "We're all friends here."

"Oh do I..." Alex's anxiety was playing up. She couldn't think straight. She couldn't think of anything else to say. "Sorry," she repeated once more cursing at herself.

Stephen giggled again.

"It's just when I'm feeling a bit anxious. I'll be OK in a moment." Alex tried to concentrate on her breathing. "Carry on I'll keep up. I don't think it's actually possible to die from embarrassment."

"Isn't it?" Stephen said.

Alex was just about to explain why, when she

spotted his smirk.

"So how much did Stacy tell you about what we do here?" Stephen asked.

"Oh, I think I just got the sales pitch," Alex replied. "She seemed very busy, just had time to run through the basics with me. She looked really stressed out, she was very polite though."

"Yeah, like I said, we need all the help we can get," Stephen said. "Some days there's only a few of us that can make it and there's never a let up in the demand for help," Stephen added, a little withdrawn looking off into the distance. "Well anyway," he shook his head "all the food we have here has been donated either directly from the public or been collected via churches or schools. You know those sorts of places. Sometimes if we have enough people we can arrange a stand or two somewhere special."

"I take it all the items get brought here to be sorted?" Alex asked looking around at the stacked shelves. "That must mean you're never sure what stock you're going to receive? Must be hard to deal with, at least in the supermarket we always know what to expect?"

"It can be a little tricky to sort out but it's not too bad once you get used to it. I'm sure you'll be able to cope."

Stephen continued to show Alex around, making

sure to point out how the goods were collated and stored in groups ready to be packed. He also stopped to introduce her to a few other members of the team that were helping to make up food parcels.

Three young looking fresh faced volunteers were busy sorting out various tins of soup and preserved fruit, dividing them between different cardboard boxes. They couldn't have been more than twenty. The trio took the chance to have a brief rest from their duties as Stephen and Alex approached.

"These hard workers are Melissa and Jennifer, Mal and Jen for short and this is Garry. They're all students from the university. They come in when they can. Hey guys, this is Alex she's offered to lend us a hand," Stephen said knowing they would be glad of the help. "I'm sure you three can teach her the ropes next week."

"Great, the more the merrier," Garry said as he wiped his forehead with the back of his sleeve.

"What course are you doing?" Mel asked smiling at Alex. "We're both in first year social studies."

"Oh, I'm not a student anymore," Alex said a little perplexed. "I finished a few years ago, I did a business degree."

"Oh, sorry. You look young for you age then,"

Mel replied with a cheeky smile. "I thought you'd have still been studying."

Alex's face beamed, it wasn't often she got complimented by strangers. In fact she wasn't sure that it was sincere, but she was taking it anyway.

"See I told you everyone's friendly here. You'll fit in just fine," Stephen said continuing the tour. "Next I think I'll show you the canteen, you can have a look at what happens in the front of the building and meet a few of the other people."

Stephen, with Alex dutifully in tow, completed the circuit around the store room and back towards the way they'd come. Alex was trying to concentrate, trying to be attentive taking mental notes as they went, but her thoughts were wandering. What was it about the man in front of her that she was so drawn to? His good looks, his husky voice, she wasn't that shallow, was she? It had to be more than that, it had to be, she couldn't think straight.

"How did you hear about the Foodbank?" Stephen asked.

"I saw the coloured sign in the window the other day on my way home from work. It kind of caught my eye."

"Ah ha, I told her that would work!" Stephen said grinning. "It's the usual policy not draw too much attention from the street. It makes it easier for the needy people. You know... if the building blends into the background. Most of the public don't know we're here so the people who need us aren't afraid to be seen coming in."

"Yeah, you're right about that. It's definitely plain from the outside. I must have passed it hundreds of times on my way home and never noticed it."

Stephen chuckled as the pair continued to walk.

"I usually make my way straight home. I need to care for my mother. She finds it difficult to look after herself. But I suppose that day was different, I was in a good mood for a change. I thought I'd call in just to have a look if I could help and, well, here I am back again."

"Oh I see..." Stephen said. "What's wrong with your mother, if you don't mind me asking? Maybe there's someone here who could help."

"Oh, she's got Alzheimer's," Alex's heart sank. "Some days are worse than others, some days she can almost be back to normal and then the next she's completely gone again."

"What about the rest of your family, can any of them lend a hand?"

"No," Alex sighed. "My mother and I are the only ones left I'm afraid, there's no one else who could help."

"Oh dear," Stephen frowned. "Well then, maybe you could bring her here for an afternoon, after the rush that is. There's a few people here I'm sure wouldn't mind keeping her out of trouble for you for a few hours. It'd give you a break. Don't worry she'll be fine. We're used to dealing with difficult situations."

"Yeah, that would be nice." Alex felt her mood lighten.

"I've only got one parent as well," Stephen said with half a smile. "I can't remember my mother. She died when I was very young. It's just me and my father now. He never met anyone else. I think losing her affected him too much."

Alex's heart skipped a beat, they had something in common. OK it wasn't a great thing but at least it was a start.

As they approached the door to the canteen Stephen came to a stop and turned to face Alex. "Hey, you know that thing I should have warned you about earlier?"

Alex nodded in agreement.

"Well this is another one, remember to knock." He grinned and pushed the door inwards. "You'll see why."

The door opened directly into the small busy kitchen. An elderly lady stood with a stern look on her face just outside the doors reach with a large saucepan of hot soup in her hands. She kept her eyes locked onto Stephen as they entered.

"Sorry for the interruption ladies. I'm just showing the new volunteer, Alex around." He turned back towards Alex covered his mouth with his hand and whispered. "She's never forgiven me for knocking the cake out of her hands a couple of months ago."

"Oh, I better remember to knock then," Alex chuckled. Perhaps the door banging wasn't so embarrassing after all.

Alex looked out through the large serving hatch into the canteen. Quite a large number of people sat huddled in groups around different dining tables. A few of them seemed to be going through notes on their clip boards. Alex soon realised those must have been the other volunteers Stephen mentioned.

Alex's attention was brought back to the kitchen as the two cooks introduced themselves.

The elderly lady was first to speak.

"Oh, now I remember you dear," her face lit up. "You came in at the beginning of the week. I'm glad you decided to come back to help out."

"Ah, was it you? Sorry, I didn't recognise you there for a moment," Alex replied. "You've had your hair done, it looks nice." Alex raised a hand up to her own hair and twisted some between her fingers. "I haven't had time to get mine done yet."

"You two are just in time," the elderly lady grinned as she passed two bowls of hot soup towards Alex and Stephen.

"Oh no, I'm not hungry thanks," Alex blurted out.

"It's not for you silly," Stephen laughed. "It's for the people out there, it's serving up time."

Alex's face started to warm up again.

Stephen led the way out into the canteen and over to the nearest occupied table. "We need to bring them some bread and butter. Oh and today we can offer them some cheese on toast if they'd prefer. We try to give everyone that comes here a warm meal but some days we've more to offer than others. It depends what perishable items the supermarkets have donated."

Alex and Stephen soon finished serving the visitors. At the last table Stephen asked if the volunteer would mind coming to join them. Alex followed Stephen and the middle aged man towards a vacant table in the corner of the room. He introduced her as they made themselves comfortable.

"This is Alex, a new volunteer," Stephen said to Graham before turning back to Alex. "Graham is a part time social worker. He likes to help out from time to time and we're very grateful to him for it." Stephen patted him on the shoulder.

"He's able to help out with the more challenging cases." He turned back to Graham. "Would you mind telling Alex a bit about how you help out here?"

"Well, er... for a start we have to try to treat each case individually," Graham said. "People have their own stories to tell and their situations can be completely different from one another. Most of them aren't so straight forward. You'll find the people referred here are usually suffering from mental distress as well as physical. I find it helps if they have someone to talk to."

Alex nodded along as Graham continued to talk.

"Even if they aren't to blame they can suddenly find themselves in situations totally out of their control. I suppose some people just get a run of bad luck."

Alex felt herself starting to smirk.

"I try to understand what they're going through. Hopefully I can point them in the right direction, maybe help change their lives around."

Alex continued to nod along in agreement. It was nice to hear an unbiased point of view from a social worker. She had to admit it to herself, the last time she'd met one was a long time ago and it wasn't a pleasant experience.

"Take the last couple I was with. They have two small children to look after, bills and a mortgage to pay. The man was the sole provider in the family and had worked all his adult life for the postal service. Twenty years he'd been there and then six months ago they made him redundant. He's been looking for a job ever since. Recently he's had his job seekers benefit stopped. They've no savings left and are about to lose their house."

"That's horrible!" Alex said.

"I know," Graham continued. "I hear similar stories nearly every day, it's sole destroying. The Foodbank can provide them with some immediate food and some supplies for the next couple of days, but we're only supposed to help them out three times, after that they need to be dealt with by a different organisation."

Alex's head dropped as Graham rose from his seat. Stephen thanked him for his time before he strolled back over to the other table.

"Hey, keep your chin up. It's not always so depressing here," Stephen chuckled. "The visitors are always so appreciative of us helping them. Anyway we find ways to amuse ourselves when it's quietened down, you'll see."

Alex looked up at Stephen and his mischievous grin, transfixed again by a man she hardly knew.

"Will you be able to come in tomorrow?" Stephen asked.

"Sorry I can't I'm afraid," Alex smiled. "I

usually take my mother out around town on Fridays. Helps get her out of the house for a few hours. We call in at the library so I can exchange a few books and then spend the rest of the afternoon in the museum. It's a lot quieter in the week than at the weekend, so I can let her wander around on her own for a bit.

"Ah OK," Stephen muttered.

"Are you open at the weekend?" Alex asked.

"No, afraid not, we don't have the funding to open every day. It's not for want of trying though. It's hard to close up knowing people will go hungry," Stephen sighed. "But we can only stretch ourselves so far."

The pair made their way across the canteen towards the public access back into the waiting room.

"Well that's it for the grand tour, not much else I can show you," Stephen said before stopping and turning to face Alex. "So what do you think? Do you think you'll fit in here?"

"I'll be back, don't worry. The people seem really nice..." she lingered looking up at the handsome man in front of her. "I've got plenty of spare time to fill."

"Good," Stephen laughed.

"What do you do for the rest of the time, when you're not volunteering here I mean?" Alex asked. "You look quite fit, do you work out?"

Stephen glanced down smiling.

Realising she was reaching her hand out towards Stephen's arm Alex quickly snapped it back towards her waist, her face began to flush again. "Sorry, I er... you had something on your sleeve." Alex cursed at herself under her breath.

"Yeah, you could say that," Stephen chuckled. "I work for my father. He owns his own gym so I get to work out a lot. You should come over sometime. Maybe we can help put some muscle on those bones."

"I used to work out you know, I haven't always been this skinny." Alex frowned. "It's only since I've had to look after my mother," she snapped. "Sorry I've got too much to worry about at the moment and hardly any spare money as it is."

"Hey don't take it the wrong way, I didn't mean it like that. Working out is good for you, it helps improve your mood." Stephen smiled again. "Look if you feel like it you're welcome to come along, no charge, while you're volunteering of course. Bring your friends along too. We could do with the extra numbers."

"Hmm... we'll see, maybe if I can persuade some of my friends to come along too," Alex offered. "I'll think about it." It wasn't such a bad idea. She used to work out when she was younger, she used to enjoy it.

Alex's mother had made her go to self defence and mixed martial arts classes for years despite how often she'd protested. She'd excelled well beyond what her small stature portrayed, never losing a fight no matter how much the size difference. The problem was though people got hurt, something she'd gained a reputation for a long time ago, something that had led to her coming to the attentions of a certain thug of a lady called Cat.

Alex said her goodbyes and walked out onto the street. The clouds were still thick above her and the night was drawing in but at least it had stopped raining. She pulled her hood up, gathered it in around her cold neck as best she could and set off. She wasn't looking forward to the walk home.

CHAPTER 6

"Happy birthday sweetie," Alex's mother said as she bent down to kiss her daughter on the forehead.

Alex opened her eyes. "Mum! You remembered."

"I wrote myself a note," her mother chuckled.

Alex turned to look at the clock. It read 11:30am. She double checked, it still read 11:30am. Oh my God, she thought, I slept in, finally. Well it is my birthday after all, she smiled and stretched.

Alex's mother picked up a large soft pillow like parcel from the floor and placed it on Alex's lap.

"Here you go, I made you a present," her mother grinned. "Come on open it, I want to see if you like it."

Alex looked down at the unexpected gift. It had been neatly wrapped in shiny paper with a 'Happy Birthday' motif and tied with a red ribbon.

"Oh mum you didn't have to, thank you." Alex looked at her mother. "When did you get the gift wrap?"

"Yesterday, when I wandered off," she smiled again. "You've no idea how difficult it was to hide a role of wrapping paper," she laughed.

Alex found the seam in the corner and ripped the multicoloured wrapping paper off to reveal a bundle of knitted items. She reached in and pulled out a hat, scarf and a thick woollen jumper. They were a nice surprise, all the same colour, plain save for a simple matching decoration, but well made nonetheless. Her mother had always been good with crafts. Her condition hadn't robbed everything from her yet.

"Thanks mum, they're perfect." Alex reached up and gave her a hug. "I needed some more warm clothes. Oh, did I remind you Bob was coming around in a bit?" Alex added. "He wants to drop my present off and make the arrangements for tonight."

"Which ones Bob again honey?"

"He's the one that comes to visit, a lot. You like him, you've met him loads of times."

"Oh, OK dear if you say so," Margaret's voice trailed off as she started towards the door. "Oh, oh yes, he's the nice lad that follows you around?" She said half turning back towards Alex. "What's happening tonight?

"He's invited me out for a drink to celebrate. Nothing extravagant. I'm quite looking forward to it actually."

"Yeah that's him." Margaret was smiling again. "I can picture him now, treats you like a queen. Yes I like him, nice guy." She looked at Alex out the corner of her eye. "Still single is he?"

"Yes mum, he's still single," Alex tutted.

Alex got dressed and went into the kitchen to prepare lunch. She needed to get things ready for Bob's arrived. She glanced up at the clock on the wall. It read 12:10pm. She needed to hurry. She made up a spread of different sandwiches and a few nibbles and then retrieved the small chocolate fudge cake from the fridge and placed it in the centre of the table.

Margaret attached a banner across the living room and began to blow up some birthday balloons to make the place look more fitting for a party.

A knock at the door signalled the arrival of Alex's friend and Margaret to welcome their guest.

"Hi skinny," she teased as she opened the door. "Nice to see you again, thanks for coming."

"I won't be long," Alex waved, "I'm nearly finished."

"I'll just pop your presents down here, OK birthday girl?" Bob said raising his voice at the end.

"Yeah, thanks," Alex smiled. "Grab yourself a drink. I think there's some juice in the fridge or I'll put the kettle on in a minute if you'd prefer."

"The juice will be fine, thanks. I'm still hot from walking," Bob replied as he walked over to pour himself a drink of orange juice. "Is there anything I can do to help?"

"No don't worry, relax a bit," came Margaret's strained reply. "We're nearly finished."

BANG... the noise of an over filled balloon exploding rang out around the room.

"Damn thing," Margaret muttered under her breath. "I can never get the knot right on these."

Alex and Bob both started to chuckle.

"Oh well it was the last one anyhow," Alex said to her mother. "Don't worry about it."

Alex retrieved Bob's bag of presents and went to sit next to him on the couch. Grinning she removed a small oblong box, lifted it to her ear and gave it a little shake.

"Maybe some jewellery," she guessed.

Underneath the wrapping lay a nice surprise. Bob had got her a new mobile phone.

"Oh wow, that's, that's great, thanks." She leaned over and hugged her friend, then kissed him without thinking on the side of his cheek.

"I'm glad you like it," Bob said starting to blush. "Now you don't have to keep borrowing mine," he laughed. "It's a pay as you go. I've already put some credit on for you, enough to keep you going for a while."

Alex placed the phone down on the table then returned her hands to the bag. Two more neatly wrapped parcels remained. "The other one," Bob whispered.

Alex pulled out the slimmer more elongated package and shook it against her ear but couldn't hear anything suggestive.

"It's an eBook reader," Bob said with a smile as Alex ripped off the wrapping. "I know you like reading. I thought it might help you relax at night." He pointed to the box. "It's got its own light so you don't need to have your lamp on. I can transfer some books from my computer if you'd like, just bring it along with you when you come around."

"Thanks again it's very thoughtful," Alex

replied. "But you didn't need to spend so much money on me."

"Who else am I going to spend it on?" Bob grinned. "I just like seeing you happy that's all."

Alex considered the gift, it was thoughtful. She just wasn't sure about reading books on computers. She could see there were benefits but she still liked the idea of owning something physical. She'd give it a go though. After all, it might just make it easier to get to sleep at night.

"The last ones for your mother," Bob whispered, "I thought it'd cheer her up."

"That's sweet of you," Alex said before calling her mother over. "Here you go Mum. Bob got you a little something as well."

Margaret sat down in the vacant chair and unwrapped her unexpected present. A broad smile formed as she removed the notebook and studied the picture on the front.

"It tells you what plants are in flower each month and suggests where you might find them," Bob said leaning forwards.

"Thank you, it's lovely," Margaret said. "I'll go put it on the shelf out of the way until after we eat." She walked around the back of the settee and placed a hand on Alex's shoulder. "I like this one," she whispered in her ear, winked and carried on walking.

"You don't mind us going out later do you mum?" Alex called after her.

"No honey, it's all right. You two young people go out and have fun. I'll be fine here. I found a video I want to watch anyway."

Alex and Bob took her hungry mother's hint and followed her over to the table.

"This looks nice," Bob grinned, "but are you sure you had to go to the effort of cutting the sandwiches into dainty little triangles?" He said as he picked one up, eyeing it with suspicion.

After the plates had almost been cleared Bob pulled a small bag of birthday candles out of his pocket and arranged them on the cake.

"There won't be much room left soon if you keep ageing like this," he chuckled. "You'll have to get a bigger cake."

Alex cuffed him around the back of his head for his troubles.

Margaret stood up and still giggling went over to draw the curtains. Then brought a cigarette lighter back from the kitchen to light the candles.

Alex reached over to blow the candles out as soon as Margaret lit them.

"What do you think you're doing?" Margaret snapped. "We haven't sung happy birthday yet."

"Oh mum do you have to... really?"

"Yes," she laughed, "it's part of the fun."

"So what's the plan for later?" Alex asked Bob after the cake was finished.

"I was thinking we'd take a trip to the 'Wild Boar Inn' if you're all right with that? It's nice there, I like it. I could invite some of my buddies too if you want?"

"Yeah I like it too, it's nice and quiet there, but if you don't mind I'd prefer you didn't invite your friends. I never know what to talk to them about. I don't know anything about science fiction. They make me feel really dumb."

"OK no problem, I'll be round to pick you up at eight with a taxi waiting, so be ready." He smiled and made his exit.

Alex spent the next couple of hours trying to dye her hair in the bathroom using a sachet she'd picked up the day before. She couldn't afford the expense of getting it done at the hairdressers so this was the next best thing.

Soon it was time to get ready for the night out. It had been a while since the last time and she was out of practice. She found it more difficult than usual to pick out a suitable outfit. It wasn't easy to hide how skinny she'd become, but at least the cold weather gave her the excuse to cover up. She even struggled to choose a pair of shoes. The high heels caught her eye, but they weren't going to a club, just a themed tavern, it didn't seem appropriate.

By the time she'd chosen, her bedroom was covered in rejected clothes, thrown in frustration and left were they fell. Handbags, belts and odd shoes littered the floor making it almost hazardous to walk.

An unfamiliar noise startled Alex. It took her a few seconds to realise her new phone was ringing. She found it beneath a pile of dresses on her bed and fumbled to find the right button to answer the call.

"Hi there birthday girl, you didn't expect me to knock did you?" Bob said. "Hurry up I'm downstairs waiting in the taxi."

"OK, I just need another minute," Alex replied. "I'll be down as quick as I can." She grabbed a few things, stuffed them into her bag and rushed towards the front door.

"Are you sure you'll be all right on your own tonight mum?" Alex shouted.

"Yes I'll be fine, don't worry about me," came the reply. "I think I'll be in bed soon anyway I can feel another headache coming on. Have a good time."

"OK, bye mum, see you later."

"OK honey, love you. Have fun," Margaret shouted as Alex disappeared out of the door.

Alex rushed along the flickering corridor and leaped down one flight of stairs after another.

"Hey there precious," an unwelcome voice sounded from around the corner. "Where are you off to in such a hurry?"

"Oh, hi there Cat. Sorry I can't stop, I'm late." Alex's voice echoed along with her thundering footsteps.

"You look nice tonight," a quiet voice replied, but Alex didn't notice, she was already another two flights down ignoring the distraction.

Bob was standing against the side of the taxi tapping his wrist watch as Alex burst out onto the street.

"Sorry," Alex said catching her breath. "I tried to be as quick as I could."

A little over fifteen minutes later they arrived at their destination. The driver having taken them out of their urban surroundings and way out into the countryside. Bob tipped the driver and was first out of the taxi. He ran around to open the door for Alex, holding out a small umbrella over her head as she stepped out. Together the pair strode across the cobbled street admiring the view.

The 'Wild Boar Inn' was an exceedingly old building that had hardly changed at all over the centuries. It was about as authentic as a 'Ye Olde' experience could get. Even its location seemed to fit perfectly. Nestled at the end of a long drive that wound its way serenely through an ancient wood. The inn was part of a small cluster of buildings extending out from the side of a steep limestone rock face. The deep ochre colour of a few old fashioned street lamps bathed the front of the majestic building in a warm inviting glow, while the backdrop was lit by a cluster of spot lights accentuating the eerie shadows of trees leaning over the cliff towards them.

The flickering amber glow of candle and fire light greeted Alex and Bob as they pushed the heavy wooden front door open. The warmth of a roaring open fire hit their skin and the intoxicating smell of old wood and leather heavily laden with the sweet scent of whiskey filled their nostrils.

As Bob closed the door a waitress pointed the pair over to the last vacant spot in the busy tavern. Alex's eyes followed the waitress's finger towards the empty booth in the corner. It looked very inviting, almost like it had been fashioned in a natural stone alcove. Alex thought it strange as she scanned the heads of the already seated customers, why hadn't it already been taken? The pair sat down opposite each other on the well-warn leather covered benches. Between them half a whiskey barrel had been converted into a simple table on which sat a small flickering beeswax candle.

It wasn't long before the same pleasant waitress came over to take their order. Bob didn't need to look at the menu. He ordered a sharing meat platter and a bottle of red wine.

When the waitress returned she placed two simple silver beakers on the table and opened the accompanying ceramic flagon which surprisingly contained the wine. Then came the food, a spread of various cuts of roast and cured meat with a freshly baked round loaf of bread alongside.

"This is lovely!" Alex said. "It's perfect, thank you."

"Save room for desert," Bob grinned as he offered her a piece of bread he'd just carved.

When they were finished the waitress cleared away the table and asked if they'd like another drink. Alex smiled and nodded.

"Can we have the other bottle please?" Bob asked grinning again.

What seemed like only a few seconds later, the sound of people clapping made Alex turn around. Her mouth dropped open. The whole tavern was watching the waitress as she walked towards them carrying another birthday cake. She was being followed by a minstrel playing a familiar tune on his lute. Alex's face changed to a colour closely matching the fire as all at once the tavern burst out into a chorus of Happy Birthday.

After a brief serenade, the waitress brought

the pair the next bottle of wine and Alex took a large gulp without even giving it time to breathe. Bob leaned back and chuckled to himself with a satisfied look on his face.

"I knew you'd have a good time," he grinned.

After the last of the dishes were cleared away the conversation turned back to their real world problems.

"Your mother looked a lot better today," Bob said. "How's her treatment going?"

"Yeah, she was happy today. I think she felt good about being able to surprise me for a change," Alex replied. "Like I said, some days it almost seems like she's back to normal and then all of a sudden she'll get a bad turn and we'll be back to square one again."

"It must be tough, I can't imagine having to look after my parents," Bob replied. "Hey perhaps you'd like to come with me when I go to visit them next summer."

"I don't know. It'd depend on how my mother is and well... Spain... it's too hot," Alex said pondering the idea. "I'll think about it though. I can't remember the last time I had a holiday." Alex's expression changed, she became pale as the blood flowed away from her face.

"What's up?" Bob asked.

"Did I tell you they'd made me redundant at work?" Alex blurted out. "I only have another two weeks left. I don't know what I'm going to do. Where the hell am I going to find another job now?" she said raising her voice.

"That's awful," Bob said cringing. "I thought you were doing all right there?"

"It wasn't anything to do with me, nothing like that, just cutbacks," Alex replied. "They couldn't afford to keep paying all the temporary staff, so that was me screwed over."

"Hey come on now, don't be like that. You'll get another job I'm sure of it," Bob said leaning across the table to put a comforting hand on her shoulder. "Cheer up it's your birthday."

"Yeah, I suppose you're right," Alex sighed. "I'm sorry I bought it up, I was trying not to. I guess I'm not used to the alcohol any more. Speaking of which," Alex said grinning as she picked the vessel up, shaking it from side to side, "it's empty again."

"Oh dear," Bob replied. "Well we'd better do something about that then hadn't we?"

Another bottle of red wine and two hours later Bob's phone rang. The taxi was waiting for them outside.

"I arranged everything earlier," Bob replied to Alex's unasked question.

"You know sometimes you really amaze me," Alex said. "Thank you for tonight. I did have a good time."

Bob paid the bill as agreed and the pair meandered out into the icy cold of the night air.

On the way home Bob asked the taxi driver to drop them off a few streets early, insisting the walk would sober them up. Bob stumbled out onto the street as the taxi slowed to a stop. Alex followed a few seconds later trying to maintain her composure.

"I guess some of us can't handle our drink," she teased.

Bob was still refuting his drunken state and fumbling with a loose shoe lace as the taxi drove off into the distance. Alex stood still, arms folded across her chest trying to retain a little warmth, amused at his plea of innocence. She took a moment to take in her surroundings. The night sky above was clear. The reflected light from the full moon brightened up the sleepy street. It was quiet, empty, still. Not even wind broke the silence.

"Are you ready to get started then?" Bob asked as he stood up.

"Yeah we'd better be getting back, it's getting late," Alex said glancing down at her shoes, glad she'd decided against the heels.

Bob put his arm around his friend and the pair started their slow walk home.

"How's the volunteering going?" Bob asked.

"OK thanks," Alex replied. "They've shown me

around the place and I've found out what I need to do. I'll start properly next week."

"That's good. What are the people like?" Bob asked. "I hope you can make a few more friends, I don't like seeing you lonely."

"They seem nice and anyway I'm not lonely," Alex grinned and punched him in the arm. "I've got you haven't I?"

"I was just a bit worried," Bob smiled. "I'm saying this as a friend, so don't take it the wrong way, OK? You've been on your own for a long time now. I just think you could do with someone to help out now and again. When was the last time you had a serious boyfriend?"

Alex's face started to redden. She had to admit to herself it'd definitely been a long time. "Oh don't you start as well. I have enough of it from my mother, I'm fine honestly."

"If you say so," Bob chuckled. "What type of man do you like?"

"You're not going to let it go are you?" Alex tried to protest. "Did my mother put you up to this?"

Bob's expression didn't change. He just kept his teasing stare up. Alex gave in.

"Well there's this one guy I met the other day, he's tall handsome and really fit," Alex's eyes lit up. "You should see his arms they're like tree trunks."

"Ah, OK, you like guys like that do you?" Bob's shoulders sagged. "Well at least you've someone in mind," Bob's voice trailed off as he quickened the pace. "Let's hurry up a bit shall we, it's getting cold."

They were still chatting together as they neared Alex's apartment block. The road ahead was empty apart from one black SUV parked right outside the entrance to the building. Even the taxi Alex had noticed in the street every night was nowhere to be seen. As they got closer to the vehicle, she could hear its engine idling but its blacked out windows prevented her from seeing any movement within.

"That's odd," she said turning to her friend.

People didn't hang around in these parts unless they had a good reason for it, or a bad one... she flinched at the thought. As the pair passed the rear of the vehicle Alex heard the passenger door open. She griped Bob's arm.

A tall, bald man in a dark business like suit stepped out. He strolled around the back of the SUV and onto the street behind them. Alex glanced behind her at the stranger. His piercing stare was familiar. She'd seen him before. She felt her heart starting to race. The front door to the apartment block swung open in front of them. Another smaller man in a suit stepped out into the street blocking their path. Alex glanced back again. The tall man continued to close from the rear.

"Miss Forster," A deep voice said. "We'd like to have a word with you."

Alex's heart stopped.

CHAPTER 7

Alex froze, she thought about running but they were boxed in. The door to the SUV's rear compartment swung open.

"Miss Forster, we need to have a word with you." The command came again, more forceful this time.

Alex heard the engine start to rev.

"Please step into the vehicle Miss Forster," a different voice called from inside.

"What, who are you?" Alex shouted. "What do you want?"

Bob, now feeling suddenly sober, had found his phone in his pocket and was desperately trying to make his fingers find the right keys to dial for help.

"Miss Forster I won't ask you again. Please step into the vehicle." Another warning came as the suited men closed to within reaching distance of their intended target.

The smaller man snapped his head towards Bob. "I wouldn't do that if I were you," he growled, grabbing Bob's shoulder with his free hand. The other stranger started to reveal the unmistakable shape of a handgun concealed within his jacket.

Alex's mind raced. Whoever these people were she didn't want to find out and she damn well wasn't going to get in that truck without a fight. She felt the familiar pounding in her chest as adrenaline began to surge through her blood stream. She knew what she had to do, she'd done it before, but she only had a split second to react.

With far more power than what her diminutive stature portrayed her arm swung out towards the smaller man's face. Throwing all of her bodyweight behind the well practised manoeuvre her elbow connected with a sickening thud. It found its target, the stranger's soft exposed vulnerable throat. The assailant collapsed unconscious unable to breathe. Through her peripheral vision Alex saw the shot coming from behind but couldn't avoid it. She reacted instinctively with a reverse hook kick, her heal connecting with a crack on the tall strangers temple.

She felt her feet connect with the tarmac as she landed. She tried to regain her balance but it was more difficult than it should have been, something was wrong. She looked around, both men were unconscious. The squeal of complaining tyres distracted her, she watched as the SUV disappeared into the distance. It was over, for now at least. In that moment, as her mind allowed her body to relax, a wave of unbearable pain began to sweep through her body. She looked down at her chest. Warm blood was soaking through her jacket. Her knees began to buckle. The street lights began to dim as her vision narrowed. Alex thought she heard the fading voice of her shocked friend as she slipped into unconsciousness.

"Oh my God Alex. Are you all right?" The voice echoed from far out into the darkness and then everything was gone.

Bob was trembling as he caught her falling body. He laid Alex down, she'd stopped breathing, a slow trickle of blood flowed from her mouth. His brain searched his memories in desperation for anything to do with first aid. He checked her pulse. There was still a faint heart beat. He locked his lips over her mouth and began to blow. He watched as her chest raised and fell. A horrible gurgling sound emanated from somewhere beneath her clothes. He began again watching as her chest rose. A sudden spluttering cough stopped him. Alex wheezed. Her eyes fluttered. Bob leaned back wiping the blood from his mouth. His friend was alive.

Alex began to open her eyes. Again and again her face was bathed in a strange blue light. She could hear a muffled siren. Someone must have been hurt. Her tired confused mind tried to make sense of what was happening. Her body ached.

"You'll be all right, don't worry," a comforting voice whispered in her ear from out of the fog. "We'll have you fixed up in no time."

Her memory was hazy. She tried to get up. A sharp shooting pain ran up her back. She tried to move her arms, something was holding her back. What was going on? She tried to clear her thoughts. Where was she? Her vision was beginning to clear. The blurred images started to come into focus. She was lying on a bed... in the middle of the street... surrounded by people. She was moving, being carried. Anxiety started to replace the confusion.

The sweet voice of a paramedic grabbed her attention.

"Hey there, glad you could join us. It's lucky your friend was here, I don't know how he managed to stop the bleeding."

Her memory was clearing, images flashed into her mind. Bob's smiling face, the tavern, and the walk home. The strangers, the fight, her heart began to thud again.

"Bob," she tried to call out, but her voice was too weak.

She coughed to clear her lungs, the wheeze was gone.

"I'm here," a hand grasped hers, "don't worry."

Alex felt herself rising. The gloomy street was being replaced by the strange clean white interior of an ambulance. The stretcher came to a stop with a slight jolt. A paramedic began attaching instruments to her body. She was being hooked up to machines. Alex started to hyperventilate.

"Wait," Alex shouted. "What about my mother? Someone needs to tell her that I'm all right." She tried to struggle, alarms started to sound.

"I'm going to have to sedate her." A voice rang out.

"Wait, no..." she struggled. The haze was returning, the pain subsiding.

A friendly face came into focus above her. Bob hushed her. She felt his warm hand stroking her forehead. She felt her muscles relaxing, the tiredness was returning. She tried to concentrate on the tear stained face, she couldn't hold on.

She thought she heard his fading voice, but the darkness was beckoning again.

"Alex, Alex, can you hear me? I've got some bad news." His voice was choked, hard to understand. Someone was closing the doors. A siren sounded in the street. A police escort, the ambulance was leaving. Alex was trying hard to concentrate. The ambulance disappeared from view as the doors slammed shut. It didn't make sense, her befuddled mind wasn't working.

"Who was that..? Wait who was in that?" Alex's quiet voice trailed off as her body succumbed to the drugs. Her head fell back limp on the pillow.

When Alex awoke for the second time, the journey was all ready over. The room was quiet, the white lights dimmed. The bed sheets smelled clean, fresh, and clinical. She eased herself up and looked around. A hospital ward, people were sleeping. It must have been sometime in the night. Something tugged at her hand as she tried to move the sheets. Her hand throbbed. She looked down and studied her body. Needles and tubes were in her skin. She still felt dazed but there was no longer any pain. She wondered how close to the edge she'd been.

It was an unfamiliar environment to Alex. She'd always been the healthy one. She'd never needed any sort of treatment herself before. She never got sick, not ever, not even a cold. As a child she'd watched as the other children around her at school were overcome by illness after illness and still nothing. She never suffered when there was the outbreak of measles. She'd never even managed to pick up chickenpox. She recalled how other parents would warn her mother about how it would have been better to get it out of the way while she was still young. She'd been lucky once or twice with car accidents, narrowly avoiding serious injuries. No broken bones, just a few minor sprains and strains. It always seemed to be someone else who got hurt, not her.

Alex heard the clinking footsteps first as a nurse made her way towards her. The quietness of the ward accentuating her steps across the hard cold surface. Alex greeted her with a smile.

"I'm glad you've woken up dear," the nurse said. "You gave us all a bit of a fright last night."

"Wha... What happened?" Alex croaked.

"Don't you remember dear? You were shot. We didn't think you'd make it."

Alex clutched her chest remembering the searing pain.

"Your condition is stable now. The bleeding had stopped by the time you arrived. The doctors said they didn't find any internal bleeding either, just a bit or residual soft tissue damage. It was strange but the wound just seemed to have closed itself up."

Alex ran the nurses words through her mind.

"The doctors said you were incredibly lucky. How the bullet managed to miss your lungs they don't know. Must have got deflected by your ribcage." She smiled. "Still, you're back with us again now. That's all that matters."

The nurse picked up the clipboard at the bottom of Alex's bed and wrote down a few unseen notes. "Try to get some rest, breakfast will be here soon. I'll be back to change your dressings in a couple of hours."

"Is anyone here with me?" Alex asked in a hushed voice.

"There was a nice young man that came in with you." The nurse smiled again. "You only missed him by an hour or so. He said he'd be back in the morning. He was going to go get a change of clothes and pick you some things up from your apartment."

The apartment, Alex's heart fluttered, her mother...

"My mother?" Alex's voice was slow, deliberate, pained.

What was it Bob had tried to tell her? She searched her foggy memory. He had some bad news. It was all she'd heard. "Tell me she's all right?"

"Hush..." the nurse's soft voice said. "She's resting for now."

Alex's heart sank. She struggled in vain with the sheets. "I have to see her."

"Hey, settle down," the nurse said as she placed Alex back down on the bed. "The doctors will tell you more in the morning. Try not to worry about it for the moment, she's being well looked after. Now get some rest, you need to heal yourself remember."

Alex sighed and stared up at the ceiling. She wasn't going to be able to sleep again that night.

An hour or so later the sun rose above the horizon, people began to wake and the sleepy atmosphere of the ward gave over to its busy day time activities. A simple breakfast was served and Alex indulged in the morning ritual she'd managed to avoid for so long. The boredom of the ward was only broken for her when she spotted the familiar outline of her friend walking towards her from the nurses desk.

"Morning sleepy head." Bob smiled and rubbed Alex's hair.

"I bought you something to cheer you up." He pulled out a bunch of flowers from behind his back and arranged them into the empty vase by her bed.

"Thank you, they look pretty," Alex smiled.

"I picked these up for you too. I'm not sure what you needed so I just grabbed a few things," Bob said as he placed a small backpack onto Alex's lap. "I hope they'll be OK."

"What happened?" Alex's voice broke the uneasy silence as Bob sat down. "Who were those people? How did they know my name?"

"I er... I really don't know," Bob conceded. "The police arrived soon after you were shot. I just had time to press the call button. They must have heard what was going on." He removed his phone from his pocket and waved it like a trophy.

Alex let out a quiet chuckle.

"You sure sorted those two out," Bob said as he settled down. "If they didn't have guns they wouldn't have stood a chance."

Alex gave him a half-hearted smile before her demeanour changed. "I said I wasn't going to hurt anyone again."

"Hey, don't talk like that. You did great. They were going to kill us. Well it was you they wanted I was just in the wrong place," Bob chuckled.

"What if they did really only want to ask me some questions? I might have killed them."

"Those scum deserved everything they got," Bob shouted.

"What do you mean?"

"They tried to kill her. When she was on her

own."

"What?" Alex said. "Who?"

"I only found out after the police arrived and the ambulance crew had managed to stabilise you. An officer offered to come with me up to your apartment. That's when we found her... your mother."

Alex gasped.

"The door had been forced. She was just lying there motionless face down on the carpet. After what had just happened to you I panicked, I didn't know what to do. The rest happened so quickly it's hard to recall."

"What... what did they do to her?"

"The officer was on his radio calling for assistance straight away. He ran over to try and help her. He called me over to help roll her onto her side. It was only then that we noticed the bruises. I don't know what those animals had done to her but it wasn't a pretty sight. It looked like she'd taken one hell of a beating."

"Oh my God, what the Hell did they do to her?" Alex's eyes welled up.

"Then more uniformed people rushed into the room. It was frantic. They were doing everything they could to try and keep her breathing." Bob's face creased up. "She wasn't moving, she wasn't responding. I felt so helpless, I couldn't do anything."

"Tell me please." A look of shear desperation spread across Alex's face.

Bob sighed, hesitating as he drew the courage to say what he had to say.

"Alex..." he took her hand in his, "she's in intensive care. I'm sorry. She's in a coma..."

Alex felt sick to the pit of her stomach. "B..." she hesitated this time "but she will be OK won't she? She's going to get better?" Bob didn't reply. "Isn't she?" Alex pleaded.

"I'm sorry, I don't know. The Doctors said it was too early to tell, but I'm afraid it doesn't look good. They've got her hooked up to life support." Bob's voice wavered. "But she's not responding to the treatment."

Alex slumped back into bed.

"She was already at the hospital by the time you'd got here. They wouldn't let me see her while she was in the emergency room. It took them a few hours to get her stable. I spent the best part of yesterday running back and forth between the pair of you."

"Oh," was all Alex managed.

"I'm glad you're OK," Bob smiled. "I don't know what I would have done if I'd lost you."

Alex closed her eyes and let the tears stream down her cheeks.

Bob's smile started to creep up mischievously in one corner. "Who would have listened to my bad jokes?"

"Hey, don't make me laugh." Alex feigned a slap as she coughed. "I'm glad you're here. Thanks for staying with me."

"What are friends for?" Bob chuckled. "Hey, you owe me one."

"For what?" Alex creased her face up.

"Oh I don't know," Bob grinned again, "maybe saving your life."

"Oh that," Alex's mood was improving. "Thanks. Hey... I thought I saved your butt... again?"

"Yeah, I suppose you did," he laughed.

"So what happened to the two men?" Alex asked.

"Oh, the police arrested them, but they had to be bought to the hospital first for treatment," he grinned. "You clobbered them pretty well."

Alex's face reddened.

"They've been taken into custody now as far as I'm aware. That reminds me. The police said they needed a statement from you as well. I made mine last night. They'll probably be along shortly, now they know you're awake."

A senior male doctor was surprised to see Alex so mobile when he came to check up on her progress later that morning.

"How do you feel this morning Miss Forster?"

"I feel completely fine, just still a bit woozy from all the painkillers. Doctor when can I go and see my mother?" Alex asked as he wrote on his notepad.

"Let's concentrate on getting yourself fit again shall we? One thing at a time."

"But I have to see her," Alex pleaded.

"Your mother is in a stable condition. You can go and see her in a few days."

Alex gave up. She wasn't going to get her way.

"I need to check how your wounds are doing." The doctor scribbled on his notepad again before turning to face Bob. "Would you mind stepping out for a minute? I need to draw the curtains."

Bob moved without a fuss and waited just outside.

After closing the curtains around the bed the doctor pulled Alex's robe to the side and proceeded to remove the bandage from across her chest. Alex looked down but the awkward angle made it hard for her to judge the wound for herself. She looked up and tried to read the expression on the doctor's face. It looked worried.

The doctor continued to grimace as he eased the dressing off and cleaned the dry blood from her skin with an antiseptic wipe. He paused, his eyes were wide. The colour seemed to have drained from his face.

"What's wrong Doctor?" Alex asked.

"I, er... don't understand," his troubled voice replied.

"Can you bend forward for me please? I need to check your back."

Alex felt the strange sensation of her skin being pulled as the adhesive dressing was peeled away from her back.

Alex waited for the verdict but all she heard was silence. She turned her head. The Doctor was standing up straight, rigid. He was staring at the wound on her back.

"Is something wrong?" Still yet more silence. "Tell me what's wrong with me."

The outburst broke the Doctors trance.

"Your skin, your wounds. They've gone, it's healed. It's... it's not possible."

"Is that a good thing then? Can I put my top back on?" Alex snapped.

"Oh, yes, sorry, please."

The Doctor scribbled something on his notepad, pulled the curtain back and strode as fast as he could out of the ward. Alex and Bob watched as he disappeared down the corridor.

"Your wounds have healed?" Bob eyed his friend. "Already? I don't believe him, they can't have."

"That's what he said, you must have heard,"

Alex replied.

"Here let me have a look. At least you know I'll be honest," Bob said reaching his hand out towards Alex's gown without thinking.

"Hey, the one on my back," Alex raised an eyebrow "OK?"

"Oops," he repositioned himself. "No... He was right. I can't see anything, not even a bruise. Does it still hurt?"

"I don't think so, I feel fine," Alex replied.

"That's so not fair," Bob said creasing his face up. "I only have to look at things and I'll get a bruise for a week."

A police arrived next. Bob gave up his seat and went to fetch another. She tried to be as sensitive as she could. Taking Alex bit by bit through the events she could recall leading up to the incident. All the while making notes until she was satisfied she had a satisfactory statement. She stood up to leave.

"Aren't you going to ask me if I want to press charges?" Alex asked.

"I'm sorry. We can't bring charges against the men in question in this instance." The police woman turned to leave.

"Wait, what do you mean?" Alex said raising her voice. "I want them sent to prison."

"It's not possible I'm afraid. We had to

release them early this morning. They're most likely already out of the country by now."

"But that's ridiculous," Alex shouted.

"They were travelling on diplomatic papers. They have immunity. We couldn't hold them."

Alex's face reddened, this time in anger.

"There was nothing we could do about it I'm afraid. The best we can do is offer assistance with relocation. If that's what you would like?"

"I can't I need to be here, for my mother. She's in intensive care. I'm not leaving her here."

"I didn't think so," the police women said in a soothing tone to try and calm the situation. "I'm sorry, really I am." She passed Alex a card. "This is my direct number, if you change your mind or you just need to discuss things give me a call. I'll try to help out if I can."

Bob was still there later that day when the Doctor returned, this time along with three silver haired serious looking suited men. They discussed Alex's condition at length, seemingly unable to come to a unified conclusion. They took turns again and again to check instruments and scribble down notes. After roughly twenty minutes of this indecision, the chatter slowed down. The tone of their conversation became more positive. The younger Doctor stepped forward.

"Miss Forster, we're not sure how, but you

seem to be in perfect health." He appeared genuinely shocked at the diagnosis. "The results from every test we've run on you have come back within normal levels."

Alex and Bob looked at each other.

"I suppose there's only one thing we can do for you now. You're free to go, I'm discharging you. There's no medical reason that we can think of to keep you here in this bed any longer."

"Oh... OK," Alex said. "If you're sure?"

"I'll have one of the nurses come over to disconnect you from the machines. Now, I want you to make an appointment to see your GP in the next couple of days for a check up just to be on the safe side. If for any reason your condition deteriorates I want you straight back here, do you understand?"

"Thank you Doctor," Alex nodded. "So I'm free to go see my mother then?"

"It'd be better if you gave it another day or so, you've been through a lot."

Alex sighed.

"But Yes, you can go and see her," the Doctor added. "I don't think I could stop you anyway. Just try to remain calm, we don't want to risk any relapses."

Alex turned to Bob and asked him to get her things together.

"I'll give the ward a ring for you to let

them know you will be arriving shortly," the Doctor said. "As next of kin I think the Doctor in charge there will want to discuss things with you." He stopped to speak with a nurse on his way out who came to release Alex from her wires.

"Take it easy for the rest of the day dear," the nurse said after she was finished. "Those painkillers you've been on are pretty strong. I wouldn't try anything too strenuous." She smiled and turned to Bob. "Have you got transportation?"

"I'll call a taxi when she's ready," Bob replied. "Don't worry. I'll make sure she gets home safe."

Alex took a sharp intake of breath. The sudden thought of coming so close to where it happened took her by surprise. How could she go back to where that terrible thing had happened? How could she be on her own in the very same room where her mother had been left helpless on the floor? What was she going to do now? The disturbing thoughts were starting to overcome her. She was starting to feel sick again.

"Are you sure you feel all right?" Bob asked studying Alex. "You still look a bit pale."

"I don't think I'm up for going back to mine so soon," Alex replied. "Would you mind if I stopped at yours for a few days? You know just until I get myself together again."

"Of course you can," Bob smiled. "I've been

waiting for an excuse to use the spare room."

"Thanks," Alex said. "I really appreciate all the things you do for me."

"Steady now!" Bob said as he helped Alex onto her feet. "You've been lying down for a long time. You don't want to rush things."

He closed the curtain around the bed to give Alex some privacy while she got changed. When she was ready, Bob led Alex away from the ward as the pair made their way towards her waiting mother.

CHAPTER 8

Alex lagged behind Bob as they meandered their way through the maze of hospital corridors. She could feel the anxiety inside her starting to build. She desperately wanted to be reunited with her mother but what would she look like? She knew it would be bad but how bad was bad? She tried to imagine it, tried to mentally prepare herself for the shock. Were the injuries Bob described accurate? Had he told her the truth or was he trying to shield her from it? Alex tried to control herself as the fear rose.

Each claustrophobic corridor Bob led her down seemed to end in yet another. Bright white, sterile, all similar but subtly different. She tried to read the numbers overhead, tried to follow the directions as they led her ever closer to the moment she was dreading. She could feel herself getting light headed.

"Nearly there," Bob said with a smile. "Not too far now."

Alex tried to concentrate on where they were going. She needed to remember the way for the next time she visited. When she'd be on her own, without her support.

"Do you need a rest for a minute?" Bob asked as Alex's pace began to slow. "You're dragging your feet."

"No I'll be all right, it's fine," Alex replied. "I need to get this over with."

"If you think it's for the best," Bob added putting his arm around her waist for support.

"I can have a rest after I've seen her."

Alex saw the sign she'd been looking for, the intensive care ward.

"She's just in there," Bob said pointing to a closed door with a small rectangular window. "It's a private room."

Alex took a deep breath and walked up to the glass. Bob lingered a few paces behind.

"I'll give you a minute," Bob said in a hushed voice.

Alex turned to face him, tears streaming down

her face. "OK," was all she could manage.

Bob made his way over to the nurse's desk to confirm Alex's arrival.

"Hi, er... my friend Alex Forster is here to see her mother. She was told the Doctor needed to speak with her."

"Ah yes, Miss Forster," came the reply. "Yes we were told to expect her. She can go straight in that's no problem."

Bob looked around just in time to see his friend disappearing.

"The doctor has been informed," the nurse added. "He should be with her shortly."

Bob returned to the door and glanced through its window. Alex was hunched over her unconscious mother weeping. He turned away, not wanting to intrude. A few simple plastic chairs lined the corridor, he took a seat.

Sometime later the door creaked open. A weary Alex emerged and came to sit by her friend. She hardly acknowledged him, her numb tear stained face kept low. Bob didn't speak. He just placed his arm around her, drew her close and hugged her. Alex rested her head on his shoulder.

A solemn looking Doctor came to greet the pair soon after, introducing himself as Dr Hunter.

"Hi, Miss Forster I presume."

Alex lifted her head and nodded.

"Do you mind if I take a seat?" The Doctor motioned to a seat across from them. "We've been informed that you're next of kin for your mother, is that correct?"

Alex tried to speak but the words wouldn't come.

"Yes she is," Bob answered for her. "There are no other relatives."

The Doctor nodded and made a note on his pad. "Your relation to Miss Forster?"

"Oh, I'm just a good friend," Bob replied. "Here for support."

"Miss Forster, have you been informed of your mother's condition?" The Doctor asked.

"No... Not really. Something about a coma and her being attacked..." Alex grimaced, "by the same men who attacked us."

"Yes, I'm afraid she was in a bad way when she came into us. Unfortunately she is still in a coma and unresponsive," the Doctor replied. "We've managed to stabilise her condition for the moment but I cannot guarantee for how much longer."

Alex felt tears begin to roll down her face again.

"Her external injuries are consistent with a sustained violent assault," the Doctor said. "We've been attending to them as best we can, but her lack of response to the treatment has been problematic."

"What do you mean?" Alex asked.

"We ran some routine blood work tests as soon as she arrived and have since run a full toxicology screen. Those results have proved surprising."

Alex raised her head.

"Of course the screen found substances consistent with her prescribed medicine," the Doctor said. "But it also picked up an extremely large amount of an old and very powerful anti-psychotic drug in her system. One used in psychiatric hospitals decades ago. In small doses it worked well as a sedative, but it has since been superseded by newer safer drugs due to its side effects."

"What are you saying Doctor... I don't understand?"

"It's early days yet but I personally believe your mother had been drugged, possibly over a long period of time. I believe she was given a final overdose on the night she came in to us."

"But how?" Alex blurted out. "When? I would have known. I would have suspected something."

"The drug was most probably given via intramuscular injections," the Doctor added.

Alex gasped.

"The results from other tests we've ran aren't promising either I'm afraid." The Doctors face looked pained. "It appears the drug has had a much worse effect on your mother than we first thought."

Alex took out a tissue to wipe the tears from her face.

"Most of her organs are beginning to shut down. We were hoping they would've shown signs of improvement by now but unfortunately they are still in decline." The doctor took a deep breath. "If it was just that, we could try to aggressively treat her to keep her stable. It would involve her being on life support indefinitely, at least until we could find donor organs. Machines would need to take over as her organs failed."

Alex raised her hands to cover her face.

"What are you saying Doctor?" Bob asked for his friend.

"As part of her analysis we sent her for an MRI scan. I'm sorry to have to tell you this Miss Forster. Your mother is also suffering from a large tumour deep within her brain. It's inoperable."

The corridor was silent save for the quiet sobs of a heartbroken Alex.

"Is there no hope Doctor?" Alex managed.

"We will try to keep her stable for as long as we can, keep her comfortable," the Doctor replied. "She won't feel any pain."

"How long does she have?" Alex mumbled.

"It could be as little as a few days, a week at most."

"OK, thank you," Alex sobbed.

The Doctor stood up to leave. "We have counsellors here if you need to talk to someone."

"No, thank you," Alex's voice wavered. "I've been preparing myself for this moment for a long time now. I just didn't expect it so soon."

Bob put his hand on Alex's shoulder.

"I'll be all right," Alex took a few deep breaths. "I just need a minute." She stood up and made one last look through the glass at her mother. "I need to get away from this place. I can't take it any longer."

"Come on let's get you home." Bob put his arm around her again and led her away.

The taxi came to a stop outside Bob's apartment block. Bob tipped the driver as usual and walked around the car to let his friend out. Alex sat motionless staring out of the window. The sound of her door opening seemed to break her trance and she turned to look at her friend, her face numb, expressionless.

"Let's get you inside shall we?" Bob said.

Alex swung her legs around and stumbled out onto the street.

"Easy now," Bob said. "You've been through a lot in the last couple of days."

Bob's apartment was similar to Alex's but it was well looked after and in a more respectable part of the city. It was incredible how much the appearance of the city improved over the relatively short distance of a few streets. His apartment was located in a privately owned complex accessed through a gated area and a secure car park. His parents had purchased it for him a number of years ago to help him whilst he was at university.

Bob led Alex up to the security booth where they were greeted by the pleasant young man on duty. Bob made a point of introducing her to the security guard and signing the form to allow her access over the next couple of days.

Alex followed Bob through the front door. He checked his mail box as they passed on the way to the lift. Alex let out a sigh as the lift doors slid open. It was nice to be somewhere where things worked like they were supposed to. She wasn't looking forward to returning to check what damage had been done to her own apartment.

Bob's apartment was set out in a neat fashion, very sparse, minimalistic. Nothing cluttered its clean lines, everything had its place. Alex knew he was fussy and asked him where she could drop her things. He showed her to the spare room and told her to make herself comfortable. The layout of the flat was different to Alex's, almost opposite. Something she'd have to remember when hunting for the bathroom in the middle of the night.

"I wondered what was in here," Alex said as Bob opened the door.

Bob shrugged. "I haven't had any reason to use it before." He disappeared whilst Alex was looking around. When he returned he had clean towels and his dressing gown in his hands. "Here, you'll feel better after you take a shower," he said smiling as he handed them over. "I'm sorry I haven't got anything more appropriate for you to change into, unless you want one of my t-shirts and a pair of shorts. I er... don't have many female visitors."

"That'll be fine," Alex said. "Thank you."

"If you want we can go over and have a look around your apartment tomorrow? It'll give you a chance to pick some clothes up," Bob said. "I've already called in work to tell them I need a few days off."

Alex nodded.

"Anyway, I'll leave you to settle in. I'll be on my computer," Bob said smiling. "I need to log in, tell my friends why I haven't been online."

The next day Alex woke up early. Unsurprisingly she hadn't got much sleep. The strange environment didn't help and she could still just about hear the train rumbling passed in the distance.

Alex went to put the kettle on before sitting down in front of the television. She flicked the station over to the local news and waited but was disappointed there was no mention of the incident.

Bob came into the living room still yawning at just passed eight. "Anything on the news about it?"

"No, nothing today," Alex replied.

"There was a small section about it in the newspaper the day after it happened," Bob said then rushed back into his room. He emerged with the paper in his hands. "Here you can have a look if you'd like. I think it was on page six."

Alex snatched it from his hands and thumbed through the pages until she found the right one. "Here it is. Mother and Daughter Attacked in Suspected Double Murder Attempt. The police statement says they're still looking for the suspects." Alex turned to Bob looking confused.

"They probably didn't want to admit they'd had to let those men go," Bob replied.

"What if they're still around?" Alex said screwing up her face. "What are we going to do?"

"Try not to worry about it," Bob replied. "That police officer sounded pretty convinced they'd already left the country. I can't see them being allowed back in any time soon."

"Yeah, I suppose you're right," Alex sighed. "I've got too much on my mind at the moment to worry about them as well. What's the plan for the day?"

"Do you want to go and get the apartment out of the way first? Then we can grab some lunch," Bob said. "After I can go with you to visit your mother again if you'd like?"

Alex agreed and strode off to the kitchen. "What do you want for breakfast?" She asked as she went.

"Hey, I'm supposed to be looking after you remember," Bob replied, laughing as he rushed passed.

Alex made another cup of tea, this time for the both of them, while Bob placed a couple of slices of bread in the toaster.

"Are you sure you won't have anything?" Bob asked. "There's plenty in." He opened the cupboards to prove his point. The noise of the toast springing up from the toaster broke the silence. Bob shrugged as he turned back to remove it, tossing it onto his waiting plate. "What are you thinking about?" He asked as he coated the toast with a liberal amount of butter.

Alex shook her head as she continued to stare down at her tea. "I'm fine, don't worry."

"Ouch," Bob grimaced.

Alex raised her head. Bob's hand was rubbing

his throat as he tried hard to swallow his toast.

"Are you all right?" Alex asked.

"Yeah, my throats just a bit sore," Bob replied. "I probably just picked up a bug while we were in the hospital. Every time I go to those places I seem to pick something different up." He shook his head in dismay. "Remind me to get some lozenges on the way will you."

Alex found herself wandering into the living room leaving

Bob to finish up his meal. The view out of the window wasn't much to look at but it gave Alex's mind a chance to roam as she stared down at the street.

"Are you ready to go?" Bob asked.

Alex sighed deeply before turning to face her friend. "I suppose, let's get it over with."

Bob looked her up and down. "Follow me." He strode off into his bedroom beckoning Alex to follow.

Alex dragged herself away from the window and traipsed after him. She came to a stop in the doorway and leaned against the frame.

"Aren't you coming in?" Bob asked.

"It's a bit late to try and get me in here," she replied with a chuckle.

"No stupid, here put these on." Bob threw her one of his jackets, a woolly hat and scarf. "I don't want you to catch a cold on top of everything else."

"But I'm fine, I won't," Alex protested.

"Humour me will you."

"Fine, if it'll stop you fussing."

Bob wrapped his own scarf tightly around his painful throat and coughed.

Bob began to shiver as the pair left the corner shop. "I hate colds," he sniffled. He pulled a honeyed sweet from the packet, popped it into his mouth and waited for its soothing liquid to coat his rasping throat.

"Are you sure you're going to be OK?" Alex asked. "Your lips are going blue."

"It's just a cold, nothing I can't handle." He sneezed. Bob was starting to feel sorry for himself. His whole body felt cold, his head was throbbing and he could swear his bones hurt.

A little while later the pair entered Alex's apartment block and made their way up the many flights of stairs.

"Here, you'll need this," Bob said handing a key to Alex.

"The police arranged to have the broken lock fixed. They said they couldn't leave the property unsecured. I sorted the remuneration out for you."

"Ah," Alex said rolling the key over in her hand, "thank you."

Alex raised the key towards the door and

pushed it into the lock. She took a deep breath before turning it and pushing the door open.

The air smelt stale, unnatural. Alex ran over to the window almost forcing it open. She stood there, her hands on the frame breathing in the clean outside air. Bob walked over to his friend and patted her on her back.

"Come on now, it's OK, you can do this."

Alex allowed herself to be turned around. Her eyes scanned the room unable to take in the sight. The once tidy room was now a total mess. It looked like the place had been ransacked. Clothes, magazines, even her mother's paintings lay strewn carelessly across the floor. The TV screen had been smashed. The set now lay on its side in pieces. All the panels on the leather suite had been ripped by what looked like a knife. Draws were pulled out, their contents spilled beneath them in heaps on the floor.

Alex bent down and began to try and put things back in their correct places. Angry tears welled up in her eyes. All but numb she collected up the clothes and began to fold them, arranging them into a neat pile. All of a sudden she lashed out. The pile of clothes scattered across the floor again.

"I can't do this." She clutched her hands to her face and dropped to her knees. "Why would anyone do this? What could they have possibly wanted?" She sobbed. "We had nothing?"

Bob turned intending to comfort his friend but Alex had already frozen, her sobbing stopped. She scrambled to her feet and rushed into her bedroom. They were still there. It didn't make sense. Her birthday presents still lay untouched where she'd left them on the bedside cabinet. Alex looked around. Her draws had been emptied. The contents of the wardrobe littered the floor. Boxes had been thrown up against the wall in a big pile.

Alex felt the panic taking hold, she was starting to hyperventilate. She allowed herself to collapse onto the bed. Tried to get her breathing back under control, tried to calm her anxiety.

The sound of the kettle boiling drew Alex's attention back to the outside world.

"I figured we were going to be here a while," Bob said as he popped his head around her bedroom door. "Do you want a brew?"

"Ye... Yes, I'd love one thanks," Alex replied wiping her eyes. Alex took a long deep breath. She wasn't going to play the victim any more.

Alex walked out of her bedroom and into the kitchen. Bob had been clearing things away in there while she'd been in her room, to her surprise it didn't look that bad. A little more optimistic now she joined in with the cleaning operation.

"It'll soon get done, don't stress about it," Bob said. "We just need to focus on one room...." A coughing fit interrupted him mid sentence. "Sorry, at a time. It doesn't seem as bad that way."

"What do you think they were after?" Alex said struggling to think things through in her head.

"Honestly, I haven't got a clue. Did they steal anything?"

"Not that I can think of," Alex replied. "They didn't touch the presents you gave me. They were the only things of any real value."

"Did they take anything of your mothers?" Bob asked.

"I haven't checked yet, but I don't think so. I don't think she had anything worth stealing," Alex sighed again. "Why did they do it, I don't understand? We had so little and the thought of what they did to my poor mother when she was here all on her own. It makes me sick to think about it."

"Did you or your mother have any enemies?" Bob asked.

"No, we kept to ourselves, we never bothered anybody," Alex replied screwing her face up.

"What was it your mother did again?" Bob

asked. "Before she got ill I mean."

"Nothing special, she used to run a small gallery near to where she used to live. Why?"

"Maybe she got involved with the wrong people."

"I don't think so and anyway it was a long time ago now," Alex replied. "Surely if she'd had any such dealings they'd have come to a head before now."

"Yeah I suppose you're right," Bob shrugged.

After the kitchen and living room were cleaned Alex and Bob made their way to her mother's bedroom. Alex gasped as she pushed the door open. The bedroom had been turned upside down. Every wardrobe and cabinet had been completely emptied. Draws had been yanked out, emptied and then thrown across the room. All of her mother's remaining sketches and paintings were spread across her bed. Her mother's notebooks lay open on top surrounded by now frame-less photographs. Alex walked over to the bed and picked up a random photograph.

"That's weird," Alex said as she looked at the jumbled pile. "Some of these are from other rooms. They must have collected them together and brought them here."

"Are you sure?" Bob asked joining her by the bed.

"Yes," she replied still looking at the

photograph in her hand, "this one's from the living room."

Bob looked at Alex puzzled.

"Look here," Alex said grabbing another photograph from the pile. "This one's from my bedroom."

"That is weird," Bob replied. A crease formed in forehead as he raised an eyebrow. "Maybe they were looking for something specific. Something that wasn't valuable. Information maybe."

"I don't know. Why would they?" Alex sighed. "What could they have possibly hoped to find?"

"Well it seems they spent most of their time in here," Bob replied. "I think we can assume they were after something of your mothers."

"Yeah but what? She didn't have anything and she'd forgotten about most of her life."

"Ah, maybe that was it," Bob blurted out. "Maybe they were trying to find out about something that happened in the past." His voice was getting faster more excited. "She couldn't remember. That's why they drugged her..." He paused. "That's why they beat her. Oh no, your poor mother." His hands covered his mouth. "I'm so sorry."

If the pair of friends were going to have time to visit Alex's mother they wouldn't have time to finish cleaning the whole of the apartment in one go. Instead they got as much of the apartment back to normal as possible but left the rest for another day. Alex gathered together a suitcase full of clothes and essential bathroom items to take back to Bob's. She wasn't sure when they'd be back so she crammed in as much as she could just to be on the safe side.

Bob was first to walk through the door. "Are you sure you've got everything you need?" He turned back towards his friend. "Are you sure there's nothing missing, nothing you want to report stolen?"

"Wait," Alex paused in the door. Her heart started to pound again. Her mind was racing. "Oh please, no, no please, please be here."

"What's wrong?" Bob shouted as Alex disappeared back into her mother's bedroom.

"Please be here, please," Alex said to herself as she scattered the items on her mother's bed. It wasn't there. She ran back into her bedroom, to her bedside cabinet. The draw was empty. "Oh no, not that. No."

"What's wrong?" Bob said again.

"It's gone. It's not here," Alex's voice was shaking. "I... I can't find it."

"What's gone? You're not making sense," Bob said screwing up his face.

"My photograph."

"A photograph doesn't matter that much does it? It's not worth stressing about," Bob replied.

"I'm sure you'll find it. It's probably mixed in with the others."

"You don't understand," Alex's voice was pained. "It's the only thing I had of him, my father. I always kept it in here, they must have taken it."

"I'm sure it meant a lot to you," Bob replied, "but what on earth could they have wanted with a tatty old photograph? Try to calm down, you're over reacting a bit don't you think?"

Alex took a deep breath. "I suppose... maybe I am."

"We can have a good look for it next time we're here," Bob offered.

"Yeah, you're probably right," Alex sighed. "Let's head back shall we?"

CHAPTER 9

The pair of friends were making their way back to drop the suitcase off at Bob's apartment when Alex stopped in the middle of the street. Bob came to a stop a few paces ahead as he struggled to halt the heavy suitcase.

"Hey, wait a minute I've got an idea," Alex said as she pulled her purse out from her pocket and searched it. With a smile she pulled out the card she was after, the card the police woman had given to her at the hospital. "Yes, this is it. Can I borrow your phone again?"

"What happened to yours, Hmm?" Bob replied

"Sorry," Alex said looking at her shoes. "I'm

not used to having one yet. I keep forgetting to bring it with me when I leave the house."

Bob unzipped his coat and reached into its secure inside pocket. He shivered as the cold autumnal air rushed in.

"You should stay at the apartment, you're looking worse," Alex said as he passed her his mobile. "I can go visit my mother on my own, don't worry."

"It's only a cold, it'll go away," Bob sniffled.

Alex found the number on the card and dialled. After a short wait the pleasant police women answered.

"Hi, it's Alex Forster you came to see me at the hospital the other day. You gave me your card."

"Oh yes, I remember," the police woman said. "How are you feeling?"

"I'm fine now thanks," Alex replied. "Er... the reason I was calling, well it might seem a little strange, but did the two men you arrested have anything on them? Did you confiscate anything?"

"I'm not sure, they did leave in quite a hurry," the police woman replied. "I'll go check if you'd like. Was it something in particular you were looking for?"

"Well, you see, this is the strange bit,"

Alex said. "I think the only thing they took was an old photograph of mine. It was important to me. It's of my mother when she was young with a gentleman friend."

"Hang on a second and I'll go to have a look. I'll call you back in five or ten minutes on this number."

While they waited for the return call, the pair continued their journey. They'd only just gone through the gates when Alex felt the phone vibrate in her hand. Alex checked just in case but its screen simply flashed up unknown number. Alex held it to her ear and accepted the call.

"You're in luck, I think I've found what you were after," the police woman offered. "I'll set it aside for you to pick up."

"Oh, thank you so much," Alex replied. "That's brilliant."

"Good news?" Bob asked.

"She has it down at the station," Alex said turning to face Bob. "See, I told you I wasn't imagining it," Alex added holding her gaze until Bob turned away.

"I still think it's weird," Bob muttered.

"I wonder why they took it," Alex said with added tension in her voice, "and if it was so damn important to them why leave it behind at the station?"

"Yeah, what a strange thing to want to

steal," Bob replied with a frown. "They didn't look like the average criminals you see around here did they?"

Alex shook her head.

"They were more prepared, they must have planned it in advance." Bob's voice was getting panicky. "They must have known you'd be out of the apartment that night. They were probably waiting for you to get back."

Alex remained silent.

"They'd spent a long time searching through your things. It didn't seem like they were looking for things to sell. It must have been the information they were after. It's very strange how they picked that item out from amongst everything else. They must have needed it for something."

"I don't know, it was just an old photograph," Alex replied. "What could anyone possibly want with a tattered old holiday snap?"

"Maybe it showed something more than you thought," Bob said raising an eyebrow again.

"I can't think what. Unless it was something to do with the man in it."

"Didn't your mother tell you anything about it when you were younger?" Bob asked.

"No, I'm afraid I only found the photograph after the dementia had taken hold. She'd completely forgotten about that part of her life by then."

"Wait a second," Bob blurted out. "Do you mean you found it as in you came across it whilst you were cleaning, or you found it as in it was hidden?"

"Oh... it was behind one of my baby portraits. I did think it was a bit strange at the time, but I just thought my mother had put it there and forgotten about it."

"Is there anything else in the photograph other than your mother and the man?" Bob asked. "Anything that sticks out? Anything that could have a hidden meaning?"

"No... It's just a simple old snap shot. Nothing interesting about it at all other than the people."

"Oh well, have a good think about it. We'll never know why they took it unless you can find out more about it."

Alex felt the welcoming warm air on her exposed face as she entered Bob's apartment. She took a deep breath. The sweet smell of mulled wine on the air warmed her cold nose. Bob hesitated and watched for her reaction.

"It's a plug in," he said. "I thought it would cheer the place up a bit." A few seconds later Bob returned Alex's smile and strolled off towards the kitchen. "I'll put the kettle on, there's no point in us rushing straight back out into the cold."

Alex sat down on the sofa and relaxed. It must be nice being able to have the heating on when you want. Alex shivered at the thought of her cold apartment. She sat back and tried to think things through in her mind.

A few minutes later Bob passed Alex her piping hot cup of tea before wrapping both of his hands around his.

"You look a bit better now we're back in the warmth," Alex said.

"Yeah, I feel a bit better too," Bob replied. "At least I think I do."

Bob took a seat in his normal spot and turned the TV on with the fancy remote control. "Do you like it? I've set it up to control everything."

Alex nodded humouring her friend.

Bob's gaze was concentrating on the screen as page after page of the program guide flashed by. His eyes didn't land on anything he particularly wanted to watch and so settled on a documentary he'd seen before.

"Have you come up with any theories yet?" He said trying to start up a conversation.

"No, I'm afraid not," Alex replied. "I don't even know where to start."

"Hmm, do you know anything about what your mother used to do before you came along or when you were little?"

"Not really, she never spoke about it. She always used to cut me off when I brought the topic up."

"Well how about other family members?" Bob asked. "I know you don't have any left now but can you remember anything about them from when you were small?"

"I can just about remember my grandparents," Alex offered. "They were killed in a car accident when I was very small. I was never told anything about the extended family."

"There must be something we're missing," Bob sighed.

The conversation went quiet. Neither of the friends had anything left to add. They sat in silence, sipping their tea, transfixed by the images in front of them on the screen.

"Have you ever tried to trace your family tree?" Bob asked, sitting upright grinning. "It might give us some clues."

"Er... no, I haven't tried. I've never given it much thought," Alex replied.

"We don't really have time now, but I can do some research for you on the internet," Bob said. "I should be able to help you find out a bit more. Maybe we can find some details about your parents. Maybe we can find out who your father was."

"I don't know if I should," Alex's expression

changed, she tensed up. "I mean what if I do find him? What if I find out he's not like I imagined? What if he turns out to be a criminal or a murderer even or worse, what if he doesn't want anything to do with me?"

"Well if you don't try to find out you'll never know," Bob replied. He rushed off to grab a pad and pen, scribbled down a note for himself and stuck it to his computer screen. "I'll get started when we get back. Have you finished your drink?" He asked.

"Do you mind if we call into the Foodbank on the way, you know, to tell them what happened? I was supposed to be going in today, I don't want them to be worried," Alex asked trying to make it sound as innocent as she could. "Anyway, it'll give you a chance to meet the people there. Maybe they can persuade you to volunteer as well." Alex started to laugh as Bob sneered.

"Had you better call into work as well then, to tell them?" Bob grinned.

It was Alex's turn to grimace this time. "To tell you the truth, I can't be bothered with them anymore. I don't feel up to working with how things are. The doctor gave me a sick note anyway so I could spend time with my mother. It'll be easier if just gave them a call instead."

"If you're sure?" Bob replied shrugging his shoulders.

"I'm sure I can make them understand," Alex said with a harsh tone in her voice.

Bob hung back as Alex opened the front door of the apartment block, taking the time to gather up his scarf around his sore throat. Alex recoiled as the sudden icy chill of the outside air hit her. The abrupt temperature difference took them both by surprise. Alex turned away and struggled to pull her hat down further over her ears.

"Looks like winter is just around the corner," Bob said shivering again.

"God I'm getting sick of this weather," Alex replied. If it isn't raining it's freezing, you can't win."

"I hate to break it to you, but the bad weather hasn't started yet," Bob said in a hoarse voice. It's just going to get worse."

"I know, don't remind me," Alex replied, her head lowered as she marched outside.

Alex led the way to the Foodbank, it wasn't a long walk but she had to keep stopping to allow Bob to catch up. He was lagging behind feeling sorry for himself. His head was throbbing and his nose was blocked. "Sorry," he kept repeating between sneezes.

The waiting room was full when they reached their destination. Alex eased the door open and held it for her friend.

"Oh hi Alex," Stacy's welcoming voice rang out. "We saw it on the news. We were all so worried about you."

"Yeah I'm OK, no need to worry," Alex replied feeling her cheeks begin to flush. She placed her cold hands on her face hopping it wouldn't turn a deeper shade of red.

"God, it's cold out there today," Bob said trying to distract the attention from his embarrassed friend.

"I'm glad you're OK," Stacy replied. "Do you want to go through and find some of the others? Don't take this the wrong way but I've got a whole lot of people to deal with today. I can't really spare the time to chat I'm afraid."

"No problem, I'll see who else's about," Alex replied. "Is Bob all right to come through with me?"

"As long as he doesn't hurt himself," Stacy chuckled. "I don't want any more forms to fill in."

"I'll look after him," Alex laughed. "I promise."

Alex made her way through into the corridor, Bob following behind. She stopped outside the staffroom and opened the door to see who was in. She froze as she saw him inside.

"Oh, er... hi Stephen," Alex stuttered. "I was expecting to find James hiding in here."

"Oh, hi Alex," Stephen said surprised. "Thank God you're OK. It said you were shot. I didn't think we'd be seeing you again so soon."

Alex cursed silently in her mind. News travels quick around here, she thought. She tried hard not to be the centre of attention and now it seemed she was famous all of a sudden.

"Yeah, I'm fine now," Alex smiled. "My friend Bob, he's hiding behind the door, managed to call the police in time."

Bob felt Alex's hand tugging at his sleeve. He took the hint and bent around the door to wave.

"He's got a cold. He's trying to stay out of the way. We're going to visit my mother at the hospital. I just wanted to call in to let everyone know I was OK."

"Well I'm glad you did," Stephen smiled. "It looked horrible on the news, all the police cars and the ambulances everywhere. The entire street was closed off the next day you know. I suppose the police were looking for evidence."

Alex felt her heart starting to thud, her ears began to ring. Her breathing was getting short.

"Are you sure you're all right?" Stephen asked. "You look a bit faint."

"It's just I haven't heard about it in detail before," Alex replied. "I don't really know what happened. It's still a bit of a shock."

"Do you know why they attacked you?"

"I have no idea," Alex replied. "None of it makes sense at the moment."

Stephen's normally happy demeanour turned sorrowful. "How is she, your mother? It said on the news the police were treating it as attempted murder. The last I heard they said she was in a critical condition."

"She's not good. She's hanging on but..." Alex's voice trailed off as she became tearful. "The Doctors told me she's not going to make it. I don't know what I'm going to do without her. She means the world to me."

"There's no hope for her?" Stephen inquired.

Alex shook her head.

Stephen moved to try and comfort her but Alex cut in.

"Just give me a minute, I'll be fine. I don't want people to tell me how sorry they are and they know what I'm going through. You don't, nobody does OK?"

Stephen backed away at the harsh words.

"I'm sorry," Alex offered. "I didn't mean to snap at you. I'm just feeling a little vulnerable. I'm not used to it. I've always had to be the strong one. It's hard for me."

Stephen sat back down, adjusting himself as he tried to get comfortable again.

"I think you need something to take your mind off things for a while. Give you a chance to wind down."

"Maybe you're right," Alex took a deep breath. "I do need something to take my mind off things."

"Well the offer's still open at the gym," Stephen replied. "It's nice and quiet in the day, just what you need. You can take your frustration out on the weights."

"But I've never lifted weights properly before," Alex admitted. "I don't know how. When I used to train we just used bodyweight exercises."

"Ah... you'll be fine," Stephen dismissed her concerns with a wave of his hand. "You'll have me to teach you."

Alex's head rose. "Well if you're going to help me I'd feel better about it. Where about is it? You never got around to telling me."

"It's just around the corner, in the old church. It's called the Iron Temple. You must have seen it."

"Oh, yes I've seen it, lots of times in fact," Alex replied. "I thought it was a strange name for a church. Every time I walked passed I thought to myself it's made out of stone not metal. I just always assumed the metal was on the inside."

"I guess I'll have to persuade my dad to have

some clearer signs made up," Stephen laughed.

A quieter laugh joined in from outside the room. Alex turned to see Bob covering his mouth with his hand. She tried to stare at him but he couldn't help himself and carried on laughing. She clipped him on his shoulder with her outstretched hand as he tried to escape.

After things calmed down again, a less embarrassed Alex returned to speak to Stephen.

"Sorry about that," Alex said, still a little uneasy. "He likes to make fun of me."

Stephen remained silent, smiling at her.

"What?" Alex said. "What?" She said again. The room suddenly felt very small, she felt exposed.

Stephen was grinning but still remained silent. Alex stood there transfixed. She could feel his gaze on her. That handsome face, those welcoming eyes locked on hers. She couldn't move.

"You're funny, you make me laugh."

Alex's mind was racing. What does he mean funny? Is that good or bad? It wasn't what she wanted to hear. She swallowed.

"I think we're going to get on just fine," he added in a calm voice, watching for her reaction.

Alex felt her heart flutter. She let out a nervous giggle. "I hope so." She cringed as she heard the sound leave her mouth. What a dumb thing to say she thought. He's going to think I'm desperate now. Alex only relaxed a few seconds later when he broke the awkward silence.

"Well I can't sit around here all day. I'd better go and see if the others need some help," Stephen said as he glanced up at the clock.

"Do you think you'll be up to helping out again this week?" Stephen asked. "Listen I totally understand if you can't."

"We'll see," Alex replied with a little hesitation. "It depends on my mother. Anyway I think I'll see you at the gym. Maybe tomorrow. Like you said the exercise might take my mind off things."

"Yes, please do," Stephen replied. "It would be good for you to come."

Alex swallowed hard again.

"I'll try to persuade Bob to come with me too. If he's well enough that is."

Another waving hand appeared from around the door.

"Nice to meet you Bob," Stephen said smiling before breaking out into a quiet laugh.

"Do you want to talk to anyone else while we're here?" Bob asked. "You know, to tell them you're all right as well."

"No it's OK, I'm sure Stephen can tell them for me," Alex answered still distracted by her thoughts. "We should be heading off."

"So that was the guy you were talking about

the other night?" Bob asked.

Alex raised her head to look at her friend. Bob raised an eyebrow.

"You know, when we were walking back home after the taxi dropped us off."

Alex tried to remember but the night was still a blur for her. "Sorry, I can't remember," she conceded. "What were we talking about?"

Bob looked at her with a strange cheeky grin on his face.

"Well he does fit the description doesn't he?"

"I still don't have any idea what you're talking about," Alex said shaking her head.

Bob stared at her, his eyebrows raised again.

"Hey, I got shot remember," Alex snapped. "Give me some slack."

"If you say so," Bob said and began to laugh again.

When the pair got back out into the open air the sky was starting to darken. Bob coughed as the cold air hit the inside of his rasping throat.

"You're getting worse," Alex said looking at her friends pained expression. "I can go to the hospital on my own, don't worry about it. You need to get yourself back home and out of the cold."

"No don't be silly, I said I'd go with you,"

Bob said coughing again.

"I'll be fine, I'm a big girl," Alex said staring directly at him. "Get yourself home. You don't want to be spreading your germs around the hospital."

"But that's where I..."

"I'm not asking," Alex cut him off.

"All right, all right you win," Bob whimpered.

The two friends parted company in opposite directions. When Bob was satisfied he was a safe distance away but still within ear shot. He turned back towards his friend.

"Hey Alex," he shouted.

She stopped in her tracks. "What now?" she said turning.

"I'll nip into the police station on the way back to pick up your photograph. I'll see you back home."

"What? Are you sure?" Alex shouted. "Won't you need me to be with you for that?"

Bob chuckled, "They know who I am, I was there remember?"

About twenty minutes later Alex arrived at the entrance to the Hospital complex. She made her way across the massive car park, weaving between the mass of parked cars towards the main building. She stopped for a moment distracted by one of the metal signs at the edge of the maze.

She glanced down at the parking terms.

The sign read: Up to 1hr £3, 1hr to 4hrs £4, over 4hrs £5

Alex chuckled to herself at the irony. If she'd been able to afford a car she wouldn't have been able to afford to park it. She was better off walking anyway she told herself. At least it was healthy.

Alex entered the towering building and walked over to the map on the wall. She was pretty sure she could remember her way, but she just wanted to remind herself exactly where the ward was just in case. She scanned the map, found the room she was after and headed off. She hadn't noticed what the visiting times on the ward were but she'd ask one of the nurses when she got there.

Alex rounded the last corner and entered the final corridor. The nurse's desk at the end was empty, the lights were dimmed. The sound of her footsteps echoed down the corridor. Alex started to feel alone again. What if she isn't here? What if they've moved her? She stopped, the hospital seemed silent. What if something has happened to her? All of a sudden a wave of dread swept over her. Her hands searched her clothes for her phone. They would've called her if something had happened, wouldn't they? Her hands kept searching the same places over and over. Alex felt her heart squirm as the realisation that she'd left her phone at home started to sink in. Her breathing was erratic she was hyperventilating. They would have got in touch with Bob, wouldn't they? He had his phone. She tried to calm herself. She turned, her mind not working straight. He wasn't here, she'd told him to go home. He couldn't contact her... they couldn't contact her. The walls started to spin. Alex reached out her arms, her hands desperate, trying to find support. She felt the darkness coming again. She tried to control her breathing but it was too late. She collapsed to the floor with a thud.

CHAPTER 10

Alex gradually opened her eyes as she regained consciousness and looked around. She found herself seated in one of the plastic chairs next to the nurse's desk. She was greeted by the comforting smile of the young looking female nurse sitting next to her.

"You had a bit of a stumble dear. Nothing to worry about. We see it quite often down here."

Alex was still a bit groggy. She raised a hand to her head and ran her fingers over a small painful lump. She was still rubbing her head as the nurse passed her a warm drink of tea in a plastic cup.

"Here drink this. It'll make you feel better."

Alex thanked her and took a sip.

"I know it's not the best cup of tea in the world," the nurse giggled, "but it's got some sugar in. It'll help bring your blood sugar levels back up."

"How long was I out?" Alex asked.

"Oh not long, a couple of minutes that's all," the nurse smiled. "I was just around the corner."

"Sorry," Alex said with a sigh. "I get anxious sometimes and I start to panic, it makes me dizzy."

"Like I said, it's nothing I haven't seen before," the nurse replied. "You're not the only one it happens to. Don't let it get you down."

"Sorry," Alex said again. "I came in to see my mother. Do you know how she is?"

The nurse's pleasant expression changed, it looked pained.

"She's comfortable at the moment. I changed her not long ago. But I think the Doctor wanted to have a talk with you about her again."

"Oh," Alex said grimacing. "When do visiting hours finish? Do I still have time to go see her?"

"Yes, of course," the nurse replied. "In cases like this we try to allow close family members access whenever they're able, but finish your tea first, get your strength back."

"There's something I meant to ask while I was here," Alex said in a quiet voice.

The nurse nodded and waited for her to continue.

"I know she's in a coma but will she know that I'm here? Can she hear me? Can she feel it when I touch her?"

The nurse sighed. "It's hard to say dear. You'd be better off asking the Doctor, but from my experience let's just say there's still a lot we don't know about the human mind. I don't think anyone could give you the correct answer."

Alex wasn't looking forward to the experience. Even though she'd been assured by the Doctors and nurses that her mother was comfortable, she'd looked in so much pain the last time she'd seen her.

Alex glanced through the window before easing the door open. It was hard for her to look at first. It took a while for her eyes to get accustomed to the macabre sight. Her helpless mother lay motionless with not a hint that she recognised her daughter's arrival. Alex drew closer, averting her gaze now and then when her emotions threatened to take over. She tried to calm herself, tried to imagine her mother as though she was in bed fast asleep, just her head and arms uncovered by the clean sheets, something she'd seen many times. It wasn't working, this time it was cruelly different, she almost didn't recognise her.

Margaret's eyes weren't sleeping they were welded tightly shut from the swelling. A clear plastic mask covered the lower part of her face. Alex's trembling eyes traced the breathing tube over to the noisy artificial respirator in the corner of the room and across to the humming monitors with their blinking lights and their occasional beep.

Alex stood by her mother's side in silence stroking her forehead. Eventually she plucked up enough courage to cast her eyes over her battered mother's arms. Tube after tube pierced her skin and Alex watched as the different coloured drips made their way into her body. The large welts she'd seen yesterday had spread. Her mother's once pale skin now looked almost completely covered in shades of purple and blue. Alex fought hard to keep the images of her mother been attacked from flooding her mind, but she was losing the battle, she couldn't keep them out. Tears began to roll down her face.

A glimpse of sudden movement at the door distracted Alex from her thoughts. Her eyes automatically locked onto the white coat of the Doctor as he walked past the glass window.

Remembering the conversation with the nurse, Alex picked herself up and tried to dry her eyes before following the movement out of the room.

"Ah Miss Forster, I'll be with you in just a second. Could you take a seat for me?"

Alex watched as the doctor placed a stack of files down onto the nurse's desk, he was obviously on the way through and hadn't meant to stop. Even though his back was turned Alex could have swore she saw him take a deep breath. Her eyes followed him as he returned.

As he walked towards her Alex became aware of how quiet the corridor had become. How long had she been in there? Where were the other people? She glanced around trying to find the time. It must have been past midnight. Alex got a sinking feeling when she looked at the understanding expression on the Doctors face.

"I've been meaning to talk to you about the progress of your mother's condition." He took another deep breath. "I'm sorry to have to tell you this. Her condition has deteriorated considerably over the last twenty four hours. I'm afraid we can no longer keep her stable."

Alex cringed.

"We were hoping her liver and kidney functions would improve with treatment but they appear to have been too badly damaged. We can keep trying to increase the intensity of the treatment but I think in her case it will just be prolonging the inevitable. I don't think we should be putting her through any more suffering, I think she's been through enough."

Alex looked up at him through her bleary eyes.

"For the dignity of your mother I think we should consider withdrawing treatment."

Alex ran the Doctors words over in her mind. His soft voice did little to appease the meaning. Her head dropped and she let out a muffled sob. She didn't want to listen. She wanted to shut the world out. She wanted to be somewhere else, anywhere but here in this situation, hearing what she was hearing. She didn't want it to be real. She wanted it to all be just a bad dream. She wanted to wake up and find her mother still with her.

"It will be fast, she won't feel anything," the Doctor added. "She won't be suffering any more. There are drugs we can give her to ease the passing. The machines are all that's keeping her tethered to this world. Once we remove life support it will happen quickly."

Alex managed to nod.

"Is there anything I can get you? Is there anyone we can call to make it easier for you?"

Alex nodded again without opening her tearful eyes. "I'd like my friend Robert to be here with me. I don't think I can do this without him."

The Doctor scanned his clipboard. "Yes we have a contact number here. I'll have one of the nurses give him a call for you. We can arrange for things to happen in a few hours. Is that OK?"

Alex nodded once more.

The whole event had taken just over half an hour although Alex hadn't been aware of the passing time. She'd watched in a daze as the doctor had made the necessary preparations and undertaken the procedure. Things seemed to have gone OK, like he'd promised. After things had settled down Alex asked Bob for a moment alone. He left to wait for her in the corridor. Alex stood at her mother's side in the now quiet room, the noisy machines were resting. Her mother looked peaceful. The unsightly tubes and wires no longer penetrated her delicate pale skin. She looked down at her mother's sleeping face and stroked her hair for the last time.

Alex emerged from the room a few minutes later, her head hung low. "It's over," was all she managed to say.

"At least she's at peace now," Bob said in a quiet voice. "She isn't suffering anymore."

Alex nodded but continued to whimper.

By the time the pair had made their way to the exit the sky had brightened once more marking the dawn of a new day. The unobstructed sunlight glistened brightly off the morning dew. A few brave overwintering birds twittered in the sparse trees. Alex lifted her head. The numbness she felt inside seemed to thaw along with her surroundings. She took a deep breath and held it a moment before releasing it all at once in a large sigh. Bob held out his arm for her to link and the pair started their slow walk home.

"What do you want to do for the rest of the day?" Bob asked trying to break the awkward silence. "Do you feel up to anything?"

"I just want to go back to the apartment and rest for a while," Alex replied. "Maybe we can do something later to take my mind of things OK?"

"Yeah it's fine. I was just thinking, well you might have wanted some alone time. There are things I could be keeping myself occupied with if you want."

Alex grasped her friends arm. "I'm already alone... I've no family... there's no one left," she stuttered. "What am I going to do?"

"Don't worry, you'll get through this, you're strong," Bob replied choked.

"She's gone, what am I going to do without her?"

"You've still got me, I'm not going anywhere." He tried to smile. "Come on now. Try to keep your chin up. I hate seeing you upset."

Alex tilted her head. "I know you're still

here... You're always here for me." She managed a one sided smile.

"So what happens now?" Bob asked.

"The Doctor said I need to wait for the coroner to sign off on her body, after that I can start with the funeral arrangements... Will you help me? I don't think I can do this on my own."

"Whatever you need, I'll be right beside you," he smiled.

Alex awoke later that afternoon and found Bob sitting in front of his computer. Bob turned distracted by the noise. "Hey you're awake."

Alex wandered to his side. "I couldn't sleep much I kept waking up. I couldn't stop thinking about it."

Bob got to his feet. "I'll go get you a warm drink. Do you want tea or coffee?"

"Coffee, please," came the quiet reply.

Alex sat down in his vacated seat and stared unthinking at the screen.

"Do you want anything to eat? Cereal or toast, I could rustle something up quick in the kitchen if you'd prefer?"

"No I'm not hungry, thanks."

"Are you sure because it's no problem, it won't take a second?"

"I'm fine, please stop fussing, you're running around is starting to make me feel dizzy."

"Here you go," he said a few minutes later as he handed the warm drink to her. "So what do you think?"

"Of what?" Alex replied.

"About what I've been working on. I've been trying to track down the rest of your family."

Alex eyed the computer screen. "It's just my mothers and my name with a few numbers next to them." She turned to look at her friend. "There's nothing else here."

"That's the strange thing, I hardly got anywhere. It was easy to find you. I just looked you up on the birth records. I only needed your name and your date of birth. Here look." Bob leaned across the desk to move the mouse. "There that's your mother's name isn't it and your date of birth?"

Alex nodded.

The screen changed as Bob clicked on the link to what looked like a black and white photocopy with a long list of names.

"It doesn't show your father I'm afraid and your mother is still listed as Miss Forster, so she obviously wasn't married at that point. Oh, by the way what does the 'E' stand for?"

"Sorry?" Alex said confused.

"Your name, your records just show it as Alex E Forster."

"Oh, it's Eve," Alex replied. "I never use

it, it sounds horrible."

"Oh, OK," Bob chuckled. "I was just curious. Anyway, then I tried to find out about your mother. That's when things started to really get strange. I can't find any records for her from the time before you were born."

Alex stared at him confused.

"On this website I've checked through all the relevant marriage and birth records with no luck. I couldn't even find her birth certificate. On other websites I've looked at voting and tax registrations."

Alex stared up at him.

I also tried to look up your grandparents. I couldn't find any records for them either. Everything I could think of has drawn a blank." He shook his head frowning. "I'm sorry. I don't know what else I could try. I'm all out of ideas."

Alex sat for a while thinking. "Are you sure you can't find her birth certificate?" she asked.

"No, there's no births listed under her name anywhere near those dates."

"What if it's not the right name?"

"What do you mean?" Bob replied

"Well think about it. If someone were to change their name a long time ago and didn't officially record it. It would explain things wouldn't it? Surely you would need their original name to find out about their past. There'd be no paper trail."

It was Bob's turn to think things through. "Yes that would make sense. But why would she change names? Unless... Unless she wanted to disappear." The speed of his talking started to increase. "She'd have to have had a very good reason, wouldn't she? Maybe that's why those men were looking for her, that's why they were trying to find information in your apartment."

"But why would she have kept it a secret from me?" Alex added. Her voice was tense.

"Why indeed?" Bob replied. "Why would a mother lie about something so important to her daughter and keep it a secret for so many years."

Alex looked shocked. "We could be just jumping to conclusions though couldn't we?"

"Hmm we could be, but I've got a feeling we're on the right track," he spun around. "I've just thought of something that may help us, but I can't do it from here."

"What is it?" Alex asked.

"Do you know where your grandparents are buried? Their gravestones may give us some more information."

"Ah no, I'm sorry, I never knew where they were buried. My mother never took me to visit their graves."

"Are you sure they were your grandparents?"

"What?" She snapped "Of course. Who else could they have been?"

Bob remained silent studying his friend.

"You can't be serious?" Alex snapped again.

"It would explain a few things," Bob replied.

"I don't like where this is going."

"How old were they?" Bob asked.

"I don't know. It's hard to remember."

"What did your mother used to call them?"

"I don't know! I can't think, I don't want to think about this at the moment," Alex shouted. "Please stop with the questions."

"OK... I'm sorry," Bob replied. "I was just getting a little over excited that's all. I didn't mean to upset you."

Alex sighed. "My mind is messed up at the moment. I can't think straight. I need to do something. I don't want to sit still. I need to keep moving."

"Try to calm down, it'll just make things worse," Bob said.

"How could things possibly be worse," Alex snapped yet again.

"Please, settle down... for me."

Alex's stern expression started to soften.

Bob's face was turned towards the door. "Perhaps Stephen was right," he said out loud as he thought.

Alex could only just make it out. "What do

you mean?"

Bob's gaze turned back to his friend. His glum expression was changing. "You need to take your frustration out on something that won't get hurt," he said becoming excited once more. "Get your things together, come on we're going to take him up on his offer."

"But... but," Alex tried to speak.

"No ifs or buts, we're going. If you let things get the better of you now God only knows what will happen to you. It's a long dark road you're on but I'll be dammed if I'm not going to hold a light out for you."

Alex stood rooted to the spot for a second or two, her mouth held open to protest but no words would come. She couldn't remember the last time Bob had spoken to her like that. The makings of a smile began to creep across her face.

Bob ran over to his computer with his phone in his hand and found the Foodbank's website.

"What are you doing?" Alex's soft voice asked.

"Just finding the number to ring." He held a hand out to block Alex as he pressed the numbers on the keypad. "Oh hello, is that Stacy? Could you put Stephen on the line for me?"

About 30 seconds of silence went by with Bob still holding his hand out. "Oh hi Stephen, it's Bob, Alex's friend, we met yesterday. Listen,

Alex has had some very bad news and I think she could do with burning off some of her nervous energy. Would it be OK if we came along to your gym in a little while..?"

Alex stood behind him frowning.

"Great, you'll be there just after three. OK that suits us fine. See you in a bit." Bob pressed the end call button. "You see, that's that sorted. Now you can't get out of it." Bob checked the time on his phone before placing it on the desk next to his computer. "It's just gone a quarter past two. If we get changed now, by the time we get over there it'll be nearly the right time."

Alex followed Bob into his bedroom and sat on the end of the bed while he searched though his wardrobe for something suitable to wear for physical activity. Alex began to chuckle at his fumbling efforts. A few seconds later his hands found his one pair of tracksuit bottoms, the ones he'd not touched since PE at school. Reluctantly he tried them on for size but he needn't have worried. He'd hardly grown at all since the last time he'd worn them, if anything he looked like he'd just been stretched a bit.

Alex continued to laugh as he pulled on a tatty old pair of trainers with too much force resulting in the appearance of his big toe as it poked through the mesh at the end.

"Hey, it's not my fault," Bob said with a frown. "When was the last time you saw me doing something that remotely resembled physical activity?"

Alex couldn't help herself from chuckling. She watched as her friend started to smile back at her.

Bob disappeared into his wardrobe again. "I can't find a single suitable t-shirt. I'd be too embarrassed to wear any of these in a place like that."

"Just put that hooded sweatshirt on over the top," Alex said, "nobody will see what's underneath."

"It's all right for you, at least you're used to those sorts of places," Bob grimaced. "I'd normally avoid them like the plague."

"I know you're uncomfortable going there," Alex said with a smile. "I know you're only going because of me. Thank you."

Bob's grin was interrupted by a sudden unexpected cough.

"Are you sure you're up to it though?" Alex asked. "You looked really bad yesterday."

"I actually feel much better today," Bob smiled. "It was probably just one of those twenty four hour bugs. It's almost gone now. I honestly feel back to normal. I feel good even." He rolled his shoulders around feeling the movement of his child like muscles.

Alex chuckled again.

"I do feel more energetic," Bob added. "It's weird but I could swear I'd been working out. I feel healthier than normal... No there's no need to worry about me," he smiled.

Alex wandered off to get changed herself. After all she couldn't walk around in her pyjamas all day. Since she'd only brought a few of each type of garment with her to Bob's apartment, she managed to put her hands straight on the clothes she was after. She pulled her stretchy yoga bottoms out of the bottom draw and removed a tight fitting stretchable sports top and jacket that were hanging in the wardrobe. Her trainers were underneath. They were nowhere near new but at least they looked clean. She got changed without a fuss. She didn't have the luxury of changing her mind.

As she turned to leave the room she caught her reflection in the mirror. Her eyes ran up and down her body. She was sure she used to fill her clothes out a lot more. She quickly zipped her jacket up. Maybe he wouldn't notice if she didn't take it off.

Bob was sitting at his computer flicking between different songs when Alex emerged. "Ah you're ready?" He said as she walked over to the bathroom.

"Almost," she replied. Her voice seemed a little higher than normal.

"I don't believe it!" Bob said shocked.

"What?"

"You're actually putting make up on to go to the gym," he laughed.

"My eyes are still puffy," a bashful voice replied. "I'm just trying to cover it up."

"Hmm, if you say so," Bob replied still laughing.

As soon as Alex was ready the pair headed off away from the apartment complex in the direction of the park. Alex knew the way. She'd seen the old church many times whilst wandering through the park. She'd sat across from it on one occasion. Her mother had even sketched it. Her mind was wandering. She tried to picture how the now tired old building would have once looked, sat prominently on top of a small hill overlooking the formerly small village.

The modern day image wasn't so romantic. The church now sat surrounded on three sides by a sprawling housing estate. It's once large grounds having been sold off gradually over decades past. The only remnants still visible from the road were a few tree tops sticking up over what Alex imagined was a walled garden.

A busy main road now cut the church off on its fourth side, dividing it from the tranquil rolling landscape of the park. Alex thought about it. It's a shame what happens to attractive scenery when modern development takes hold. Still, if no new houses were built people wouldn't have anywhere to live, so needs must she supposed.

It didn't take long for the pair to reach their destination. They had already turned off the main road and were walking up the path to the front door. It was a lovely building, full of character. Constructed out of a mixture of dark coloured bricks and etched stone work. It still had a number of beautiful lead lined stained glass windows. Alex's eyes were drawn upwards towards it's steeply angled slate roof and the religious stone carvings that stood above at its corners. She wondered how long it took the craftsmen to construct, how much would it have cost.

The original entrance into the church was through a large set of heavy wooden doors inset into a stone archway. The massive doors themselves however didn't look as though they'd moved in millennia. Instead a much smaller modern door had been cut into one side.

Just as they reached the entrance, Alex stopped and turned to Bob. "Are you sure about this?" She asked. "Last chance to back out."

Bob nodded and grabbed his friend by the

elbow. "We're going in, it'll do you good." He smiled and coaxed his friend towards the open door. "What's the worst that could happen?"

CHAPTER 11

Bob led the way through the open front door, only releasing his grip from Alex's elbow once he was sure she was safely inside. Alex glanced around. They were stood in a small corridor with a low ceiling. The walls looked new, fragile even, like fibreboard. On them hung a few framed magazine cuttings. Black and white images of famous Bodybuilders and portraits of Olympic Powerlifters showing off their medals. The waiting space was just big enough for three or four people to stand together, any more would have been a tight squeeze. The nearest wall was bare except for a rectangular sliding window at chest height. Alex noticed the button for the electronic bell and pushed it.

The sound of an old fashioned metal bell rang out from somewhere within the building. It somehow reminded Alex of her school days, the familiar noise used to beacon the children in from the playground. The pair stood chatting waiting for the glass in front of them to slide open, when the adjoining door opened instead.

"Hi guys, sorry I was getting changed," Stephen said as he wedged the door open. "My dad's upstairs sorting through some things or there would've been someone in the office." He turned to look at the visitors. "So you made it then? No trouble finding us?"

"Oh, no, it's easy enough to find," Alex replied. "We knew where we were going."

"We just never thought of coming in before," Bob added.

"Yeah I can tell," Stephen said grinning as he looked them up and down. "Still we'll soon help you put some meat on those bones."

"Oh ha, ha," Alex smirked.

"Come on, follow me, I'll show you around. I need to point out all of the potential things to trip over. The health and safety busybodies have demanded it," Stephen said rolling his eyes. "I wouldn't want you hurting yourselves through a lack of common sense."

Alex was last through the door into the main open area of the old church. She stood for a moment admiring the impressive view. The building had literally opened up before them. Gone were the low ceiling and confines of the fibreboard walls in the entrance, instead they'd been replaced by the original ornate carved stone pillars and arches supporting the impressive angled ceiling, itself covered in beautiful carved wood. Most of the wooden floor had been covered by the same quite unattractive but necessary rubber matting Alex had seen in nearly every gym she'd visited. Around the walls stood various pieces of what looked like metal scaffolding. Ah ha, I told you there was metal on the inside she thought, chuckling at the private joke. Alex let her eyes work their way around the room until lingering at the masses of iron weights.

"Er... where's the cardio equipment?" Alex asked.

"Hey we don't allow swearing in here," Stephen laughed.

"No but seriously where is it?" She asked again.

"My dad likes to keep the place old school. We just have the weights and bars in here. He always says 'if you want to do some cardio work, go for a run outside'."

"Have you got any of those machines?" It was Bob's turn to ask a question. "You know, the ones that help you do the exercises?"

"You've got everything you need right here," Stephen laughed again. "Don't worry I'll soon get you up to speed."

After the short obligatory safety briefing that Stephen had seemed so glad to get over and done with, he took them into the small office.

"Take a seat please. This'll only take a few minutes."

Alex's eyes followed his exaggerated motion towards the two simple metal chairs in front of the desk.

"I just need to run through a few terms and conditions and get you to sign this form," Stephen said whilst rummaging through a draw in the desk. "Then we can get on with what you came here to do."

Instead of the confident movement Bob had planned, in his haste to draw the chair back he'd caught one of its legs under the table and pulled harder than he'd wanted. He watched as a pile of stacked papers spilled over Stephen's desk and onto the floor.

Stephen raised his head from his work and glared at him without a word. Bob apologised, fumbling with the papers as he tried to get them back into order. Alex was about to speak up for her friend until she noticed the cheeky grin forming in the corner of Stephen's mouth.

"Relax," Stephen began to chuckle. "It's fine, I don't need them anyway."

After a few questions Stephen had what he needed and finished the paperwork. "Thank God that's done. I hate that part of my job," he said with a frown. "I just want to get on with training people."

Stephen turned back to face Alex after he'd placed the completed forms into one of the draws behind him. "Bob said you'd had some bad news on the phone. Do you mind me asking what it was?"

Alex's head dropped along with her shoulders. She closed her eyes and took a deep breath. "It was my mother," her voice was slow controlled, "she passed away this morning."

"Oh..." Stephen struggled to find the words. It was his turn to look uncomfortable. "Oh, that's terrible. How awful," he cringed. "Are you sure you want to be here? I mean, I think I'd have just locked myself in my room."

"I need to do something," Alex sighed. "I don't want to stop and think. I can't deal with it at the moment." Tears began to form in her eyes. "Look, can we get started," Alex's voice had turned harsh. "I've sat down too long."

Stephen nodded.

Alex stood up and made for the door wiping

her eyes as she went.

Stephen and Bob looked at each other before finding the nerve to follow.

When they were all back in the main room Stephen led them towards an open area of the floor. Standing in front of the pair he began his speech.

"We try to focus on improving overall body strength here. We don't really cater for people who just want big muscles. If you take our advice you're going to get a lot stronger, you're not necessarily going to look like a bodybuilder any time soon." His eyes scanned the pair. "So if you're serious about training here keep that in mind."

"I just want to get fit again," Alex butted in. "I'd be a lot happier if my clothes fitted me better," she tried to smile.

"I'm not interested in looking like a bodybuilder either," Bob added.

"You don't have to worry about that," Stephen started to laugh. "The famous Bodybuilders you've seen on TV have taken many, many drugs over many, many years to look like that. It costs a serious amount of money to get that big."

"Well I don't think that's going to be us then," Alex laughed this time.

"Anyway first things first, you guys need to get warmed up and have a bit of a stretch. Go have a jog around for a few minutes, loosen your muscles up," Stephen said smiling. "There are some diagrams on the wall over there that'll show you some stretches. Come back here when you're ready. I'll be setting a few weights up for you in the mean time."

Alex and Bob jogged off trying to look like they were busy rather than putting any real effort into it. They tried out a few stretches while they read some of articles on the wall.

"I think I met this guy once," Alex said pointing towards a photograph of a chubby man who looked like he was about to burst out of his tight deadlift suit, "in a book store of all places. Apparently he won the regional qualifiers with this lift."

Bob was trying to look at it as Alex burst out into a laugh.

"I've just thought of something. You know when you hold a frog up by his front legs and his pot belly just hangs down over his thin back legs?"

Bob didn't react he just stared at the photograph. "That looks so heavy. I hope Stephen isn't going to make us try that."

Alex tapped him on his arm. "Come on, looks like he's ready for us."

"Now Alex you said you've worked out in the past, but not with weights?" Stephen asked.

Alex nodded.

Stephen turned to Bob and grinned. "When we spoke earlier it sounded like all you've done for the past ten years is sat in front of a computer screen."

Bob shrugged his shoulders and let out a chuckle towards the ground.

"Well then, as you're both novices, I think it's best to start you off by getting you comfortable with a few of the basic compound movements," Stephen added. "Specifically the ones used in most powerlifting meets. They should help get you up to speed."

Alex and Bob looked back and forth between themselves.

"The three moves I'll be showing you are the squat, deadlift and bench press. Once you're comfortable with them we can bring in the standing military press."

Bob gulped.

"I'll show you the deadlift first as it's one of the easiest things to get to grips with, excuse the pun, as you don't have to worry about any equipment. You just need a bar, some weight and a clear area to work in."

He motioned to the space around them where he'd placed the necessary things.

"We aren't interested in the amount of weight to begin with, we just need to focus on getting the technique right." Stephen turned around, picked up two coloured plates from the weight rack and placed them on either side of the bar. "I'll show you what it looks like first," Stephen grinned then proceeded to pick the bar up and placed it back down a few times.

Alex winced. Stephen bent his head up to look at her.

"Don't worry the weights aren't heavy," he said. "They're practice plates, designed to be the same size as the heavy ones so the bar is the correct distance from the floor."

"Oh," Alex said, "that's all right then."

Stephen grinned. "Now since you've just volunteered yourself, will you come over here and stand behind the bar please?"

Alex stood for a moment looking back and forth between Bob and where Stephen was pointing. Bob motioned for her to move.

"Now, you need to set yourself up behind the bar. You need to centre yourself first so stand behind it with your feet a comfortable distance apart, toes pointed out slightly."

Alex nodded and tried to do what she was told.

"Your shins should be close to the bar. Sit down into the lift. It helps if you think of sticking your backside out behind you."

Alex swallowed hard.

"Place your hands on the bar just outside the span of your feet. They need to be far enough apart to allow your hips to pass through as you stand."

Alex braced herself and tried to follow Stephens's commands.

"Most people use a mixed grip but as you're starting I want you to keep both of your palms facing towards you. I think it's safer to teach you that way in the beginning."

Alex watched as Stephen strolled around her. He seemed pleased with what he saw although at one point she wished she hadn't worn her tight yoga bottoms.

"Try to arch your back slightly upwards. It's easier to keep it straight as you lift. When you stand try not to think of pulling the weight up off the ground, try and concentrate on keeping the weight on your heels and drive yourself away from the floor," Stephen said smiling as he continued to walk around. "I like to keep my head up with my eyes out in front of me. Do you feel comfortable?"

"Not really," Alex replied.

"You'll get used to it," Stephen chuckled. "Now, I want you to start to stand up as I showed you."

With a little trepidation Alex did as she was asked. The weight moved easily.

"Now this time try to keep your shoulder blades together," Stephen added. "Grip the bar as tightly as possible and tense your muscles before you lift."

Alex repeated the lift once more as instructed.

"Try to do it in one controlled movement, don't snatch it from the ground, try and ease into it. Try to keep the bar as close to your body as possible."

She tried again.

"Good, it's getting better," Stephen said. "Try to pull back onto your heels more and once the bar goes passed your knees push your hips forward. Stand up tall, try to lock your knees. Yeah that's it, you've got it now. Try a few more, and then we can let Bob have a go."

Bob didn't pick the technique up as easily as Alex, he wasn't used to co-ordinating his body. His muscles weren't used to working in unison and he felt awkward and out of place. Nevertheless he persevered and with Stephens coaching eventually got the hang of it.

"Good, now that you're both happy with the technique, let's put some actual weight on the bar shall we?" Stephen said before replacing the learning plates with a couple of ten kilogram ones. "It'll feel a bit heavier but it's still well within what you're both capable of."

"How heavy is it?" Bob asked.

"Well the bar weighs twenty kilos on its own, so it's forty kilos in total," Stephen replied. "With the extra bit from the clamps you're probably still only looking at ninety pounds in old money."

Bob grimaced.

"Just roughly multiply it by two point two."

"No it's not that, it's just forty kilos still sounds heavy to me," Bob replied.

"It's nothing you'll be fine," Stephen laughed.

Bob stood there still looking worried.

"What are you?" Stephen looked Bob up and down. "I'd say around a hundred and fifty pounds. It's only just over half your body weight." His gaze drifted over to Alex. "Think yourself lucky Alex only looks about a hundred tops."

Alex swallowed. She thought she was at least one twenty.

"Come on Alex, show Bob how easy it is," Stephen said with a smile.

Alex walked up to the bar and lifted the weight with relative ease before putting it back down with a sigh.

"What's wrong?" Stephen asked. "You're doing fine."

"I know you're trying but it's not working," Alex replied then took a deep breath. "My mind keeps wandering. I keep thinking about my mother. I feel so helpless, maybe I could've done more to help her. Maybe if I'd realised earlier I could have stopped those horrible men."

"Hang on a second, she hasn't finished," Stephen said stopping Bob as he began making his way over to take his turn at the bar. He turned to Alex. "Wait there a second."

Alex looked up at Stephen as he walked over to the weight rack, picked out two twenty kilo plates and returned to replace the ten kilo ones on the bar.

"We need to up the weight," Stephen said, his voice was louder than before. "Try to give you something to take your mind off things."

Alex sighed again, returned to the bar and completed the lift. "Sorry, it's still not working."

Stephen bent down to put the ten kilo weights back on. Alex again picked the weight up feeling little difference.

"Hmm... hang on," Stephen said frowning before walking over to the weight rack again. When he returned he replaced the ten kilo plates for two more twenties. "There that's just over a hundred kilos. That's well over double your body weight," he said frowning this time. "People usually train for a long time to be able to do that. It shouldn't be possible for a novice."

Alex couldn't tell if he was telling the truth or just trying to encourage her, but she got herself into position again. The weight still came away from the ground albeit a little slower than before as she stood up.

Stephen stood for a moment looking at her. "Well done," he said after a few seconds. "I wasn't expecting that. Do you feel all right to continue?"

Alex nodded.

"Do you think you could handle some more weight?"

She nodded again without a word.

"Hey liven up, you're supposed to be taking your frustration out here," Stephen laughed. "You can't hurt these weights put some emotion in to it."

"I can't, I just feel numb inside," Alex replied sighing again.

Stephen returned to the weight rack and brought two handfuls of plates back with him. He placed them all on the bar.

"Now Alex, look at me," Stephen said in a slow deliberate voice.

She turned her head to face him.

"I want you to psych yourself up. This is some serious weight. If you try and lift this without concentrating you're going to hurt yourself, OK?"

Alex nodded, again without speaking.

Stephen froze in thought before placing his hand on Alex's shoulder. "What were those men like...? The ones that attacked you. What did they do to you...? What did they do to your mother...?" He let the words sink in.

Alex's jaw clenched, her teeth grinding together. She turned away staring out into space. With a slow and controlled movement she lowered herself into the starting position. Her knuckles turned white as her hands gripped the bar. All of a sudden in an explosion of movement she ripped the bar from the ground. She stood still for a moment with it held fast in her vice-like grip before abandoning it to gravity.

"Wow," Stephen gasped. "I don't believe it. You just lifted well over three times your body weight. Most people can't manage that after a lifetime of training."

"Yeah, well I'm not most people," Alex smiled.

"Bob," Stephen said turning towards him. "Do you think you'll be all right getting some practice in on your own for a bit?"

"Yeah, I think so," Bob replied glad of the privacy.

"Come on," Stephen said taking hold of Alex's arm, "I want you to meet my dad. I want to tell him what you just did."

Stephen led Alex back across the room towards the staircase in the corner. "We have a few extra rooms up here. Mostly we keep them empty, but we do get a few people that like to take private classes in them," he smiled. "It's normally just some variation on a meditation thing, it doesn't interest me much but it keeps a few of our regulars happy."

"Where is your Dad anyway?" Alex asked. "I was expecting to see him walking around the place."

"Oh he should be up here somewhere. He said he wanted to sort some gear out."

Stephen opened the first door, the room was empty save for a large wire framed box full of what looked like oversized rubber balls in the corner. It seemed nice Alex thought, a polished wooden floor surrounded by full length mirrors. She'd used rooms like it for her training when she was younger. The second room was similar but much smaller and still empty. Alex realised it'd been divided into two.

"It's the massage stroke alternative therapy room. It's a good source of revenue," Stephen smiled again. "My dad hates it, took me a few years to persuade him."

Alex continued to follow as Stephen led her about. Alex could only see two more doors. The first had a simple 'Private' sign at head height.

Stephen checked the door but it was locked.

"This doesn't look promising," Stephen said as he reached into his pocket to pull out a bunch of keys.

It was dark in there. Alex could just make out the shapes of the first few cardboard boxes.

"He must have already finished," Stephen said sighing.

The sign on the final door read 'Toilets.'

"He might be cleaning, I suppose," Stephen said as he held it open with one hand. "Dad," he called out. He stood still for a moment waiting for a reply.

Alex looked passed him, to her relief there were two more doors inside segregating the male and female facilities. "That's strange," Stephen said. "He definitely said he'd be up here... unless... If he's already finished he could be hiding out in the living quarters."

"You live here?" Alex said surprised.

"No, I don't, not any more anyway," Stephen replied. "I used to when I was younger. My dad still does though. There's an annex next to the main building. Dad had it converted into an apartment when he bought the place. It's really nice actually, I miss it sometimes."

"Oh, I didn't notice," Alex replied.

"Sorry about this, he's normally easier to find," Stephen said as he led her back down to the main room. "Hey look, Bob's doing all right," he added pointing over to her friend.

Alex looked across the room and waved. "Keep it up."

"He doesn't look that strong, does he?" Stephen asked with a smile as he turning to face Alex.

Alex smirked.

Stephen gave Bob another once over. Bob looked exhausted but he was trying and there was a respectable weight on the bar. "Hey Bob," he shouted, "looking good."

Alex continued to follow as they made their way towards the entrance until Stephen made a slight detour. He stopped in front of a plain white door Alex hadn't noticed before, placed a silver coloured key into the lock and used the small metal lip below it to pull the door open. A light flickered on as the pair stepped into the small corridor. With a satisfying clunk the door closed behind them, locking itself. Alex looked towards the other end of the corridor. Another door faced them. It looked like any other door you'd see at the front of a normal house.

"This is the side entrance," Stephen said. "It's quicker through here than walking outside and all the way around the other side of the building." He looked at her and smiled. "You don't get wet either."

Stephen rang the doorbell and waited. "Dad gets a bit cranky if I just barge in."

"It's all right, you can come in." A rough rasping voice from somewhere behind replied.

Stephen unlocked the door and held it open. "Hi dad, sorry to bother you, I want you to meet someone."

"Who is he, I'm busy?" The deep voice boomed.

"Actually it's a she," Stephen replied. "It's only her first day and she's just pulled three thirty on deadlift." Stephen waited a few seconds before speaking again. "I think I've found you another one."

"Oh well now you're talking." Came the voice again, its pitch increased.

Alex watched as the figure of a tall heavy set man appeared from behind the door.

"Well where is she, let's have a look?"

Alex stepped out from behind Stephens back. "Hi," she said in a quiet timid voice.

Stephens's father dropped his eye line. "What? Is this it, where's the rest of her?" He laughed. "You can't be over a hundred pounds." The man turned to look at his son. "Are you sure you added the weight up right?"

Stephen didn't reply he just stood there grinning.

"Does she know what she's just done?" The man asked.

Stephen shook his head this time but still continued to grin.

Stephen's Dad smiled down at Alex.

"See what I mean dad?" Stephen finally broke his silence.

The man's stern expression softened. "Nice to meet you." He held out a large weather beaten hand towards Alex. "What did you say your name was?"

"Er... I'm Alex." Her voice was still nervous. She cast her eyes over the aged man's distinguished features as he stood assessing her. His all but white hair had a few remaining blonde streaks from his youth. Alex's gaze wandered over his chiselled muscular jaw line and towards those eyes. Alex felt herself drawn into those dark blue eyes. It was obvious where Stephen had got some of his good looks from.

"Well Alex, I'm Eric," the man said.

Alex felt the grip of his rough hand tighten.

"I'll be keeping an eye on you. I haven't seen Stephen so impressed in a long time." He turned back to his son. "If she's as good as you say, take good care of her. Maybe we can get that trophy back some day."

CHAPTER 12

Stephen and Alex continued chatting as they made their way back into the main room of the gym.

"I think my dad liked you," Stephen said. "He's normally more annoyed than that when I disturb him."

"He seemed nice enough to me," Alex grinned.

"I think you surprised him, you look so delicate," Stephen smirked. "I mean there's nothing to you, you look like the wind could blow you away... and yet you just pulled above the national record for your weight."

Alex stopped. "I did what?"

"Yeah, your first day as well," Stephen

chuckled. "You're one strong little bag of bones."

Alex screwed her eyes up and glowered.

"Speaking of which, we need to get some meat on your frame," Stephen added rubbing his hands together. "Then we'll see what you're really made of."

"What did he mean by get that trophy back?" Alex asked starting to walk again.

"Oh, you caught that did you?" Stephen said. "We used to keep a few mementoes in a cabinet by the entrance," he sighed, "from my competitive days. I won a few powerlifting meets when I was younger."

Alex stared at him. It was the first time she'd seen him look really troubled. Why would that make him look so unhappy? "That's good isn't it?" She asked.

Stephen just sighed again and looked away.

"Why, what happened?" She added.

"Oh, I gave up in the end," Stephen said with a huff as he turned back towards her. "I was a strong kid, but I couldn't keep up after a while. The enhanced guys started to catch up. It wasn't long till they overtook me."

Alex frowned.

"They kept finding new ways to get round the doping tests. Eventually I just couldn't compete any longer."

"Oh, you mean they were taking drugs?" Alex asked.

Stephen nodded. "You see, I'm very strong for a natural guy. I had a seven hundred pound deadlift in me at one time," he tried to smile. "My dad said he's never seen a stronger natural competitor, but I didn't want to use the drugs."

"That sounds heavy," Alex said trying hard to make it sound like a compliment.

"It sure felt heavy," Stephen laughed.

"So why not be proud of what you achieved? I know I'd be," Alex added with a frown again. "Why take the trophies down?"

Stephen sighed once more. After a short pause he began to speak again. "I couldn't cope with it any more. I was obsessed with it. It was driving me to pieces." He shrugged his heavy set shoulders. "I stepped away, tried to make a clean break of it, but I had to keep coming back to this place.

"Oh... that's a shame," Alex said with half a smile.

"Dad removed the cabinet last year," Stephen said with a huff again. "I don't think he's forgiven me for giving up yet."

When they got back to the main area they found Bob sitting on a bench gasping for breath, his face bright red. Alex and Stephen both glanced at the bar at the same time. There was obviously a large amount of weight judging by the amount of plates. Alex looked back across to Stephen as they both started to chuckle.

"Nice try," Alex said continuing to chuckle. "It almost worked."

Bob looked up and scowled. "What? I've just lifted that," he said between breaths.

"Yeah, sure you have," Alex replied.

"Honestly, I've just done it twice."

"Well go on then, show us again," Alex said with a sneer.

"But... I can't, I'm exhausted," Bob managed. "I need a rest."

"Ha-ha, I thought so," Alex smiled. "Nice try."

Bob didn't protest any more he just concentrated on getting his breath back.

"Take a seat," Stephen said motioning to the bench where Bob was sitting.

Alex could feel another rehearsed speech coming on.

"You two have done well today, especially as you're completely new to all this." Stephen looked at both of them and smiled in turn. "Now what you need to do is to go home and get some rest. Recovery time is very important with strength training. Your bodies need time to repair the damage you've just done to your muscles. You'll probably be sore tomorrow so a soak in a warm bath or two won't hurt." He rubbed his hands together and grinned. "You also need to get some fuel in your system. Both of you look like you've never seen a square meal before."

Bob and Alex looked at each other.

"I want you to eat," he continued. "Eat more than you normally would. Your bodies need nutrients to grow. As long as you avoid processed products and things with lots of sugar in, food isn't bad for you." Stephen looked back and forth between the pair again. "As long as you're working out regularly I promise you, you will not get fat."

Alex cringed, she didn't like the way she looked and she didn't like it even more when someone else pointed it out to her. It wasn't her fault. She couldn't afford to eat lots of food. She had to get by on what she could. She had to make it last as long as possible for both of their sakes.

All of a sudden a thought she wasn't expecting flashed into her head. Her mother wasn't here anymore. She didn't have to split the food. She'd have more to herself. Alex's face twisted up in agony. What a horrible thing to think. She tried in vain to banish the image from her mind. Just an instinctive reaction she tried to tell herself, like a hungry dog possessive of its food. But it was true, the food wouldn't have to stretch so far any more, the money would go further. Alex didn't like where her train of thought was taking her. She sighed out loud trying to distract herself.

The sound of the old school bell ringing as a few of the gym's regulars came in was a welcome distraction. Alex and Bob took it as a sign that the gym would soon be filling up and made their excuses to leave.

By the time the pair had got home again the sky had grown dark once more.

"Did you have a good time?" Bob asked as he opened the front door to his apartment.

"Yes I think so," Alex replied. "It kept my mind off things for a while."

"I know it's too soon but do you feel a bit better?"

"Yes, thank you," Alex smiled. "I think I needed to get out. I feel OK at the moment, but I'm not looking forward to tonight. It'll be the first night without her."

"Things will be all right," Bob said trying to smile, "you'll see. Eventually things will be OK."

"I don't think I'm going to be all right for a long time," Alex said with a heavy sigh.

"I'll go run you a nice hot bath," Stephen said. "It'll do you good."

"That... would be lovely," she replied as she

wandered over to the couch and slumped down.

Bob smiled and walked straight into the bathroom and got to work running the water, he'd have a shower later.

"It's ready for you when you are," he shouted. "Do you want anything to drink? I think there's some red wine left."

Bob didn't quite hear what Alex said but he went to fetch the wine anyway and poured her a large glass. Alex was already in the bathroom when he returned.

"Thank you," Alex said with a smile as Bob handed her the glass. "It's really nice of you."

Bob stood in the doorway smiling back as Alex took a sip from her glass before placing it down on the edge of the bath. Alex started to remove her top and then stopped.

"So, are you going to give me some privacy or are you just going to stand there and watch?" She said grinning.

"Do I have a choice?" Bob replied.

"Go on, get out of here," Alex said as she threw her top at him.

"Do you want to watch a film?" Bob asked an hour later from the couch as Alex emerged from the bathroom.

"I don't think so," she replied with a sigh. "I'm going to try and get an early night if you don't mind. I need to think some things through."

"OK, I'll keep the volume down."

Bob watched as his friend disappeared behind the bedroom door then filled up his glass with the remaining wine. He took a large sip before sinking back into the couch and began to flick through the channel listings, preparing for yet another lonely night.

As his mind wandered Bob's gaze drifted across the room towards his computer. He was trying to cut down but he was finding it hard. He hadn't logged into his online game since the incident. In fact he'd tried to stop himself thinking about it. He forced his eyes back towards the TV, tried to find something to watch. What had the rest of his clan been up to without him? The thoughts were in his head again. Were they all right? He was already walking over. Just ten minutes he told himself. He'd login to have a talk with them, nothing more, just a quick chat and that'd be that, he'd turn it back off again. His fingers were already typing in the memorized user name and password. He just wanted to find out what he'd missed out on, where was the harm in that? But it wouldn't just be that and he knew it. His mind stopped protesting as his character appeared in front of him on the screen.

Alex was up and about early the next morning and was already busy in the kitchen when Bob shuffled in.

"What's up with you?" She asked. "You look like you had a worse night's sleep than me?"

Bob tried to focus his blood shot eyes. "Oh, it's nothing, I couldn't sleep," he tried to smile. "I thought I smelled coffee."

"Did you do too much at the gym yesterday?" Alex asked starting to chuckle at her sorrowful looking friend. "I bet your muscles are killing you."

"They aren't too bad actually," Bob replied in a rough voice easing his head from side to side, "a little sore maybe but nowhere near what I was expecting. Usually whenever I've tried to do anything physical I've been in absolute agony the next day. This time it's nothing a few aspirins won't cure. How about you?"

"Oh, I'm fine," Alex smiled. "I guess I'm lucky in that respect. My muscles seem to heal faster than most people."

Alex placed another espresso mug on Bob's elaborate silver machine. With a few hisses and whistles the freshly brewed liquid dispensed a double measure into each.

"Here, you look like you need it more than I do," Alex said as she passed the first mug to her sleepy friend, still amused at his stupefied expression.

Alex grabbed hers then walked passed her friend into the living room. She was already seated on the couch with the TV on before Bob had realised and followed her.

"Do you think anything interesting has happened?" She asked as she flicked the channel over to the news.

Bob mumbled an uninterested reply.

Alex didn't notice at first, she wasn't particularly interested in the images she saw before her. It was only when she heard her name spoken that she sat up straight, alert. The news reporter was speaking to a senior member of the police force. Alex wasn't expecting to hear what was said next.

"Unfortunately this has now become a murder investigation and we have stepped up our investigation accordingly." The policeman on the news was stern. "All efforts will be made to apprehend the culprits. We would like to hear from any member of the public who has information on the whereabouts of the perpetrators. However, and I need to stress this, they should not be approached. They should be considered armed and extremely dangerous."

The video had obviously been edited down for the broadcast but still, Alex couldn't believe what she'd heard. They wouldn't need to find them again if they hadn't released them in the first place. She tutted under her breath. That police woman told her she'd thought they wouldn't even be in the country by now. What hope had they got of catching them again now?

"I'm going to go freshen up," Alex said with a sneer as she tossed the remote to the still groggy Bob who fumbled the simple catch.

Alex heard the sound of her phone ringing just as she'd begun to get undressed for the shower. "Bob," she shouted, "can you get that for me?"

He must have heard as the ringing stopped a few seconds later and she heard his muffled voice answer. Whoever it was she could call them back after she'd finished. It can't have been that important she thought as she turned the hot water on.

"Who was it then?" Alex said to Bob, who was staring at her with a confused look on his face when she walked back into the living room.

"Which one?" He replied.

"Huh," Alex said narrowing her eyebrows, "what do you mean which one?"

"There were two calls for you," Bob said frowning. "The first was the hospital. They need you to get back in touch with them as soon as you can."

Alex ran over to pick-up her phone as Bob continued to speak.

"The second one was strange. A man called, said he worked for some solicitors or other.

Apparently your mother was one of their clients."

"What?" Alex interrupted.

"He knew a lot about the situation. Said he needed to come talk to you, to sort things out," Bob said with a shrug. "I didn't know what to say, I just suggested he should visit if it was that important. He's on his way, said he wouldn't be long."

Alex stared back at him confused herself now. "I don't know anything about any solicitors. I haven't even got round to thinking about it yet," she snapped. "He probably saw what happened on the news and he's trying his luck. He's just hoping to get a sale out of it."

"Yeah, you're probably right," Bob replied with a sigh. "Sorry, I didn't know what to say and you were busy."

"It's all right," Alex said, "I'll find a way to get rid of him, don't worry about it."

"There is one thing I don't understand," Bob spoke up again. "Where did he get your number? I'm sure only the hospital and the police know what it is."

"Forget about it for the moment," Alex snapped again. "I need to call the hospital back, that's more important."

Alex dialled the number for the hospital and the extension Bob had given her. After a short wait a pleasant female voice answered and Alex introduced herself.

"Hi Miss Forster, I take it you got the message I left for you?"

"Er... I'm not sure," Alex replied, "my friend just said you wanted me to call back."

"The Doctor asked me to contact you as a matter of urgency. It's about your mother." There was a short pause before the lady continued. "The police have requested a full autopsy be carried out and the coroner is holding off on the death certificate until it's been completed."

Alex grimaced.

"As next of kin will you give your consent to have the autopsy undertaken?"

Alex stayed silent.

"It's all right if you need a while to think it over, but if you could get back to us with your answer as soon as possible?"

"It's OK," Alex cut her off, "you can do what you need to. I want to find out what happened to her as much as you."

"OK, thank you. I'll inform the Doctor he can precede."

"Do you know a rough time scale?" Alex said then took a deep breath. "When will I be able to start preparing for the funeral?"

"Well the police want it done as quickly as possible, so it should be done within the next couple of days. The results will take longer to come back of course," the lady replied. "The coroner won't want to sign off on the body until they've come back I'm afraid. I'd hold off on your preparations for at least the next week."

"Oh OK, well thank you anyway," Alex replied.

It wasn't long before the intercom at the door to the apartment buzzed. Alex had just had time to get changed when Bob answered the call.

"Mr Underwood it's security. There is a gentleman here, a Mr Wiessenburger, says he has an appointment with you."

"Yes I was expecting him," Bob replied. "Oh, would you mind checking his ID for me before you send him up thanks?"

"Saves me doing the awkward bit at least," Bob said after releasing the intercom button.

The door opened a couple of minutes later to a very confident, immaculately dressed man.

"Mr Underwood, we spoke on the phone," the man said reaching into the inside pocket of his tailored suit and removing a small silver container. From it he produced a very professional looking silver embossed business card.

Bob welcomed the stranger into the apartment. That was when he noticed the subtle earthy scented cologne, the type you don't find on the high street. He didn't strike Bob as your average salesman, he at least wanted to hear what this man had to say.

"Ah, Miss Forster I presume," the man said in a confident voice. "I'm sure what I have to say to you will interest you greatly."

Bob motioned to the man to take a seat in the single chair as he and Alex sat down together on the couch. The man sat and proceeded to place his briefcase down onto the coffee table between them. As he opened it Bob's eyes were drawn to its simple gear logo stamped neatly in the top corner of its supple calf skin leather.

"I've travelled quiet a long way to be with you today Miss Forster," the man begun. "Your mother had been one of our most valued customers for many years. I presume like most people in this situation you are unaware of the work we do?"

Alex nodded, but the look on her face was of utter confusion.

"Our firm is very selective. We only deal with a select few multinationals. Your mother must have been highly valued."

Alex simply stared back at the stranger. Something must have gone wrong somewhere, she thought. Surely he'd realise his mistake sooner or later.

"My section handles the accounts and legal affairs of our more demanding customers. Those that would rather retain a low profile," he continued to speak as he sorted through unseen papers in his briefcase. "We keep all of their details anonymous as per their wishes. Not even their employers know about the accounts or whereabouts."

"I'm sorry I'm not following you," Alex interrupted.

"Miss Forster, I'm not surprised that you have not been informed. The only reason I am here talking to you now is due to the instructions that your mother left with us the last time she made contact."

"Er sorry, just when exactly was that?" Alex asked.

"A little over two years ago," the man said as he checked his notes. "When she made her final will and testament."

Alex sat back in her seat thinking.

"Ah, here it is," the man said withdrawing a formal looking document and passing it to her. "This is your copy to keep."

Alex reached over and took the paper from his hand before slouching back into her chair. She ran her eyes over the print, scanning it to the bottom. It took her a few seconds to work out what she was looking at. It was definitely her mother's name and even her signature. What was going on? Why hadn't her mother told her? What had she been keeping from her?

"As you can see, you stand to inherit her entire estate, which includes her accounts with us," the man said. "That is the main purpose of my visit to see you today."

"Oh, I'm sorry," Alex replied. "I hadn't even got round to thinking about that as yet."

"Due to the nature of our business we do not allow any of our client's accounts to roll over to other family members," the man continued. "Her accounts will therefore be closed and all monies will be transferred to an outside account of your choosing." He waited for Alex's response.

If this was real Alex thought, and it certainly looked that way at the moment, she wasn't going to turn down the opportunity of receiving some well needed money no matter how small the amount. Hopefully it'd at least cover the funeral costs.

"But I don't understand," She replied. "If this is real how did you find out so fast and how did you find me? I haven't even received my mother's death certificate yet."

"We have our ways." The distinguished gentleman smiled. "Let's just say we like to keep an eye on our client's health issues. Some of our team know their way around a computer system or two."

"Oh," Alex said studying the form again.

The man pulled a sleek looking black laptop

out from his briefcase and plugged a Wi-Fi dongle into one of its USB slots. "Could I have your bank details and I will transfer your money."

"When you say money, how much are you talking about?" Alex asked as she passed him her card.

"Hang on a moment please, this won't take long," the man said as he typed something unseen onto his laptop. "Your mothers account has remained inactive for the last twenty five years. I'm just adjusting it for compound interest. Ah, here we are. It's up to date now."

Alex leaned forward.

"You stand to inherit a little over three point two million pounds."

Alex choked.

"I'm sorry," Bob butted in. "I don't think I heard that right did I?"

"It's correct the total amount is a little over three point two million pounds Sterling."

Alex didn't know what to think. What the hell was going on? Her head felt like it was spinning. How could her mother have possibly earned so much money? Why had they living like this if she had that much saved away? It could've made things so much better before she lost her. Why didn't she say something about it before it was too late? Alex started to cry.

"I'm sure you have a lot of questions to ask, but alas I am not the one to answer them for you," the man continued. "It must be a very troubling time for you. I'm sorry for your loss."

Alex nodded.

"I have set the transfer up for you. You should receive the funds within the next forty eight hours." The man smiled. "I would advise a trip down to your bank to discuss the possibility of opening an account more relevant to your new found status." He smirked to himself as he placed the bank card down onto the table. "I am sure they will be more than accommodating."

Alex sat still studying the document in her hand as the man returned his laptop and locked his briefcase.

"Now if you excuse me I must bid you farewell. I have a long journey ahead of me and flight back to Switzerland to catch. Good day to you both."

"What do you think?" Alex asked Bob as he closed the door on their visitor.

"It seems legit," he replied. "You'll just have to wait and see what happens. If that money turns up, that'll solve a lot of your problems."

"No, I mean, why would she have been involved with something like that? It sounds so unreal like the type of thing you hear about in films. My mother wasn't like that. She couldn't have been."

Alex's body slouched in the couch as she

lowered the form, uncovering her tearful face.

"I know," Bob added, "but perhaps she had another life, one you didn't know about, one before you were even born." Bob was getting excited again, his mind was racing. "Come to think of it, it does go a long way to explain some things if she did."

Alex frowned at him.

"I mean think about it, if she was trying to hide from someone or something in her past. If she did try to make a new life for herself or for the pair of you even, she'd need somewhere to hide the money wouldn't she? The man did say the account wasn't traceable."

Alex tilted her head up towards him.

Bob froze. "What if they found her, found you?" his face went white. "What if the people who attacked you weren't the actual ones who wanted to get rid of your mother? What if they'd been hired? They might have been assassins. There might be more on the way. Oh my God, what are we going to do?"

Alex looked at him through her bleary eyes. "But if that's true then they already know where I live. They can find me whenever they want.

"But maybe they don't know where you are at the moment. I'm sure it won't take them long to find out though but they'd have to get passed security first." Bob was pacing back and forth.

"You can't use that money, not if you want to stay hidden. You've got to keep a low profile, like your mother did. At least not until we can figure this mess out.

CHAPTER 13

Little could be accomplished over the next few days. Alex had agreed to stay out of sight as much as she could and so simply spent her time locked in the apartment waiting for the phone to ring. Bob on the other hand had cut his holiday short and returned back to work.

After three frustrating days Alex gave up on staying in, it was driving her stir crazy. She had to find out if that man was telling the truth, she had to find out if the money was there, it sounded so implausible, but what was she going to do if it was?

Alex waited until Bob left for work. She knew

what he would've told her. She'd call him if she was going to be back late, she didn't want him to get even more distressed. When she was sure it was safe, she sorted a few things together into a backpack, put on her big coat and tried to cover as much of her face as possible with a hat.

The trip to the bank was easy enough, not even Cat and her minions seemed to notice her while she waited at the bus stop. Alex made it to the bank by mid morning and was pleasantly surprised to find only a few customers waiting in line before her. It was a welcome change from trying to get things sorted out in her lunch hour. She paused as long as she dared at the door, wondering if her pursuers knew where she banked. If they did, she hadn't seen any sign of them so far. Once inside she lowered her hood, she wasn't going to wait in line looking like she was up to something. The cashier smiled her usual friendly but neutral greeting as Alex offered over her card.

"I'd like to check my balance please," Alex said trying to keep as calm as she could but her hands were starting to shake.

"Couldn't you have checked it at the cash machine outside?" The cashier asked looking at her as if she was making her life difficult.

Alex was caught a little off guard, she wasn't expecting questions. "I er... thought it was safer in here." It wasn't a lie at least.

"Do you have some ID please?"

"Will my driver's licence do?" Alex said struggling to get her purse back out of her jacket.

"Yes that's acceptable, sign here please."

The cashier disappeared with the ID for a few seconds but handed it back over when she returned to her desk. Alex sighed. She was relieved there didn't seem to be any problems with it.

"Now then," the cashier said as she looked at the name on the card, "Miss Forster. I'll get that balance for you."

Alex watched her, waiting for the reaction as she ran the card through the scanner on the computer. She was used to how she'd normally be treated here. She'd spoken to the lady in front of her on many occasions. The cashiers hadn't changed since the first time Alex had gone into the bank to set up the account.

This time something seemed different, something was wrong, the cashier's face froze. She typed Alex's details into the keyboard again and waited for the machine to start over. Again the shocked expression came across her face.

"Is everything all right?" Alex asked in a wavering voice. The question seemed to shock the lady back to reality.

"Oh, everything is fine. I'll just print your

balance off for you," her voice was unsteady. "Is there anything else we could help you with today? We have a wide range of services we could offer you. I could arrange for the branch manager to take you through them."

"Not at the moment thank you," Alex replied. "I just wanted to check my balance."

After a few more silent seconds Alex pointed to the paper waiting in the print tray.

"Ah... sorry, if you could take a seat, I'll bring it over to you?" The cashier's voice wavered. "I'll send for the manager. Would you like a tea or coffee while you wait?" The cashier was already pressing the top extension on the phone next to her.

"Er... I really have to be going," Alex replied frowning. "I didn't want to spend much time here today."

"Please take a seat, he'll be right down. I'll have someone bring your drink over right away."

Alex sighed, she didn't want to cause a fuss and she could hear a few people in line behind her starting to grumble.

The cashier passed her the paper with the account balance on as Alex sat down at the table. Another lady approached her from the other side. "Was it tea of coffee you wanted Miss Forster?" The smile on the woman's face seemed exaggerated.

"Tea please. Thank you. White no sugar," Alex smiled back. She was starting to feel very out of place.

When she was left alone Alex picked up the paper and ran her eyes down the page. The money was there, it'd been there for the past two days. Alex felt her heart flutter. She looked down further. Her available balance still showed a pitiful eight pound sixty. Alex tried to calm herself down. There was still time for this to be all a lie, the money could bounce. The bank was still withholding it until the transfer cleared. Alex tried to slow her breathing. It'd get sorted out she told herself, she'd find out in a few days. It'd all turn out to be a mistake.

"Miss Forster."

Alex looked up. A well dressed man was standing before her with his hand out stretched.

"Allow me to introduce myself. My name is Gavin Murphy, I'm the Branch Manager."

Alex reached up, her hand was trembling.

"Would you like to follow me through to my private office?"

Alex got to her feet. This was taking far longer than she'd anticipated.

"Ah, could you bring it through please Karen?"

Alex noticed the woman returning with her tea change direction.

"We like to look after our customers." The smug face of the manager was smiling back at her.

Alex cursed under her breath. Why are they treating me like this? Just because they think there's some money in my account for a change. Maybe she'd have felt better about it if they'd made more of an effort before, when she needed their help. Why was it people went out of their way to help others when they thought they had some money? She smiled her fake smile to Mr Murphy and followed.

The chairs were comfortable enough and Alex tried to relax as the sucking up continued.

"I'll get straight to the point Miss Forster. We like to extend our hospitality to our more valued customers. We like to keep them happy, it's good for business," he chuckled. "There are many ways in which we can help you Miss Forster. I'd like to offer you the chance to transfer onto a more suitable account, one that will, let's just say meet more of your needs."

Alex's head was spinning. She didn't want to be hearing this. All she wanted to do was to get out, to be free of this charade. Alex agreed hopping it would suffice. He started to go over some other products but Alex cut him off.

"I'm sorry I don't mean to be rude but I really need to be going," Alex tried to smile again. "I hadn't planned on spending this long here today." She tried to sound serious whilst remaining elegant, like she'd seen from her favourite actresses so many times on TV. "Perhaps we could arrange this chat for another time."

"OK, until next time," the manager replied passing her a few select pamphlets. "Have a look through these when you get the chance. They will give you a better understanding of the other products available to you."

It had already gone lunch time by the time Alex managed to get free from the confines of the bank. Although she wasn't feeling particularly hungry after the breakfast Bob had insisted she eat, Alex decided to grab something while she was out. Stephen had told them they needed to eat more and if it was going to make him happy, she was going to give it a try. Alex didn't think she could manage anything heavy just yet so avoided the temptation of the burger van. She didn't have enough cash on her anyway, but if she walked home instead of using the bus, she knew a place that would make her a simple fresh tuna salad for a couple of pounds. She could eat it on the way to the Foodbank. At least she'd have the evidence to show to Stephen.

The front desk was empty when Alex walked into the waiting room. The chime on the door didn't seem to get any of the volunteers attentions either. A few waiting people turned their heads to see what the disturbance was but no one spoke. Alex felt a little uneasy as she walked up to the desk. She noticed a new small brass bell had been placed in the centre with a small sign that read 'press for assistance'. Alex thought it odd but rang it and waited. Still no one came to greet her.

"The woman said they are very busy today," the voice of a helpful stranger said behind her.

Alex turned and smiled. "I'm a volunteer here, don't worry I'll go check what the holdup is."

Alex eased the staff door open and walked into the quiet corridor behind. No one was in the staff room either. Something isn't right, Alex thought. Where is everybody? She finally found some signs of life in the store room where Stephen was busy trying to sort box after box of food out.

"Oh, hi," Stephen said looking up. His face was bright red. "I'm so glad you've come. We're really short staffed today and Stacy has had to rush off to a meeting."

Alex walked up to him as he continued to speak.

"She seemed really worried, wouldn't tell me exactly what was going on. Just said we might be losing our funding. Something about the government making cutbacks and certain charities being affected."

"Oh, oh dear," Alex said. "What's she going to do?"

"I really don't know," Stephen replied wiping the sweat away from his forehead. "Listen could you do me a big favour and pack some of these boxes up? You can remember how to do it can't you?"

"Yes I think so, it wasn't too difficult."

"OK thanks, I need to go sort the front desk out. Some of the people have already been waiting nearly an hour. I'll come back to help you after I've eased the backlog a bit."

Alex looked around at the stacks of boxes in front of her and the mountain of tins waiting to be packed. The day wasn't turning out quite the way she'd planned. Still, she'd said she wanted to be a volunteer and she didn't mind really. She just wasn't expecting to get lumbered with so much work.

Alex watched as Stephen disappeared out of sight. She was at least expecting to have some company, even if it wasn't the good looking one she'd had in mind.

It was too quiet in this massive room all on her own, every noise she made seemed to echo. But it wasn't too long until the sound of the door swinging open again distracted her.

"Hey, look who's here," Stephen said in a

loud voice as he stood in the doorway at the other end of the storehouse. "I managed to persuade a friend to come join you."

Alex watched as a familiar face appeared from behind him. It took her a few seconds recognise the girl as one of the students she'd met before the incident. What was her name? She searched her memory. There were two of them, Melissa and Jennifer, which one was she? She didn't want to make a mistake.

"Hi Alex," the girl said smiling, "I'm glad you're better. Stephen told us all about what happened. We couldn't believe it."

"Yeah, I'm OK now thanks," Alex replied. "Well as long as I don't think about it too much that is."

"Oh good," the girl said with a smile again. "We were really worried about you. I'm Jen by the way in case you were wondering. I'm the one that talks too much," she grinned. "I couldn't get here any earlier. I've only just finished class."

"Well I'm glad you could make it," Alex replied. "Stephen said no one else could. Apparently he's been running around all day trying to get things sorted by himself."

The girl joined in with Alex filling the boxes. She was obviously well versed in what needed to be done.

"Yeah, it's like that here sometimes, he

tries his best." The girl's happy demeanour seemed to wane. "Most of the volunteers have other commitments to juggle. It's just unfortunate the way things work out from time to time. That's why we're glad you decided to stay." Jen's energy was back again.

Alex felt her mood starting to lift. She wasn't used to feeling accepted and the girl's spirit seemed to be catching.

"What do you get up to in your spare time?" Jen asked.

"Not a lot really, I haven't had the cash to do much lately," Alex replied. She didn't want to think about the new money that may or may not be in her account.

"Yeah, talk to me about it," Jen said with a laugh. "I've just had to pay my tuition fees. I'm going to be broke for the rest of the month."

"I read," Alex added quickly. "I read a lot. It helps me to unwind."

"Ah, me too," Jen said beaming. "Hey, you should come join us at the book club. They hold one once a fortnight down at the town hall."

Alex wasn't expecting the positive reaction. She'd got used to people thinking she was just boring. "It's nice to have another girl to talk to."

"Well there's plenty more of us to meet at the club," Jen added. "Come along you'd enjoy it."

Alex thought about it. "It would be nice to get away from all the testosterone for a while."

"You'll fit in just fine," Jen laughed.

"Hey Stephen are you going over to the gym again today?" Alex shouted. "I've been stuck inside for ages. I need to burn some more frustration off."

"Yeah, same old, same old," Stephen replied. "Dad only really needs the help later on in the day when it gets busy."

"Have you been Jen?" Alex said turning back towards her.

"What, to the gym? Oh, no no no... I don't want big muscles," she replied shaking her head and screwing up her face.

"It's not that bad," Alex laughed. "Come on, it's good for you and you'll be helping Stephens dad out."

"Sorry I can't," Jen replied, "I haven't got enough money this month, and anyway I don't have anything to wear."

Alex gave Stephen a look of encouragement.

"Oh don't worry about the money Jen," Stephen said in his loud voice again. "Dad lets the volunteers use it for free. He says it's good to keep the numbers up."

Jennifer still didn't look convinced.

"Come on Jen, you can keep me company," Alex

said smiling at her. "I promise you'll feel better afterwards, a little sore maybe but definitely better."

"Hey Alex," Stephen shouted. "Your friend Bob called in to do a session yesterday. He's getting better, I was impressed. Normally it takes a while for people to improve but he seems to have taken to it like a duck to water."

Alex ran what she'd just heard over in her mind. "He never mentioned anything to me about it."

"I'm sure he doesn't tell you everything," Stephen laughed.

Alex was exhausted when she eventually got back to Bob's apartment. She'd only intended to make a short trip. Instead it had turned into a full day. She hoped Bob had listened to the voice message she'd left him when she was on the way to the gym.

She was on her way to the bathroom to take a well deserved shower when something grabbed her attention out of the corner of her eye. Next to the wash basin pedestal, sat a neglected object she hadn't noticed before. What was the harm in trying she thought as she pulled the glass bathroom scales out? She stepped on one foot at a time and watched in horror as the needle shot up passed its normal resting place. She must have put on nearly eight pounds in as many days. She stepped back off the scales in disgust and shoved them back in their hiding place.

Alex looked down at her stomach, it didn't look any bigger. She ran her fingers over her hips and thighs, her skin felt thinner if anything. She raised her head to look in the mirror. Her face seemed more rounded, her skin looked healthier. Even the hollows under her eyes had disappeared. She smiled. It'd been such a long time since she'd liked what she'd seen in the mirror. She'd almost forgotten what it felt like.

The sound of Bob's voice and the door shutting broke her concentration. "I'm in the bathroom," she shouted before stepping into the shower.

Bob was in the kitchen preparing a meal for them both when Alex finished getting changed.

"Hey, er..." Alex said making the last syllable linger as she walked over to him.

"Yes...?" Bob copied her waiting for the inevitable favour to be asked.

"Would you mind if I invited a friend from the Foodbank over for dinner one evening?" Alex asked. "I'll help with the cooking if you want."

"Don't you see Stephen enough at the gym?" Bob sighed.

"Eh...?" Alex looked at him puzzled. "No silly. It's a girl called Jennifer. We seem to get on really well and I know you like cooking."

"Oh, well in that case, yes it's fine," Bob smiled, his voice lifted. "I'm glad you're making friends."

"Would it still be OK if she bought another female friend with her?"

Bob grimaced but nodded.

"Are you sure you're going to be all right having a group of girls in your apartment?" Alex added. "I know you don't feel that comfortable around women."

"Hey I can talk to you can't I?" Bob said with a laugh.

"Yeah but you've known me for years, that's different," Alex grinned. "You couldn't even talk to me in the beginning remember."

"Don't worry about me, I'm sure I can cope," he said with a laugh. "I'll take one of my brave pills."

Alex had grown that used to having him around that she'd forgotten about the medication the psychiatrist had given him. She leaned herself against the door frame and took a long look at him. He was a good friend. She couldn't imagine not having him in her life.

It was then she noticed something different about him. It was subtle but it was definitely there.

"You look different somehow," Alex said, "but

I can't quite make it out. Did you have your hair done?"

Bob looked at her with a puzzled look on his face. "No, why?"

"Let me have a look at you," She said. "Turn around and face me."

Bob turned his body away from the oven.

"Did you put on some weight?"

Bob screwed his face up.

"No, in a good way I mean," Alex added. "You look better. Your face has filled out a bit and your shoulders... I could swear they're bigger."

"Oh," he laughed. "I hadn't noticed. Speaking of which, you don't look bad yourself. Must be all my great cooking."

Alex joined in with the laughter. She had to admit it, he was much better in the kitchen than she was.

"Maybe it's the exercise?" Bob offered after he'd calmed down.

Lost in thought Alex ran her fingers across her hardened stomach. "It shouldn't be happening this fast though, should it?"

"Well you don't hear me complaining," Bob said starting to laugh again.

"No, I suppose not," Alex said in a quiet voice as she turned and drifted off into the living room. Something was bothering her, something didn't seem right, but she couldn't work it out.

Ten minutes later Bob brought the meal in and set it down on the table.

"So how did it go at the bank?" He asked.

Alex looked at him, her face blank.

"You said you went in your message."

"Ah sorry," Alex said shaking her head. "I had something else on my mind. Yes I went."

"And?" Bob encouraged.

"It was there," Alex said smiling. "The money, it was already in my account. The bank hadn't cleared it yet, but it was there, all of it." Her expression changed, she cringed. "What the hell am I going to do?"

Bob's mouth was open, he looked like he was going to reply but no words came out.

"Where did my mother get it from? Why was she hiding it, hiding us? What if she was involved with something bad, I mean really bad?" Alex was starting to shake. "What if we're in big trouble? Oh my God, we need to find out what she did."

Bob took a deep breath. "Yes we do, but I'm at a loss as to where to start. Let's try and think things through calmly shall we. Maybe it'll give us some ideas."

Alex nodded and tried to calm herself down.

"Try and eat some of your food before it goes cold," Bob added with half a smile. "It'll help you think."

Alex sighed and picked up her fork.

"Let's try and look at the facts we already know," Bob said, his voice sounded serious. "We've tried unsuccessfully to trace both your mother's and your family's past." Bob was waving his knife back and forth, his eyes looking up at the ceiling. "So we can suggest either no records were made, or more likely, they were altered."

Alex nodded whilst she took a mouthful of food.

"We also think your mother had possibly changed her name," Bob lowered his eyes towards Alex. "If she hadn't recorded it officially, it'd go a long way to explain the dead end in the paper trail."

She nodded once more.

"The people who attacked you appeared to be searching for information. Maybe we aren't the only people trying to track down the rest of your family," Bob added cutting another piece from his steak. "But that doesn't help us either. We need to think of a way to find out what she was up to."

"Oh no," Alex said grimacing.

"What's wrong? Bob asked. "Was I talking too fast?"

"No, I've just thought," Alex replied. "My apartment, they're going to want it back."

"What are you talking about?" Bob asked

frowning.

"I'll need to declare the money and when I do the council will want the apartment back. I'm going to have to find somewhere else to live."

Bob motioned around him.

"Thank you, but I mean somewhere permanent," Alex added smiling at him. "Not that I'm going to miss it that much, it holds too many painful memories."

"I'll help you to move, and anyway you can find a really nice place now," Bob said placing his hand on his melancholic friend's shoulder.

"I can't go splashing the money about," Alex snapped. "You told me not to remember?"

"Well maybe we can find you somewhere nice and discreet," Bob offered.

"But look at me. I'm not used to being able to afford nice things. I didn't ask for this, I'm not ready for it, I don't deserve it."

"Come on now, don't be like that. There's a lot of good that can come out of this," Bob replied. "Think of all the people you could help with all that money. Think of all the people we've met who were in a worse position than yourself."

"But my life is going to completely change now," Alex said with a sigh. "I'm not sure if I want it to."

"You're a good person," Bob replied with a

pause. "I'm sure it's not going to change who you are."

CHAPTER 14

Alex tried to keep herself occupied with her volunteering and trips to the gym over the next couple of days. It wasn't easy. She was beginning to lose hope. The thought of her mother's lifeless body lying in cold storage in the morgue made her feel sick. Then from out of the blue the telephone rang. The hospital had received the results back from the autopsy and the coroner was now happy to sign off on the death certificate. Alex breathed a sigh of relief, she could at last prepare for her mother's funeral. She'd be able to make sure she was peacefully laid to rest.

Planning the event was relatively

straightforward. Alex knew it was going to be a simple affair, but it'd taken a toll on her emotions nevertheless. It was bound to she kept telling herself, there wasn't anything wrong with letting it affect her. The grief she felt was real, she couldn't keep it locked away like normal.

Bob helped her choose the type of service and picked out some uplifting music. Her mother would have wanted them to think of the good times, not dwell on the bad. As much as it upset her thinking about it, Alex wanted it to be about celebrating her mother's life. Well, the only life she'd really known about anyway.

The money had already cleared in her account by the time Alex had got around to checking. She used the cash machine outside the bank this time. She didn't feel up to facing the overly helpful staff again anytime soon. She'd purposefully picked a busy day to try, to blend into the crowd. Once she realised the money was actually there it was hard to keep her composure, but she managed to restrain her excitement to only one excited yelp.

It was only then that she allowed a wave of relief to wash over her. She didn't have to worry about paying the bills, she could buy as much food as she wanted, she could even turn on the heating. Alex hadn't got a clue what she was going to do with it all though. Never even in her wildest dreams had she imagined having so much.

In the back of her mind she was still worried about losing her apartment, but it was a different kind of worry now. She wasn't loosing it because she couldn't afford the rent. She was losing it because she didn't need it any longer. She smiled at the thought. She could afford to move somewhere nice. She could escape this hell hole for good. Still, something felt wrong about it. Something was there, niggling, eating away at her inside, she just couldn't put her finger on it.

The money at least meant Alex didn't need to worry about the financial aspect of planning the funeral, but that still left the guests or lack thereof. There weren't any other family members she could rely on. She couldn't even count on any of her mother's old friends. They'd drifted away one by one after the illness took hold. In any case, she was no longer sure how to or even if she wanted to contact them.

Alex made an effort to invite Lorraine from work, but in the end she'd made her excuses. The only other people she could think to ask were the volunteers she knew best from the Foodbank.

Jennifer and Melissa had agreed to come along, but as Alex had only just invited them to dinner, they didn't really have a choice. It was a little emotional blackmail but she wasn't going to spend time worrying over it. She wanted to be sure at least a few people would be there, the thought of it just being Bob and her turned her stomach.

Alex found the Foodbank's manager sorting through papers in a back room.

"I'm really sorry," Stacy replied with a sigh. "If it was another time I might have been able to put things off." She grimaced as she looked down at all the forms on her desk. "There's no chance I'm afraid, I'm up to my eyeballs in paperwork."

"It's all right, I knew you'd be busy," Alex said trying not to sound worried, but it was another person to cross off the list.

"I had some bad news at the meeting the other day," Stacy added with another sigh. "It turned out to be much worse than I'd expected."

"Really, things are that bad?" Alex said with a frown.

"Yes, I'm afraid so. It looks like we could be closing next year. You've heard about all the government cut backs haven't you?"

Alex nodded.

"Well the charity has lost most of its funding," Stacy continued. "The people at head office are reassessing each individual site in turn. They've told me I have until the end of the week to submit evidence proving we can increase revenue or else they'll close us down."

"That definitely sounds like bad news," Alex said frowning. "What is it you need to do?"

"I'm struggling to find funds to cover next year's rent," Stacy said shaking her head. "If I can prove we can at least cover that I think we'll be all right, but I've run out of ideas."

Alex thought about it for a moment, she was in a position to help out after all and Stacy looked so stressed. She thought about all the poor people the Foodbank helped out on a daily basis. How they'd be affected if they lost their support. In fact there were probably people; children even, still alive today directly as a result of the help they'd received there. She thought about the stress she herself had been through over the years, when she'd struggled to pay her way. Who knows, if her mother hadn't left her the money, she could've ended up in need of their help in the coming months.

"How much do you need to cover the rent?" Alex spoke up.

"We're short by nearly ten thousand in total," Stacy sighed staring down at the figures. "I don't know what we're going to do."

Alex smiled running through what she was going to say in her mind. "What if I knew a way out of your situation?" She said grinning. "Would it be worth say... a trip to my mother's funeral?"

"If we could find the money then yes," Stacy replied looking up at her with wide open eyes, "yes it would, but I can't see how."

"My mother left me some money, more than I could possibly need," Alex smiled. "I'm sure she'd have approved of me helping out. I'll cover the money for the rent, you just make sure you're there," Alex said still smiling.

"Are you being serious?" Stacy asked almost frowning.

"Yes, don't worry about it, think of it as an early Christmas present," Alex replied with a chuckle. "Do you have an account number? I'll take a trip down to the bank tomorrow and ask them to transfer it for you."

"Oh that's wonderful, thank you so much," Stacy said with a broad smile across her face. "It's such a lot of money though."

"Well I don't know much about how things work yet," Alex said still trying to think things through, "but I'm sure the manager at the bank said they had an accountant that could help with charitable donations, something about it counting towards my tax bill. Anyway I'm glad I'll be able to use some of it to help people out. Lord knows I've needed help myself in my past."

Alex continued to walk around the Foodbank

finding the old lady in the kitchen. She'd offered to turn up provided she remembered. Something Alex wasn't so sure about. The only other person that was a good possibility was Stephen but he'd said he wasn't going to be in the Foodbank that day. She'd have to ask him later. He'd said he was going to be busy helping his father prepare for a small monthly event at his gym, something to do with powerlifting for his regulars.

Alex remembered glancing over the records and rankings list pinned to the wall when she'd been wandering around the gym. Stephen had said it kept the regulars interested and gave them motivation to keep coming back. Alex wasn't particularly interested in it to be honest. It was probably the lack of any female names on the list that put her off. She'd meant to ask Stephen to consider doing something to attract more women there, at least then she wouldn't feel so out of place.

Alex and Bob had both offered to help out at the gym later on that day. Bob had agreed to meet her at the Foodbank after his shift. Then they'd go along together. Alex thought Bob secretly wanted a chance to show her how much he'd improved since the last time they'd worked out together. She wasn't expecting much. After all he was almost the same weight as her. She'd humour him anyway. She didn't want to hurt his feelings after everything he'd helped her with.

Of course there was another plus point to helping out that Alex had in mind. She might get the chance to persuade Stephen's father to shut up the gym for the afternoon and come along to the funeral. There still wouldn't be many people there, but if she could persuade him as well she could start to feel better about the numbers.

Bob arrived at the Foodbank a little earlier than Alex had expected and joined in helping fill a few boxes.

"There wasn't much work in today," Bob said smiling, "I'd finished by lunch. I didn't think there was much point hanging around doing nothing."

Alex smiled back at him glad of the help.

"How are things going?" He asked.

"Quite good actually, I've persuaded a few people to come along," Alex said with a grin. "Did you meet Jennifer and Melissa?"

"I don't think so," Bob said shaking his head, "what do they look like?"

"They're around somewhere, wait a second, I'll go find them." She turned back as she was about to leave. "Oh yeah, be nice, I've volunteered your services as cook tonight," Alex added with a cheeky grin, rushing off before Bob had a chance to reply.

"Here they are," Alex said when she returned. "I found them hiding out in the staff room."

"We were just warming our drinks up," Jennifer said with a giggle.

"So you're the great cook we've been hearing about?" Melissa asked.

"Hopefully," Bob said starting to blush.

"You like playing games then?" Mel asked as she studied Bob's t-shirt.

"Oh, this... er... I work in a computer shop, it helps me fit in," Bob replied stuttering.

"No need to look so guilty," she laughed. "What world do you play on? I'll try and hook you up with my avatar later."

Bob was caught a little of guard. Women usually didn't react so positively towards him.

"Sure if you want," Bob replied, "bring your laptop around with you. I'll show you after we've eaten."

"Great, it's a date," Melissa grinned.

Jennifer turned to Alex and smiled. "I told you they'd get on. She spends more time on that thing than her studies."

"At least they've got something in common," Alex laughed. "He's normally not comfortable talking to women. It's funny to watch sometimes."

Stephen had almost finished setting things up for the evening when the pair arrived. He'd already cleared a large space by the end wall and moved the three big lifting platforms into position. The middle one was clear, the one to the left had an Olympic bench set up and the one on the right was set up with massive a looking squat rack. All the equipment looked solid and extremely heavy. Alex was actually glad she'd missed the hardest part.

"Hi guys thanks for coming," Stephen shouted when he saw them. "Can you give me a hand moving some of these chairs?"

"No problem," Bob replied. "Where do you want them?"

"Ah, just line them up in a few rows so people can watch. Won't take long, nearly finished now."

"Are you expecting many people?" Alex asked.

"We normally get around fifty or so that come to watch, most of them join in," Stephen replied. "How about it, do you guys fancy it?"

"Sorry we can't tonight, we've already made plans. Well I've already made plans for the both of us," Alex said before turning to mouth sorry to Bob.

"Oh well, maybe next time," Stephen chuckled. "I was just looking forward watching the look on their faces when you joined in."

"OUCH..." Stephen shouted, dropping the metal chair with a clatter to the ground.

Alex and Bob spun around to look. Stephen was

cursing under his breath, holding his arm in some discomfort. Blood was starting to ooze out from between his fingers.

"What's wrong?" Alex yelled.

"Ah, don't worry I just scratched myself on this damn stupid thing," Stephen replied kicking out at the chair. "It's got something sharp sticking out."

"You're bleeding, I can see from here," Alex said starting to walk over to him.

"I'll be fine. It's nothing," Stephen protested trying to shield his arm from view.

"Don't be silly, let me have a look," Alex said as she tried to manoeuvre herself around him.

A few seconds later Stephen relented to Alex's concerned pleas and relaxed his grip, allowing her to prise his fingers away.

"Stephen, this is bad, it's deep. You'll need stitches."

He shook his head. "I'll be fine, don't worry about it."

"You need to let a Doctor see it," Alex said frowning.

"There's no point... See, look it's already stopping," Stephen replied looking down at his arm.

Alex stared, he was right the bleeding had almost stopped and she could swear the edges of the wound seemed smaller than when she first saw it. Stephen yanked his arm out of her relaxed grip while she was distracted.

"See, I'm fine," he said turning his arm from view.

Alex tilted her head back up to look at his face. "But the cut was deep... I saw it... it was bad."

"You must be confused, it was just a scratch," Stephen said as he started to walk away. "Can we just get on with moving these things please? Forget about it."

Alex, still frowning, went back to moving the chairs while Stephen disappeared to the bathroom to wash the blood from his hands. She could have sworn the wound was worse the first time she'd looked at it. She shook her head. It must have been the lighting in the room she told herself. It was probably just shadows making it look worse than it actually was.

Stephen retuned five or so minutes later waving a metal file in his hand. "Sorry about that," he laughed. "Won't take a second to take the edge off. We don't want anyone fragile getting hurt now, do we?"

"How are things anyway?" Stephen asked Alex as they finished up. "Sorry I haven't had time to ask. Are you still coping all right?" Did you get things sorted out? I know you said you were still waiting on the hospital last time we spoke."

"I'm getting through things," Alex replied with a sigh. "You know, slowly, taking one day at a time and all. Yes, I've had the go ahead from the hospital since then. Mother's funeral is arranged for Thursday afternoon."

"Ah, good," Stephen said nodding.

"The service starts at one pm at the Holy Trinity Church up on London Road," Alex continued. "It's the one just to the north of the park. She's been buried in the cemetery there as well."

"Yeah, I know the one. Nice place," Stephen smiled.

"I've planned a little wake in the pub next door. Mother would've wanted us to do something that wasn't too depressing, but I'm afraid there's only going to be a hand full of us going, so please come if you can."

"Yes, I'm sure I can make it," Stephen replied. "I don't think my father will mind too much if I have the afternoon off.

"Ah, is he about?" Alex asked. "I was hoping to ask him if he'd come along as well."

"Yeah, he'll be around keeping himself busy. I think I saw him on the phone a few minutes ago in the office. Do you want me to come with you?"

"No, it's fine he doesn't bite," Alex laughed. "He's just a big cuddly teddy bear."

"With you maybe," Stephen huffed.

"So Bob, do you want to show me your moves?" Stephen asked as Alex wandered off.

Alex heard what she thought was Eric slamming the phone down followed by some muffled shouting as she walked up to the office. He was sitting in the chair with his head in his hands when she reached the door. He glanced up from between his fingers when the sound of the door opening startled him. His expression softened when he saw who it was.

"Oh, hi," he said with a sigh. "What do you want?"

"I've come to cheer you up," Alex smiled hopeful it was the right thing to say. "What's wrong?"

"Oh, nothing, I'm just getting a bit old for all this. Take no notice of me," he said sitting up in his chair. "I'm just feeling a bit sorry for myself that's all. How are things with you?"

"I'm coping... I think anyway," Alex replied with a sigh herself. "Actually that's what I've come to talk to you about." She paused. "Would you be able to come to the funeral? I'd like it if you were there, it just seems right somehow."

"Hmm, I don't know. I'd have to think about it. I'd have to close this place up," he said looking up at the calendar. "When is it?"

"Everything's arranged to start at the Holy

Trinity Church at one on Thursday afternoon."

Eric looked around his office and let out a huge sigh. "What the hell, I'm fed up with this place anyway." He rubbed his face with his hands. "Some days I feel like just jacking the whole lot in and doing something else. I don't know... maybe I just need a break."

"When was the last time you gave yourself a break?" Alex asked.

"Oh," he paused. "Not for years, not since I lost Linda. I've just been trying to keep myself busy. Know what I mean?"

"I think so," Alex nodded.

"I wish things had turned out differently. We could've been so happy together. When I found out you'd lost your mother, well it brought it all back to me." He turned his face away. "Ah, look at me, acting like a fool, must be getting soppy in my old age," he sighed again. "Probably just lonely that's all."

"I don't think you're being a fool," Alex said in a soft voice. "It must've been so hard for you to lose the person you loved." A tear rolled down Alex's cheek. "I know I'm going to miss my mother desperately too."

Eric looked back at her and chuckled. "We're a pair together, you and I."

Alex smiled.

"I'll close the place up for the afternoon.

Go tell Stephen we're both going to go."

"Thank you," Alex said with a smile.

"Would you mind doing me a big favour?" Alex asked Stephen when she'd returned to the group.

Stephen eyed her without speaking.

"I need to pick some clothes up from my apartment for the funeral. I'm kind of worried those men who attacked us will be waiting for me. I'd feel safer if there were three of us." Alex smiled at him. "I think they'd think twice about it once they saw the size of you."

"No worries, if it makes you feel better I'll tag along," Stephen chuckled. "It won't be the first time I've escorted someone."

The apartment block seemed quiet when they arrived. Alex hadn't notice anything that looked out of the ordinary on the way. Well no blacked out cars were waiting for them at any rate, but she had to wonder to herself if her attackers would have been stupid enough to use the same type of vehicle. The only slight distraction came from the drunk ravings of a homeless man emanating from an alleyway and they certainly weren't in a hurry to go down there.

Alex was starting to relax as they wound themselves up staircase after staircase. Things seemed to be going well so far. In fact it wasn't until the trio rounded the last corner that they heard her voice.

"Hey famous girl, long time no see. Where have you been hiding yourself?" A big grin formed on Cat's Face. "We were starting to think you'd forgotten about us."

Alex's heart sank, she'd forgotten about Cat and her gang. She wasn't expecting to come face to face with them in the corridor. Alex looked around. They were standing between them and her door.

"These your friends?" Stephen's said in his deep voice as they maintained their pace towards them.

Alex tried hard to think of a way out of the situation, but something told her there wouldn't be any trouble this time. Daz was looking unusually sheepish. Maybe it was the sight of Stephen walking towards him. Alex smiled to herself.

"Hi Cat, how's things?" Alex said.

"I'm glad you're OK," Cat replied. "We saw it on the news."

She watches the news? Alex wanted to smirk but she managed to keep a straight face. "Yeah, the Docs fixed me up, I'm fine now thanks."

"Actually I've been looking for you." Cat's voice was getting excited. "I need your help again."

This was strange Alex thought. The last time Cat had said something similar to her was many years ago, back when she was still a teenager.

"I've got a big score planned, same sort of thing like last time but with a much bigger payload." She grinned. "If things go well we might actually be able to get away from this place. We could do with an extra man if you're up for it."

"Sorry Cat I don't think I'd be much use this time," Alex said with a sigh. "I've got my mother's funeral coming up in a couple of days. My heads all messed up as it is, I can't concentrate. I'd hate to ruin things for you guys."

"Ah well, just thought I'd offer it to you," Cat smiled. "It's going be one hell of a party."

Alex looked passed her. The rest of Cat's gang were already walking down the corridor in the opposite direction.

"You're missing the chance to change things you know?" Cat said with half a smile before turning to follow.

Bob got straight to preparing the meal for the four of them as soon as he and Alex got back. They were expecting Jennifer and Melissa to arrive any time now. Bob set some potatoes he'd peeled and sliced to boil for a Spanish Omelette while he went to have a quick shower, he could finish it once their guests arrived. Alex set the table and pulled out a bottle of wine from the rack. The alcohol did seem to help Bob with making conversation.

Alex wasn't particularly looking forward to the meal under the circumstances, but hopefully it would help distract her from her morbid thoughts a little while longer. If she admitted it, she was actually more interested in watching Bob try not to make a fool of himself. He always seemed to try just that little bit too hard. There was however the prospect of nurturing a well needed friendship, which did have its own appeal as well.

The meal seemed to be a success, although Alex did end up sitting on the couch talking to Jennifer for most of the night. Melissa had indeed brought her laptop around as Bob had requested and the pair had mostly spent the evening glued to their computer screens. Alex kept chuckling to herself whenever Melissa tried to impress him with her geeky knowledge of the game. It was amusing to see the pair type notes to each other on their computers rather than actually talking to each other, but it did serve to get around Bobs awkwardness. They certainly seemed happy enough together.

Alex smiled to herself as she looked over at Bob. She'd miss his company if the pair did strike it off, but he was going to need someone else to look after him if she moved away. Alex didn't like the thought of moving from this place but the houses around here weren't suitable given the circumstances. She was looking for somewhere less busy, away from the trouble she'd lived with for so many years. She was really going to miss him.

CHAPTER 15

When Alex drew back her curtains on the day of the funeral the sun was shining bright in the cold cloudless sky. Shivering she pulled her dressing gown in tight and hurried out of her bedroom to turn the heating up. She pressed the switch without thinking, it wasn't until she was on her way back to her room that she realised how different things used to be. She stopped in her tracks as the thought hit her. Not too long ago she wouldn't have been able to afford to waste money on something as trivial as heating. She smiled to herself, she was starting to adjust to not needing to worry about the bills, but it wasn't something that came naturally to her. At least now she could afford to give Bob a fair share of what she used, even if he wouldn't accept it.

Alex spent most of the morning pacing around the apartment in silence. Even after all of the preparations had been made she couldn't seem to rest. Agitated, she'd jump up from her chair and run off to check something else she'd remembered mere moments after sitting down. Bob tried his best to calm her down, but in her distressed state little he could do seemed to work.

Alex had plenty of suitable clothes to choose from and had picked out a simple outfit for the event. She'd already decided to wear her long plain black coat which would mostly cover things up, so went with a fitted white blouse, her black skirt, the one which finished just above her knees and her knee length black leather boots. Bob on the other hand didn't have to think about what to wear at all. He just plucked out the same faithful dark suit and black tie he'd worn on many such occasions.

A police car was waiting for them as the pair emerged from the apartment block. It was one of the many conditions stipulated by the police officer in charge of her mother's case, when Alex was making the arrangements. For the safety of all those involved Alex had also been asked to keep the funeral a quiet affair. She hadn't even been allowed to announce the event in the local paper, not that she minded too much, but it did seem to be part of the normal convention.

Without a word spoken the pair of friends made their way over to the car and got into the back. It wasn't the first time Alex had been in the back of a police car but it was the first time she'd agreed to it. The driver waited for the pair to get settled, gave them a small nod when he was sure, then began the slow trip to the church.

Alex stared unblinking out of her window for the entire ten minute duration it took them to reach their destination. Time was passing in a blur to her. Alex's eyes saw the images in front of her but her mind didn't register them. It was like the outside world didn't exist anymore, her thoughts were with her mother.

It took Alex a few moments to realise they were no longer moving. As she turned away from the window she realised they had arrived. The police car had pulled up with only the quietest of murmurs behind another already stationed outside the church that morning. With an expressionless face Alex looked out of the opposite side window towards the towering dark Gothic entrance of the church. Her gaze drawn through the large open wooden doors and into the waiting congregation. It looked like the majority of her friends had already taken their seats and were waiting in silence for the service to begin.

Alex felt a little comfort knowing that at least there were some people to say goodbye to her mother. Through her bleary eyes she thought she made out the shape of Stephen disappearing inside, another man was in front but she couldn't make him out. His father lagged a few steps behind pausing to acknowledge her arrival.

It was as Bob held the door open for Alex that she noticed the police cars at either end of the street. She tried not to think of the trouble they were expecting, she couldn't deal with it today. She forced her vision to pan back towards the familiar sight of the church. She stopped, looking in awe through her tear filled eyes at what she saw. Behind the church Golden rays of sunlight lit up the remaining leaves on the ancient trees in the tranquil graveyard. The glorious display of autumnal colours was a beautiful thing to see. It was something her mother would've taken great pride in trying to paint. Alex's eyes welled up even more, the place she'd chosen for her mother to rest seemed perfect.

Alex's numb body felt a tug as Bob's hand squeezed hers. She looked up at him without comprehending and followed his gaze. The hearse carrying her mother's coffin was heading down the road towards them. Alex felt herself begin to tremble, she let out a quiet whimper, but as always Bob was there to hold on for support. She looked up at him again. He was tense, trying to hold himself together for her. He turned briefly to acknowledge her gaze, trying to force a small comforting smile as he did.

As the pallbearers walked past helping her mother along on her last journey Alex and Bob fell into step. Alex didn't notice the people in the church as they entered. Her tearful eyes were fixed solely on her mother's coffin. Her world had been reduced to just the pair of them. She didn't notice as Bob guided her to her seat. She didn't hear what was being said to her, her mind was elsewhere.

The church service was pleasant enough under the circumstances. The vicar tried not to linger on her mother's illness as he read her eulogy, instead he emphasised the business she'd built up and her creative flair. It had taken a few days for him and Alex to get the wording right. It wasn't easy talking about someone's life when you only knew the second half of their story. The hymns sung were well judged, not too melodramatic nor to joyful. Alex had tried to pick ones she thought left you with a feeling as though things were going to be all right, that her mother's spirit would live on in people's hearts, those that seemed to offer at least a small amount of hope.

One of her mother's favourite pieces of music was played as her coffin was led out of the church towards her final resting place. Alex followed still numb but not needing her support any longer, her body seemed to have switched over onto autopilot. Alex couldn't recall how they'd made it to the graveside but she watched helpless as her mother's coffin was gently lowered into the ground and committed to the earth. Her mind struggled as it formed the last memory she would ever have of her. "Goodbye Mum," was all she could manage in her broken voice.

Alex only noticed the sad faces of her friends after the vicar had finished his prayers and she plucked up the courage to lift her head. So many people had turned up to pay their respects, many more than she'd imagined. Most of her friends had brought at least two people with them, although only those she knew best were nearest to her. In her daze she thought she heard Bob's voice reminding people they were invited to the wake at the pub, but her distressed mind could just have as easily imagined it.

Alex's thoughts seemed to come back to reality as she felt herself sit down on the hard wooden bench in the pub.

"What do you want to drink?" Bob's voice cut through the haze.

"Er... I don't care. Anything... Something strong," Alex replied in a cracked voice.

Bob slunk away to the bar relieved that the worst part of the day was over. He returned a few minutes later with two double whiskeys.

"Here you go, this should warm you up a bit," he said as he placed Alex's drink down on the table in front of her.

"What am I going to do without her?" Alex managed as she turned to face him.

Bob took a long look at his friend. Her sad face was red and blotchy. He knew that on any other occasion she'd have tried to hide the fact that she was upset. "Things will work out you'll see, just give them time." It was the best he could come up with.

"But I've no family left now. I'm all on my own," Alex said as she downed the drink in one. The lingering heat of the whisky seeming to cause little reaction.

"You'll get through this, like always. You'll find a way to cope," Bob added before following suit and downing his drink. He however, wasn't as adept at hiding his discomfort and coughed.

Alex felt her lips rise in one corner.

"Do you want a bite to eat? It might help if you have something in your stomach," Bob asked still spluttering.

"I'm not hungry," Alex replied with a sigh. "I don't think I'll ever be hungry again."

"Come on, try to keep your chin up," Bob said before standing up again, the lure of the bar drawing him back. He didn't usually drink in excess but today had taken a lot out of him. He was in need of its solace. "I'll get you some sandwiches while I'm up. It'll give you something to nibble on."

Stephen was the first to approach Alex's table and offer his condolences.

"Hi," he said in a hushed voice.

Alex raised her head to see what had distracted her from her dark thoughts.

"It was a nice ceremony," he added. "Your mother would've been proud."

Alex didn't really hear the words he was saying but the tone of his voice was soothing. She managed a half smile, her lips quivering. She watched as his face struggled to find the right expression for the situation.

"You gave her a good send off."

Alex lowered her head again but she nodded in acknowledgement.

"If you need anything, anything at all, let me know all right?" Stephen decided Alex's weakening nod was a sign she wanted to be left alone and made his retreat back over to his father.

Just one solitary police car remained when the pair shuffled out of the pub later that afternoon. The trouble they'd been expecting obviously hadn't materialised. The lone policeman looked glad to be finished with his less than glamorous assignment for the day, as he offered to take them back to Bob's apartment complex.

When Alex awoke the next morning her head was already complaining. What little sunlight there was shining through the curtains hurt her eyes. She stared with her blurry vision at the empty space on the bedside cabinet where the clock used to be. A half drunk bottle of red wine stood open in its place, she didn't see a glass. Alex allowed her head to flop back down onto her pillow. Shielded her eyes from the brightness with her arm and tried to remember what had happened. Her foggy mind could recall getting back to the apartment but nothing more.

A few seconds later her thirst got the better of her and in search of water Alex tried to swing her legs out of bed. There was something stopping them, it took her another few moments to realise she was still wearing her clothes. It was just the tightness of her skirt preventing them from moving independently. She looked down. At least it seemed she'd removed her boots. As her eyes scanned the room they found the clock upside down on the bedroom floor, its numbers blinking error on its LCD screen. Clutching her temple Alex meandered into the kitchen. Her mouth felt like sawdust as she took the first few cooling sips of water.

Alex heard the familiar sound of the front door opening and shutting and found Bob next to it with a newspaper in his hand.

"Ah, you're finally awake," he laughed. "I just nipped out to the corner shop. We were out of painkillers. I thought you'd probably need some."

"Hush, don't talk so loud," she winced.

Bob walked over to her smiling and placed the packet into her outstretched hand.

"Thank you," Alex said squinting. "Shouldn't you be in work, anyway?" She added whilst trying to open the packet one handed, the other still holding her aching head.

"I called in sick," Bob replied. "They seemed to understand the situation. What do you want to do today?"

"I want the world to swallow me up," Alex grumbled.

"After you've had a chance to freshen up a bit I mean," Bob smirked.

"I suppose I should start looking for a new place," Alex sighed. "I can't stay here under your feet forever." She cut him off before he had chance to reply. "It's very nice of you to let me stay but I need to sort myself out, I need something to occupy my mind or I'm going to go mad."

"Well go have a shower and get changed out of yesterday's clothes," Bob said giving her a sarcastic look, "it'll make you feel better. It's easy enough to search for properties on the internet. When your headache's gone we can have a look."

Bob was already sat at his computer by the time Alex had made herself respectable again. Her head was still sore but at least she no longer felt sick.

"Nice to see some colour back in that face," Bob said with a smile as she walked up to him. "I'm just finishing up. I was doing a quest with Melissa, should only be a few more minutes."

"Ah OK. Do you want a cup of coffee?" Alex asked.

"Yes please, that'd be nice," Bob said without turning away from the screen.

When Alex returned with the two cups of coffee in hand Bob had already signed out from his game.

"Have you got any idea what type of property you're after or where?" He asked.

"I hadn't really given it much thought to be honest," Alex replied with a shrug. "I've never had enough money to have a choice before. Away from those God damn train tracks that's for sure. They drive me nuts."

"I know what you mean," Bob laughed. "How about these, they look nice?"

"I don't know, they look too posh," Alex frowned. "I wouldn't feel right."

"Hmm... well then how about a new apartment?" Bob asked. "They've just built some really nice ones near the centre of town."

"I don't think so," Alex shook her head. "I want somewhere more private, somewhere with a bit of land."

"You've just said you didn't like that sort," Bob replied with a puzzled look on his face.

"No, what I meant was I do like those places but I'd want somewhere where I could be myself, you know, not be worried what the neighbours thought."

"You do know somewhere like that's going to be tricky to find around here don't you?" Bob said. "Unless you want to move way out into the countryside."

"I know," she said with a sigh. "Let me have a look." Alex motioned for him to let her sit down. "I'll probably be a while so if there's something else you need to do, feel free. There's no need for you to be stuck here as well."

"I've got a few errands I can run," Bob

replied, "if you're sure you don't mind."

"Not at all," Alex shook her head. "I need to get this sorted."

"Is there anything you want me to pick you up while I'm out?" Bob asked.

"I'll be fine honestly." Her head was shaking again.

Alex spent the next three hours in a fruitless search of the internet looking through the available properties for sale in the area. If she admitted it to herself there were actually some really nice ones, but something was holding her back. She couldn't get used to the idea of her being able to afford to live somewhere different. It troubled her somehow. She couldn't stop thinking about all the other poor people she'd met in her life that didn't have the opportunity to turn things around. She felt guilty, like she was betraying who she really was inside.

"Any luck?" Bob asked when he returned.

"No, not really," Alex sighed. "I found a few interesting looking places that I wouldn't mind having a look at, but nothing stands out to me."

"Well it's a start," Bob replied. "There's no need to rush into things."

"I need to get some fresh air," Alex said yawning as she leaned back in her chair to stretch. "Do you fancy coming to the gym with me?"

"I think I'll pass on that one today," Bob smiled. "There's a program on in a while I wanted to catch. I'm just going to put my feet up and relax for a bit."

"OK," Alex replied standing up. "I suppose I'll see you when I get back. I feel like I need to burn off some steam."

Eric was in his office when Alex walked into the gym.

"Hi," she said in a soft voice. "Thanks for coming yesterday."

Eric looked up from his desk smiling as he recognised who it was. "Oh hi," he replied. "No problem, I'm glad I went. It was a nice service."

"I er... didn't feel like staying in. I needed some fresh air," Alex said with a weak smile.

"Well a work out should help if you feel up to it," Eric replied.

"I think I'm going to give it a try," Alex sighed.

As Alex was about to walk off she noticed what Eric was up to. He seemed to be sorting through a lot of his old paperwork, placing some in neat piles ready to go into boxes, others he'd been shredding into the bin.

"What are you up to," Alex asked, "if you don't mind me asking?"

Eric let out a heavy sigh. "I'm boxing some things up, getting ready to move."

"What do you mean, move?"

"I've finally decided to do what I should've done years ago." He placed the papers in his hands down onto a pile and smiled. "I'm going to sell up and treat myself to a nice holiday."

"But... what's going to happen to the gym?" Alex blurted out. "What's Stephen going to do?"

"Ah he'll be all right," Eric laughed. "He's wanted to go back to college for years. He's just been hanging around here for my sake."

"Have you told him yet?" Alex said. She was starting to feel anxious.

"Yeah, he's out back in the garden," Eric replied turning back to his work. "Said he wanted to think things through."

Alex turned towards the door, intending to rush of to find him. "Oh er... do you mind?" She said managing to hold herself back.

"No go right ahead," Eric smiled. "He probably needs someone to talk to anyway."

Alex turned again and headed off through the door.

"Hey," Eric shouted through the open window.

Alex stopped in her tracks. "Yeah?"

"It's this way," Eric laughed.

Alex retraced her steps and carried on back out into the yard. Her eyes scanned the building.

The iron gate in the wall was open. She'd noticed it many times before but had never given it a second thought as to where it might have led, she'd never needed to. Alex wandered up to it and then carried on through the archway into the secluded walled garden behind.

Stephen was right at the other end of the path sitting motionless on a metal bench with his head in his hands. He looked up and gave a small wave when he noticed her standing there.

As Alex started walking towards him she began to take in the beauty of her surroundings. Six gnarled old looking apple trees lined either side of the main paved path, their heavy branches overhanging the walkway. One still had a few colourful apples clinging to its branches. The fruit a glorious gold overlain by a beautiful orange blush. Alex stopped a second to read the rusty metal tag around its trunk. She could just about make out the weathered etching as 'Sturmer Pippin', she wondered where it got its strange name. At the bases of the off reddish brick walls of the garden lay many separate raised beds. A few were still occupied by what looked like blackberry canes. As she took the whole view in she realised the entire area had been set out as an old fashioned kitchen garden. This was obviously where Stephen and his father liked to spend some of their spare time. She was starting to think she would too.

"Hi, your father said you'd be hiding out here," Alex said as she sat down beside him.

"I'm just thinking a few things through," Stephen said smiling back at her. "I've got some tough decisions to make."

"Yeah your father told me about it" she added. "Do you know how long you've got left here?"

"No, dad hasn't put it on the market yet," Stephen replied. "He only decided this morning."

"Oh..." Alex frowned. "So what are you going to do if your Dad sells it then? He said you were thinking of going back to college."

"Yeah, I might do," Stephen sighed. "I haven't made up my mind though yet." He looked around at the garden again. "I'm going to miss this place. I spent most of my childhood growing up here."

"Has your dad thought about what he's going to do once he's sold it?" Alex asked.

"I don't know really," Stephen shook his head. "I think he's going to be lost without it. I don't think it'll be long before he starts to regret it."

Alex remained silent for a while, looking around the garden, taking in the tranquillity of the place. Her mother would've loved it here, especially on a day like today.

"What if there was another way?" Alex blurted out. "What if there was a way that meant both of you could still be happy?" Her mind was racing. "You could both still work here, you'd just have more time to yourselves."

"I'm listening," Stephen said suddenly serious.

"How much does your father want for the place?" Alex asked still gazing into the distance. "I'm looking for somewhere to live and I wouldn't mind helping to run the gym. You and your father could stick around for as long as you wanted."

"It's a nice thought," Stephen huffed, "really it is, but it's more difficult than you think trying to get a mortgage on a business property. I'm not sure the banks would even listen to you."

"What if I didn't need a mortgage?" Alex said smiling. "What if I could just take it off his hands?" Alex turned to face him. "Seriously how much does he want for it?"

Stephen looked at her with a puzzled expression on his face. He wasn't sure if she was being serious or not.

"I er... I'm not sure..." Stephen said with almost a frown. "I think he said the property was worth about a hundred and fifty thousand and the business about fifty. If you're being serious you're welcome to go and talk it over with him. I'm sure he'd prefer to sell it to someone he knows."

"Come on then," Alex was already up beckoning him to follow, "quickly before I change my mind."

The pair made their way back along the garden path towards the entrance. Stephen picked a ripe looking apple from the tree and offered it to her. "Here take one. I saw you looking at them. It should be ready."

Alex snatched it from his hand and bit into its crunchy flesh. She grinned as its rich sharp taste filled her mouth.

Stephen chuckled as she tried to wipe away the sticky juice running down her chin.

"Bring it with you," he added, "we need to stop my dad before he sorts too many things out."

Stephen raised his fist and tapped on the glass with his knuckles until his father looked up from his sorting. "Dad, Alex wants a chat with you. She's got an idea."

A short while later all three of them walked out of the office happy and Alex would need to make an important visit to her bank. She'd need to arrange the transfer of funds with her accountant and get the legal side of things sorted out. She didn't care what her adviser would say, the arrangement seemed perfect to her and even if things didn't work out it would hardly put a dent in her balance anyway. She smiled to herself contented. Things were starting to look up for her. She only wished her mother was there with her to be part of it.

CHAPTER 16

Things seemed to have quickened pace for Alex ever since she'd decided to purchase the gym from Eric. She was starting to get used to the idea of having a new place to move into and a new business to run. She was looking forward to it, excited for the new challenges in her life. For once she'd be her own boss. She'd have control over her own destiny. Her mother's last gift had given her new hope in life, she'd become one of the lucky ones, one of the few people to escape the misery of abject poverty. She wasn't yet sure where the money had come from but she'd promised herself in time she'd find out.

Alex had spent the last couple of days busily boxing up her things from her apartment ready for the move and Eric and Stephen had been busy doing the same at the old church. Eric hadn't yet decided where he was going to move to but he'd got his eye on a few properties. He was looking for somewhere on the outskirts of the city, somewhere he'd be happy to retire to in a few years time. The commute didn't bother him, he kept saying, it'd give him an excuse to use his old 'Mustang' more.

Bob had been supportive of the move, after all it meant he'd still be able to see his friend and even though he knew Alex didn't need to find another job financially, he thought it was a good idea to keep her occupied. Having her own business would give her something to focus on instead of dwelling too much on the past. He knew she was still going through a tough time, what with losing her mother and all, but he was happy with the way things were now going for her.

As Eric was still occupying the adjoining house at the gym, Alex could only really take the things over that she intended to use in the office. She'd just finished sorting a box of items into their new places and set her sentimental photograph with its new frame on top of the filing cabinet when Eric stuck his head around the door.

"Hey there," Eric said with a big grin on his face. "I just wanted to tell you I got the money. I took a trip down to the bank this morning. It was all there waiting for me in my account. So thank you, it's all sorted. I suppose I just need to get my butt in gear now and find a place of my own."

"Thanks for letting me know," Alex replied.

Eric turned to leave but paused in the doorway. "Oh... what's this?" He said as he picked up Alex's photo, caressing the image with the tips of his fingers. "I haven't seen this in years. Stephen must've found it when he was packing things up."

"Er... what are you talking about?" Alex said frowning. Eric turned back to face her with the photograph in his hand. "This photo, I can't remember the last time I saw it. It's been so long," he replied continuing to stare into the image.

"Er... I hate to break it to you, but Stephen didn't find it, it's mine. It was my mothers. You must be mistaken."

Eric was the one to look puzzled now as he turned to stare at Alex. "It's me with Linda before she was killed," he said frowning himself. "I can remember it been taken, it was by the beach on the last holiday I took with her, my last holiday."

"It can't be," Alex snapped. "It's my mother. Her name's Margaret, Margaret Forster, not Linda."

"I'm telling you, it's me with Linda, I'm positive," Eric replied, his hands starting to shake.

"Stop it, it's not funny," Alex said, glaring through narrowed eyes. "I'm being serious."

"Look," he held the photograph up to his face. "See, it's me."

Alex stood and walked right up to him. She made herself take a deep breath before she reached up and took the photograph from his hand. She looked back and forth between it and the man standing before her, trying to fit the faces together. She tried to imagine Eric younger, maybe fifty pounds lighter, without the grey stubble and the aged skin around his eyes. It couldn't be him could it? She stared into Eric's deep dark blue eyes and wondered. Those same eyes stared back out at her from the photograph. "But it doesn't make sense, that's my mother."

Eric's legs went weak. His arms reached out to brace his large frame against the metal filling cabinet. "What are you saying?" His voice trembled. His piercing eyes locked on Alex. "Linda died all those years ago. I buried her ashes. Stephen was just a baby. The accident left us all alone. It took her away from us." His voice was manic, scared even. His deep blue eyes began to well up.

Alex didn't know what to say, her pulse was racing just the same. "Well I'm sorry, but it's definitely my mother in that photograph and her name wasn't Linda, you know that."

Alex tried to think things through. Tried to calm herself, tried to calm Eric. "How long ago did you lose her?"

Eric took another deep breath trying to steady himself. "Just after Stephen was born, just after his first birthday," he was almost shouting. Reminiscing brought the emotions back, brought more tears to his eyes.

"How Old is Stephen?" Alex asked looking at him through her own bleary eyes.

"He's just about to turn twenty seven, why?"

Alex was starting to wish Bob was here, he enjoyed trying to work these sorts of things out. She tried to work the time scale out in her head, but she'd never been the brightest with maths problems at school. Alex heard herself gasp as the numbers started to arrange themselves in her mind. "Was she pregnant?" she blurted out.

Eric's face creased up.

"Sorry, I didn't mean to be rude," Alex said eager for his answer, trying to encourage him.

Eric took another deep breath. "She'd told me a few weeks before, yes," he sighed, "yes she was."

Alex held her hands up to cover her gasping mouth. Her mind was racing again. Was she staring at her father? She backed off and froze as her back touched the wall.

"What's wrong?" Eric said, concerned by the sudden distress on her face. He walked over to her and placed one of his large hands on her shoulder.

Alex's body was stuck fast, immobile, but her eyes followed his every movement. "Dad," She said in a faint voice from behind her fingers.

Eric didn't hear.

Alex's overcome mind was struggling, desperate even, trying to cope with the situation. She couldn't move but her eyes were wide open. She'd never believed she'd find him, she'd wanted it so badly, but now it had actually happened after all those years, she found herself petrified. On the one hand she felt like passing out, she felt so nervous, but on the other she was so excited she could burst. It was all she could do to keep breathing.

"Are you all right, what's wrong?" Eric said afraid his outburst had frightened her.

Alex's mind plucked up the courage to move, out of nowhere she sprang up to hug him. The sudden force of her body hitting his caused Eric to take a few unsteady steps backwards. He coughed with relief after he'd managed to prise Alex's arms open enough to his lungs expand again.

"Hey, what's all this for?" Eric chuckled.

"Sorry," Alex said hopping up and down excited. She didn't know why things had turned out the way they had, but things suddenly made sense.

Eric was still chuckling when she spoke again.

"If it is you and my mother in the photograph and what you've just said is true, then it's more than likely you're my father." Alex heard the words coming out of her mouth but she could hardly believe she was saying them. If it was true then in the space of a little over three minute she'd gone from having no family left at all to having a father. Why were good things happening to her? Why now?

Eric caught a glimpse of Stephen pass by the window and called to him. "Hey you'd better get yourself in here lad your sister's got something to tell you."

Stephen stopped dead in his tracks and stared at his father, who was waving his arms to beckon him over, like he'd gone mad.

Like a bolt out of the blue it dawned on Alex, if Eric was her father it'd make Stephen... Stephen was her... wouldn't it? She had a brother. Her chest began to ache as her heart thumped around uncontrolled inside her ribcage. She had a family again. She wasn't alone. Unfortunately for Alex her distracted subconscious had somehow neglected in its duty to keep her respiration under control. She just about made it, slumping down like a lead weight into the waiting chair. A few deep breaths later she'd recovered enough to greet her new brother with a hug as he walked in through the open office door.

Stephen looked utterly confused. He kept looking back and forth between the smiling faces in front of him. "Well is someone going to tell me what's going on," his voice sounded tense, "or am I supposed to just guess?"

"Here, take a look at this," Eric said chuckling again as he handed Stephen the photograph.

Stephen looked it over a few times unimpressed. "So what is it? What am I supposed to be looking at?"

"That's me when I was a lot younger," Eric smiled, "probably no older than you are now, with your mother."

"Yes, well I gathered that much for myself," Stephen huffed. "I've seen your old pictures before, so what?"

"Well, the thing is," Eric continued, "it's

not my old photograph, it's Alex's."

Stephen turned towards her with a strange look on his face.

"Go on, you'd better tell him," Eric encouraged.

"Like your father said, it's my photograph. Well it is now, it was my mothers. It's her standing next to him."

Stephen started to piece the information together in his head.

"I only found it a couple of years ago when we were packing up my mother's things. It was hidden behind one of my baby portraits."

"You're sure this is your mother?" Stephen asked.

"Yes, I'm certain of it," Alex replied. "I didn't know who the man in the shot was until a few moments ago."

"But that would mean..." Stephen's mouth gaped open.

"Yeah, looks like you've got yourself a little sister," Eric butted in.

"Yeah, and I've got myself a new big brother and father," Alex laughed.

"But I don't understand, you said she was dead?" Stephen turned to stare at his father. "Why would you lie about something like that?"

"Hey, I'm as surprised as you are kid," Eric said with a shrug.

Both of the men turned their attention back towards Alex and stared in silence.

"Hey, don't look at me. I don't know what happened either," Alex said frowning.

"If she was my mother," Stephen spoke up, "what's she been up to all these years? Why would she abandon us?"

"She never spoke about the past I'm afraid," Alex replied shaking her head. "It's all still a mystery to me. If you could answer a few things it might make things a bit clearer."

"Such as?" Stephen said taken aback.

"After we were attacked Bob tried to help me find out more about her background. We wanted to know why those men attacked us, what they were after." Alex shook her head again. "The thing is. It turned out there was no paper trail to follow. We couldn't find any record of her before my birth, nor for any other family members for that matter. It was really confusing. I'd given up hope of ever finding out."

"Have you got any idea why they did attack you, why they killed her?" Stephen asked.

"I don't know if I should be telling you this, but as we're all family now, I suppose it can't hurt," Alex sighed. "A short while after her death I was informed my mother had a substantial amount of money locked away in an offshore account. I figured that was probably why."

Stephen and his father looked at each other confused, and then back towards Alex.

"How much are we talking about, if you don't mind me asking?" Eric said in a soft voice.

"It was a lot, over a million."

"Really?" Eric recoiled. "Where the hell did she get that kind of money from?"

"Oh, I was hoping you could tell me," Alex huffed.

"We never had that kind of money," Eric replied. "I knew she had a good job, but it can't have been that good, she would've told me."

"Oh," Alex sighed again. "So you don't know what she used to do either then?"

"I've got an idea, but she never actually told me who she was working for," Eric sounded rueful. "She used to disappear for weeks at a time. Said she was working on something really important. Said it'd change everything."

"Well if we're ever going to sort this mess out, I'm going to need somewhere to start," Alex replied. "I need to find out if I'm still in danger. We could all be in danger."

"Just what exactly do you mean by we?" Stephen interrupted.

"That's the thing I haven't worked out yet. At first we thought those men were just trying to rob us, the apartment was a mess, things were thrown everywhere, but nothing seemed to be missing," Alex shrugged. "For some reason they'd gathered my mother's pieces of art and all of the photographs together. It was very strange. They seemed to have been searching for something."

"Well that still doesn't explain how we fit in to all this," Stephen added raising his voice.

"That's when I realised the photograph was missing, the one you're now holding in your hand. It was the only thing in the property that possibly showed who my father was. They must have tried to get my mother to talk about it, that's why they shot her full of drugs, but it was too late by then, her memory was almost gone."

"You're trying to suggest they were after Dad?" Stephen coughed.

"Yes, it's the only possible explanation I could come up with. I don't know why, maybe they thought he had something to do with the money."

"Now wait a second," Eric cut in, "I never knew about anything about it."

"Yeah, but who's going to tell them that?" Stephen said staring at his father.

"What're we going to do?" Eric said starting to pace back and forth. "What if they find out who I am, where we are? All the strength in the world won't do us any good if they start shooting." Eric slammed his fist down onto the filing cabinet, the sudden noise was deafening in the small room.

"Let's try and calm down a bit shall we," Alex said in a soft voice. "We need to think about this rationally."

"Sorry," Eric said with a grumble. "I get angry when I'm upset."

"Now listen," Alex said locking eyes on him, "you said you had an idea about what she did. Can you tell me anything that might help to find out more about what it was?"

"It was so long ago," Eric shrugged.

"Just tell me what you remember," she encouraged.

"She'd not long finished her studying. She'd graduated top of her class in Biochemistry at Manchester Metropolitan."

"Really?" Alex exclaimed with a frown. "She was a scientist? She never mentioned anything of the sort. She was always too interested in her art."

"Well that's what she wanted to do when I knew her," Eric shrugged again. "She said she'd landed a research job for a major company. I'm sure she said it was something to do with disease control."

"Disease control?" Alex gasped. "Never." What on earth would that have to do with anything, she thought?

"Like I said, she used to disappear for weeks

on end," Eric was starting to look troubled again. "Said she couldn't leave her projects."

"How did it all end?" Alex asked as softly as she could.

"Oh..." Eric took a deep breath. "I got a call late one night. It was a man's voice, said there'd been a terrible accident at work, Linda had been badly injured. He said she'd died before they'd had chance to get her to the hospital," Eric's eyes began to tear up. "I never got to see the body before the cremation. They told me it had to be done straight away to prevent the disease from spreading."

Alex was the one to start pacing this time.

"A man I'd never seen before, nor since, delivered her ashes a couple of days later," Eric continued with a sigh. "Then it was just up to me to get on with life and bring young Stephen up on my own."

"That must have been terrible for you. Oh, I'm so sorry," Alex said as she walked up to him to give him a hug.

Eric nodded.

She turned her head slightly to look towards Stephen. "Still, look how well Stephen turned out. You must've done well to cope all on your own."

"Thanks," Eric tried to smile at his son, "if it wasn't for him I don't think I'd have made it."

"Did you happen to get the man's number or address who contacted you?" Alex asked.

"I never gave it a second thought, sorry," Eric replied with a shake his head. "I was too upset to think straight at the time."

"Oh well," Alex took a deep breath. "At least we've got something to go on. I'll get Bob to check the records at the University, maybe he can pull up some more information."

Alex lost all track of the time as she continued to reminisce with her new found family. She'd so much to talk about, to find out. What had she missed while she was growing up? What had her brother been like as a child? She wanted to know all of it, all at once. The three of them were quite hoarse after they'd exhausted themselves.

Alex felt truly happy for the first time in years. A missing part of herself had been made whole again. Of course she'd known Eric had always been fond of her, but she'd still felt the fear inside her, that her father wouldn't want her, wouldn't accept her. Before today she'd thought her father had abandoned her and her mother a long time ago, now she knew the truth, for some reason or other he'd been sold a lie. She had to try and find out what had gone on all those fateful years ago, for all their sakes.

She said her goodbyes just before closing time and made her way out into the cold night air. Eric had offered to give her a lift home but she'd politely refused, she had something she needed to sort out first.

Even though the council hadn't requested the apartment keys back until after the Christmas holidays, Alex still wanted to have everything sorted beforehand. Earlier that day she'd decided to call in on her way home from the gym to give the place a last once over. She hadn't planned on it being so late but she'd already made her mind up. It was going to be difficult enough for her to cope over the first Christmas without her mother as it was, she didn't want to have to worry about the apartment as well.

The tower block looked deserted as she walked up to it. Its old neglected lights flickering away dimly in the darkness of the night. The street seemed oddly silent, nothing really appeared out of place, but it was just too quiet. Out of the darkness the sound of a woman shouting cut through the eerie silence, it was coming from somewhere above. Alex carried on towards the entrance, keeping her head down as she went for fear of being recognised, determined to get this over with once and for all.

The lights inside were no better, constantly flickering on and off. The door to the malfunctioning lift had now been taped shut, an out of order sign hung limp by what little sticky tape still clung to the cold metal. Alex rushed over to the stairs, she didn't want to linger. Just as she reached the first step the overhead light ominously flickered off plunging Alex into complete darkness for a heart stopping three seconds. When it flickered back into life Alex quickened her pace as much as she could. The sound of her feet clattering up the tiled stairs echoed all around her.

It wasn't until she was approaching the sixth floor that she heard the noise. She paused to listen. It was definitely there. Every now and then the unusual silence was being broken by a quiet indistinguishable murmur. Alex was more intrigued than anything else. She didn't recognise it, not here. It almost sounded like a child whimpering all alone in the darkness above, but it couldn't have been. Life was hard inside these walls. People didn't cry, at least not in public, they just picked themselves up and carried on as best they could.

Alex found the girl huddled up with her head between her knees a few flights above her.

"Are you all right?" She said in a soft voice. "Can I help you?"

As the girl lifted her head towards her Alex recognised who it was. The unmistakable eyes of

Cat were looking back at her through their tears.

"Cat, what's wrong?" Alex said surprised. "Why are you all alone, where are your friends?"

Cat continued to weep.

"What happened?" Alex pleaded.

"I don't need your help," a croaky broken voice replied. "Leave me alone."

"I'm not going until you tell me what's wrong," Alex added, Cat didn't seem so intimidating to her any longer.

Cat looked up again. "It's all over, nothing matters anymore," she sobbed.

Alex stooped down and tried to put her arm around her.

"Don't touch me, get away from me," Cat shouted pushing her away. "Leave me alone."

"There must be something you can tell me, maybe I can help," Alex continued.

All of a sudden Cat rose to her feet furious, forcing Alex against the wall.

"I told you to leave me alone," she said, her face full of spite, tears still rolling down her cheeks.

Alex froze helpless as Cat held her against the cold hard wall. Cat leaned in close to her face. Alex closed her eyes. She couldn't break the mental barrier stopping her from defending herself against the bully.

It was then Cat did something Alex wasn't

expecting, something as far from her thoughts as she could possibly imagine. Alex felt Cat's soft hot lips press against hers as she kissed her. She felt the wetness on her cheek and tasted the saltiness of Cats tears in her mouth. What was she doing?

"Ouch," Alex shouted feeling a sharp pain as Cat bit her lip hard.

Alex felt the pressure on her lifting as Cat released her grip. She opened her eyes and looked at the disappearing Cat puzzled. Cat was smiling as she walked away but still tearful.

"I'll miss you, you know," was all Alex heard her say when she looked back briefly before vanishing.

Alex stood there bemused for a few seconds before she realised her lip was throbbing. She touched the tips of her fingers against it. It wasn't long until the familiar taste of iron began to spread around her mouth. She moved her hand away and looked down at her fingers, they were stained a deep glistening crimson.

Bob was sitting at his computer when Alex arrived back at his apartment later that night.

"Hi stranger, you're late aren't you?" Bob asked. "What have you been up to, anything interesting?"

"Not much, nothing interesting anyway," she replied chuckling to herself. "I just had a few things to sort out back at the apartment before I give the key back that's all."

Alex sighed, she felt all talked out for the day. She could tell Bob about her new found family members in the morning. She would however be keeping the other brief encounter to herself.

"Ah OK," Bob replied. "There's some stew left on the hob if you're hungry, just help yourself."

"Thanks," she smiled, "I do actually feel quite hungry for a change."

Alex poured herself a large bowl and sat down on the couch to eat it while staring at the TV. She wasn't really paying attention to the taste of her food, nor the noise coming from the box, she was trying to make sense of her thoughts.

CHAPTER 17

Alex heard a knock on her bedroom door. She looked up. The sunlight shone bright through her thin curtains. It was morning. She could get used to this sleeping business she thought as she rubbed her dry eyes.

"Ah, you're awake are you?" Bob said smiling as he popped his head around the door. "I've made you some breakfast."

Alex coughed to clear her sticky throat. "Thank you," she grumbled, "but I'm not hungry yet."

"You know what Stephen told us," Bob laughed. "You need to get some fuel inside you."

"What time is it anyway?" Alex asked sitting up in bed.

"Just gone ten." Her pained expression made him laugh once more. "Come on get up it's going cold. You've already had a lie in."

Alex stroked her hair and yawned. "Thank you," she repeated herself. "What did you make?"

"I've done you an omelette and some brown toast. I figured you wouldn't want porridge again."

Alex shook her head and yawned once more. "Shouldn't you be at work anyway?"

"It's Saturday, remember?" Bob tutted. "Try to keep up with the program."

Still groggy Alex rushed to the bathroom to freshen up. She didn't want to get in trouble for letting Bob's food go cold.

"There you are," Bob said, as Alex emerged from the bathroom feeling a bit more human. "Come get this down you."

It looked like Bob had already cleared away his finished dishes by the time Alex sat down.

"See, it's still warm," she said, raising another piece of the cold omelette to her mouth.

"Hmm," Bob stared at her from the couch, "if you say so."

It didn't take long for Alex to finish her breakfast. She ate it fast, more as a chore than for any sort of enjoyment. She was still finding the task of making herself eat as difficult as ever. Even though she could afford to eat better now, her mind still tried to hold her back. She hadn't realised she was developing a problem before, but it was definitely there, loosely hidden behind a veil of poverty. At least she'd managed to put some weight on. The encouragement from Stephen and Bob was helping. Even Bob himself had begun to fill out his frame a bit more.

Alex heard the news headlines begin while she was busy cleaning the dirty dishes in the kitchen. Something in the pit of her stomach told her to pay attention.

"Hey Bob," she shouted. "Can you turn the volume up please?"

Alex stacked the last clean plate in the drying rack. She hadn't heard the news reporter mention anything unusual so far. Maybe nothing worth reporting had actually happened, she thought. On the other hand it might not have been announced yet. If she rushed she'd probably just catch the tail end of the headlines. She hurried to dry her hands and ran over to join her friend on the couch.

Alex sat motionless her eyes transfixed on the screen as the images unfolded before her.

"In local news," the news reporter began to speak once more, "a police officer was tragically killed last night in what is believed to have been a failed attempt to hijack an armoured security vehicle."

Alex sat bolt upright.

"Although no direct CCTV coverage of the incident is available, footage released by the police, from the vicinity of the crime scene, appears to suggest the unnamed officer tried to intervene after noticing the disturbance while paroling the area on foot. A police report states further officers arrived at the incident within three minutes of his initial call for backup. The officer was found unresponsive and suffering from multiple gunshot wounds. Unfortunately paramedics were unable to revive him and he was later pronounced dead at the scene.

Alex's hands were covering her mouth.

"The driver of the security vehicle escaped with minor bruising and lacerations to the face. He has yet to release a statement, although police are believed to be searching for three other suspects who are well known to them. One of the culprits was apprehended at the scene suffering from a gunshot wound to the leg."

Alex looked at Bob as she recognised the first face on the screen.

"Oh no, that's Daz," she said alarmed. "They shot him, no wonder she was upset."

Bob turned to her and raised an eyebrow.

"Oh, I er bumped into Cat last night," Alex said shaking her head. "She seemed upset that's all."

The news reporter's voice cut in again.

"Police are urgently seeking information relating to the whereabouts of a certain female suspect."

Another unmistakable image appeared in front of them.

"Catherine Poole, goes by the name 'Cat', is the main suspect in the murder investigation. She is believed to have been in control of the gun that killed the officer. Police say they would be interested in talking to anyone who has information that could help them with her arrest. Although they stress she is to be considered highly dangerous and should not be approached by members of the public."

"I knew she'd get what was coming to her someday," Bob said almost laughing. "Serves her right."

"She wasn't that bad really," Alex said with a sigh. "She didn't deserve for things to end up like this."

Bob looked at her "How can you say that? You hated her."

"Yeah well maybe she had her reasons," Alex sighed again. "When they catch her she's going to go to prison for a long, long time. I feel bad for the police officer who died. Honestly I do, but her life is over now too."

"She'll get what she deserved and good riddance," Bob said laughing Alex's protests off.

"Yeah, I suppose you're right," Alex said with a huff. "I just wish things would've turned out differently that's all."

"Do you want another cup of tea?" Bob asked standing up.

"Yeah that'd be lovely," she smiled. "I'll come with you."

Alex switched the TV off before following Bob into the kitchen and picking up two mugs from the drying rack. As she stood there watching him filling the kettle she felt her mood lift. She was smiling when he turned to look at her.

"What's up now?" Bob asked frowning.

"Oh, I er... didn't tell you last night did I?" Alex chuckled.

"Tell me what?" He replied.

"I figured it out," Alex said with a big grin on her face.

"Figured what out?" Bobs frown was getting deeper.

"Who the man was," she replied.

"Are you going to start making some sense?" Bob grumbled. "Or are you just going to make me tease it out of you."

"Who the man is in the photograph with my

mother, he's my father."

"Really...?" Bob said surprised. "When? I mean who? How...?"

"Calm down a bit and I'll tell you," Alex laughed. "When I was at the gym yesterday, Eric noticed the photograph. He recognised it, said he hadn't seen it for years."

"Eric...?"

"Yes, turns out he's my father. Can you believe it?" She said beaming. "I've found him after all these years."

"Are you sure?" Bob asked. "I'd hate for you to get your hopes up."

"Yes, it's him," Alex replied. "I'm sure of it."

Bob was quiet for a moment. "So Stephen is... your brother then?" He smirked.

"Yeah turns out I've got a family again," Alex said continuing to chuckle. "I just wish my mum could've been a part of it."

"Did he have much to say about her?" Bob cut in. "Anything that'd help us figure things out?"

"Oh yeah, I meant to tell you," Alex replied lifting her hand. "Margaret wasn't her original name, but I think we'd already worked out as much. Her name was actually Linda," Alex frowned. "He never actually mentioned her last name though." She slapped her hand against her leg. "Damn it, I never even asked him if they were married."

"Well you can ask him next time you see him, it'd help a lot."

Alex turned back towards him and smiled. "He also said she was actually a scientist, said she did something involving biochemistry, but he couldn't tell me much about it though. Seems she kept him in the dark about it almost as much as me."

"She was a scientist?" Bob said frowning. "That doesn't sound much like her, are you definitely sure he was talking about your mother."

"Yes, stop worrying," Alex said dismissing his concerns.

"OK, OK," Bob frowned again. "So she was doing something involving biochemistry, that doesn't sound good." He started pacing around the kitchen. "I wonder what she got herself involved with."

"It didn't make much sense to me either," Alex added. "Do you think you could find out a bit more about what she was up to?"

"I don't know, it's worth a try," Bob shrugged. "She must have done her training somewhere. I'll try to look her up."

"Oh yeah, that was another thing," Alex cut in. "Eric told me she studied at Manchester Met."

"Ah, now then, that should be useful," Bob

smiled. "I'm sure I can pull something up from that. Hang on."

Bob rushed out of the kitchen, flopped down into his chair and booted up his computer. "Won't take a second," he shouted.

As soon as he was able Bob was searching the internet for the university's web page. "Ah got it... now I just have to find out about their past students," he said grinning. "If I'm lucky I might be able to get into their system to check the records."

Alex sipped her tea while she watched Bob work. She lingered, gazing at the screen for much longer than normal. She wanted to find out about her mother as much as he did, but in the end she decided to leave him to it. She knew it'd be a long boring process and when Bob got his mind set on a problem that was that. He'd do his best to solve it no matter how long it took. He'd just work on it nonstop until he found the solution. She was sure he'd shout her if he found something. She just wasn't expecting the call so soon.

"Hey Alex," Bob shouted without turning away from the screen.

She stopped half way across the room on the way to her bedroom. "Yeah?"

"I think I've found her," Bob's voice sounded excited. "Looks like she won an award for her work. I don't understand much of the text but it appears to be for something to do with gene manipulation."

"What's that?" Alex asked.

"Genes are pieces of DNA that affect certain characteristics. Oh my... I think your mother was experimenting with peoples DNA." He turned towards her with one eyebrow raised. "Hopefully just theoretically." He turned back to his computer. "It says here her dissertation had the title 'The Potential for Gene Manipulation within the Human Body'."

"That sounds a bit ominous," Alex replied cringing. "Why would anyone want to mess with our DNA?"

"It might not be as bad as it sounds," Bob smiled. "There's good evidence that certain diseases are directly created as a result of faulty genes. Maybe your mother was working on a new cure."

"Hmm, I'm not sure," Alex said shaking her head from side to side. "It sounds like stuff that shouldn't be messed with to me."

"You're not a scientist though," Bob smiled again. "I think most scientist's are working on ways to improve things for us."

"Something doesn't sound right," Alex said still shaking her head.

"Hey maybe your mother was on to something,"

Bob cut in. "I mean think about it. If her idea turned out to be correct, it'd be worth something to someone wouldn't it? If she did come up with a new treatment, especially for a common disease, just think how much that would be worth to a big health or pharmaceutical company. They could make millions out of it."

Alex's mind latched on to the last part of Bob's sentence.

"Hey maybe you're on to something, that'd explain how she managed to earn so much money," Alex said before taking a deep breath and sighing. "But it still doesn't explain why she apparently went in to hiding..? Why it looks like she faked her own death..? Why she abandoned my father and my baby brother?"

"No you're right, but I think we're on the right path now anyway," Bob said frowning again. "Are you sure Eric didn't tell you where she worked?"

"No," Alex replied with a shrug, "he said she never told him."

"Well then maybe there's another way of doing things," he grinned.

Bob turned back to the computer and typed Alex's mother's original name into the search engine. He sighed as hundreds of unhelpful links appeared in front of him. His fingers moved again adding various combinations of potential relevant company names but every time he did the list returned no results.

"This isn't working," he said frustrated. "Have you got any ideas?"

"Can you find anyone who knew her from the university?" Alex asked. "Was there someone who helped her work on her project? I'm sure there'd be someone who kept in touch with her after they graduated."

"It's worth a try," Bob huffed.

No matter how much he searched, he couldn't find any other names directly linked with her research. "This is hopeless," he said after a fruitless ten minutes. "I need to try something else."

Alex watched in amazement at how effortlessly he managed to find a list containing the names of all her mother's classmates. "How...?"

"Don't ask, it's best if you don't know," he smiled back.

One by one he copied and pasted the names of her fellow students into the search engine in hope of finding someone who now worked in a similar field. One name returned an interesting match.

A resume for a now Dr Kevin Ferrelli found on a dubious professional job search website listed one of his previous employers as 'DesignaPharm Int'l'. Apparently he specialised in establishing new types of viral vectors.

"I think I've found our guy," Bob said nodding to himself. "His address is listed as an apartment in London. It doesn't give a phone number but we've got his email."

Alex leaned in for a closer look. "Can you send him a message asking if he remembers my mother?"

"Already way ahead of you," Bob grinned.

Bob's email client popped up on the screen. The man's name already highlighted.

"I hope he gets this," Bob frowned. "Can you think of a title that doesn't look like everyday spam? Something he might read."

"How about 'do you remember' and then my mother's name?" Alex replied.

"No, we still need to be careful," Bob said shaking his head. "He might have been involved with what happened to her. We can't risk that just yet."

"Does it say how long ago he left?" Alex asked.

"It's quite a long time ago now, just over twenty years. It looks like up until a few years ago he worked for one of their competitors."

"So he stayed there at least a few years after my mother disappeared then?" Alex frowned.

"Yeah, seems that way," Bob replied.

"Well how about 'school reunion Manchester

Met' as the title?" Alex cut in. "I'd open it if I went there."

"Hmm, that sounds all right," Bob replied. "I'll ask him if he remembers anyone from his University days, maybe ask him if he used to work with any of them."

Alex leaned in again resting both he hands on his shoulders.

"All right that's that sent," Bob said with a smile. "Now we just have to wait and see if he replies. I hope he does, maybe we can arrange a meeting. Somewhere safe so we can see who he is," Bob said starting to chuckle. "If he turns out to be one of the men who attacked you, I'm running in the opposite direction."

Alex wasn't sure if he was joking, but in any case, she also wanted to stay as far away from those men as possible. She chuckled to herself. She could run a lot faster than him. She'd probably overtake.

"So..." Bob said. "Now the excitement's over, what do you want to do for the rest of the day?"

Alex thought things through. "Well it is your day off," she said, giving him a hopeful look. "You could come to the gym with me, keep me company on the way. Maybe we can find some more things out from Stephen and Eric. I should at least spend some time with them now I know they're family."

Bob looked decidedly unimpressed.

"Hey the exercise will do you good. Even Stephen told me you were improving." Alex gave him her best puppy-dog face. "You can't give up now."

"Oh, all right," Bob sighed, "if it'll get you off my back."

Alex chuckled to herself again as she strutted off to get her things together.

Stephen was putting a client through his paces when the pair arrived at the gym. Alex waved him a greeting before dropping off another box of items in the office.

"Thank God for that," Bob said dropping his rather heavy box in an empty corner. "I can breathe again."

"Thanks for helping," Alex said smiling at him. "There's not much else I can bring over now until Eric finds a new place."

"Don't worry about it," Bob replied. "I'm sure it won't take him long."

"Hopefully," Alex sighed, "then I'll be out of your hair. Thanks for letting me stay, I do appreciate it."

"I know," Bob smiled, "but hey, what are friends for?"

"Speak of the devil," Alex said motioning to the window.

Eric popped his head around the open door

smiling. "Ah, I wondered who was in here."

"It's only us," Alex giggled. "Just dropping some more stuff off. Then we're actually going to work out for a change," she said nodding at Bob. "I twisted his arm."

"Well good," Eric replied, "I'd hate to see all that good work going to waste."

Alex grinned.

"You're starting to fill out quick aren't you?" Eric said looking Bob up and down. "I swear you looked like a skeleton the last time I laid eyes on you."

Bob let out a nervous chuckle.

"Hey, I've got some good news for you," Eric said to Alex, releasing Bob from his critical gaze.

Alex felt her pulse quicken.

"I'm pretty sure I've found another place," Eric continued. "I'm just waiting for the paperwork to go through, but it should all be a formality."

"That's fantastic," Alex said clapping her hands.

"It's perfect for me really," Eric added. "It's a big old barn conversion on the outskirts of the city. Got a nice bit of land with it too."

"Oh I am pleased for you," Alex smiled. "I was hoping you'd find somewhere like that. It sounds great."

"The changeover shouldn't take long," Eric said. "Hopefully I'll be able to move in a week or so. The owners were selling up to move abroad. They were just waiting for the house to sell, everything else was already set up," he grinned. "Lucky for me, it meant I got it for a good price."

Alex chuckled again.

"Would you mind if I got a copy of the photograph made up?" Eric asked as he picked it up. "I'd like a copy for myself if you'd let me?"

Alex thought about it for a moment. "Sure, it's probably a good idea anyway. I'd hate to lose it and it be the only copy. Just please take good care of it, it's important to me."

Eric nodded, his head still lowered as he studied the image once more.

"We'd better be getting on with our workout while our muscles are still warm," Alex said beckoning Bob to follow.

She paused with her hand on the door frame.

"Thanks for letting me know."

Eric lifted his head up momentarily and smiled at her.

Stephen soon came over to greet the pair when he noticed them start their workout.

"Hi guys, mind if I join you?" He smiled at Alex.

"Sure," she smiled back.

"Can you show us how to do squats? I've been meaning to ask but I haven't had chance," Bob asked. He didn't feel quite so self-conscious in the gym while Stephen was there to show them how to do things.

"OK deal," Stephen grinned. "I take it you walked here today like usual?"

"Yes..." Bob replied, "Why?"

"Oh, no reason," he laughed. "You'll find out soon enough anyway."

Stephen walked them over to a vacant power cage.

"Don't worry I'll go easy on you," he grinned again. "It's a hard exercise to get right until you're used to it."

Bob breathed a sigh of relief. He felt stronger in himself physically but his confidence of this new found strength still lagged a long way behind.

"I'll just give you a quick demonstration and then one of you can have a go," Stephen added.

Bob and Alex watched as he made the movement look effortless.

"We'll just do it with the bar on its own to start with," Stephen said. "Who wants to go first? Come on Bob, I picked on Alex last time."

Stephen lowered the bar a couple of inches to a height more suitable for the smaller pair.

"Position yourself under the bar like I just

showed you," he continued. "Try to get your elbows more under the bar."

Bob shuffled into a better position.

"Grip the bar tight and arch your back," Stephen added. "Now ease the weight up and carefully take a few steps back."

Bob did as he was told.

"When you go down, try to keep the descent under control until the tops of your thighs are roughly parallel to the ground. You can go lower if you wish," Stephen said. "Then explode back up to finish."

The movement felt awkward to Bob. Maybe it was just his useless legs complaining about being used for the first time in years he told himself.

"Don't look at me," Stephen added, "just keep your eyes forward. Do it a couple more times until you get the hang of it."

After a while Bob felt himself start to relax, the exercise turned out not to be as bad as he thought it would. Nevertheless he still wasn't looking forward to Stephen putting some actual weight on the bar.

Alex herself wasn't too worried about the exercise. She'd done it many times when she was younger albeit without a heavy bar on her back.

By the time Stephen had tired the pair out, they'd both progressed to lifting a respectable weight. Something well in excess of what Stephen was expecting two beginners to be capable of.

"Well I'm impressed, well done," he said to the pair. "You've both done much better than I thought."

Bob and Alex smiled at each other.

"How's the diet going? Stephen asked. "You both look like you've got more colour to you, you even look like you might have put some weight on."

"Bob's being making sure I eat enough," Alex chuckled. "We've both been trying to eat more like you said."

"Well it seems to be working," Stephen replied eyeing the pair with suspicion. "Are you taking anything else that I should know about?" He added. "Did you buy any supplements or maybe something stronger?"

"No I've never bought anything like that," Alex said shaking her head, "I've never wanted too, why should I?"

"Are you sure?" Stephen added. "It's just you both seem to be progressing much faster than you should." He smirked. "You're starting to make the other gym users jealous."

"No, it's just us I'm afraid," Alex laughed. "Just what mother nature gave us."

"Well if you say so," Stephen huffed.

"Hey are you guys doing anything tomorrow?" Stephen asked as they made their way over to the changing rooms.

"No why?" Alex replied.

"I was thinking we could all go out," Stephen added, "give us a chance to catch up, somewhere more relaxing."

"What did you have in mind?" Alex replied.

"We could go bowling or catch a movie maybe," he shrugged.

"I er... can't I'm afraid," Bob cut in, his voice nervous. "I'm going to be busy."

"Really?" Alex said turning to her friend. "Why what are you going to be up to?"

"I er... the thing is..." Bob said scratching his head. "Well I er..."

"Go on spit it out," Stephen grinned.

"Melissa kind of well... asked me out, on a... a sort of date and er... well, I kind of said yes."

"You kept that one quiet," Alex laughed. "No... Good for you, I'm glad."

"Really, where are you going?" Stephen asked.

"I think she said the cinema," Bob shrugged, "maybe we'll go to a restaurant afterwards."

"Well we could all meet up at the ten pin bowling alley first," Stephen said smiling. "Melissa could invite Jennifer and Gary along, we could make teams. The pair of you could go off on your own afterwards."

"It's an idea," Bob said. "I'll ask her, see

what she says."

"Well I'm up for it anyway," Alex said smiling at Stephen. "I'll give you a ring in the morning to arrange things.

CHAPTER 18

Alex and Bob's legs were no longer sore the next morning but on the way home they'd definitely regretted doing so many squats. Bob was walking around the apartment flicking through the Sunday newspaper he'd just picked up from the corner shop.

He came to a stop in the middle of the living room as the article he was reading started to sink in.

"This is interesting," he said to Alex. "It says here some British scientists think they've made significant progress in the search for the cure for Cancer. It sounds complicated, I don't really understand the process, but it goes on about using phage's to replace damaged DNA inside patients' cells."

"Why is that interesting?" Alex asked with a frown.

"Wasn't it something similar your mother got an award for?"

"I'm not sure, I'm afraid I zoned out when you started talking about science," she chuckled, "sorry."

"I wonder what it was your mother discovered. I'm sure it sounded similar. It must have been a bloody good idea if they gave her all that money for it."

"Hey that's a good point," Alex said. "Check your email. See if that Dr Ferrelli's replied."

Bob booted up his computer and scanned his inbox. There it was an unopened message.

"I think we got his attention," Bob said, "but his reply is strange. He's basically suggesting he isn't happy discussing that part of his life over an unsecured connection." Bob read a bit further. "He'd gladly talk to us about the things that went on, but not over the internet." Bob turned around to face Alex. "He wants to meet us!"

"What are we going to do?" Alex blurted out. "What if he was involved? We can't trust him just like that."

"I know," Bob replied, "but if you want a chance to find out what really happened to your mother all those years ago, we don't have any other options."

"I still don't think it's a good idea," Alex grimaced.

"I could go instead of you?" Bob offered to break the awkward silence.

"Thank you but no," Alex said shaking her head. "It should be me, it's about my mother. I need to be the one to find out why they killed her."

"Are you sure?" Bob frowned.

"Yes, I'll go on my own," she said waving her hand. "You shouldn't have to risk your life as well and besides, if anything bad happens I heal fast remember," she tried to smile.

"OK, if it's what you want?" Bob said turning back to the computer. "Where do you want to meet him?"

"You said he lived in London didn't you?" Alex said. "I could catch the train down there. Where's a nice busy coffee shop near to the station, somewhere easy to find?"

"Ah, I know a place," Bob said as he began to type a new message out.

"Tell him I could meet him on Monday afternoon, if it's all right with him," Alex added. "Tell him I'll wear my purple bobble hat.

That should stand out enough."

Bob amended the message and clicked send. "Now we just have to wait for his reply again."

"Can you check the news website while you're on there, see if it says anything about Cat?" Alex asked.

"Yeah, no problem," Bob said clicking the direct link on his desktop. "What do you think it'll be under?"

"Just check the headlines," Alex replied with a smile. "I'm sure it'll be on there if they've found anything."

"Ah, I think this is it. Looks like they got her," Bob said as he clicked on the link that read 'Cop killer should get what she deserves'.

Alex leaned over Bob's shoulder to get a better look at the screen. "Oh no," she gasped as she read the text that had appeared in front of her.

'Earlier this morning, police acting on intelligence, attempted to apprehend the fugitive Miss Poole in an abandoned building by the dockside.'

Alex felt herself clenching her fists.

'Unfortunately after a short fire fight, in which another police officer was injured, the wanted woman managed to evade capture. Police are once more asking any members of the public with relevant information to come forward.'

"I'm afraid things are going to end badly for her," Bob said shaking his head. "Things were bad enough when they accused her of killing a police officer. Now it looks like she's gone and injured another one when she escaped. I don't think they'll take any more chances with her if they lay eyes on her again."

"I think you're right," Alex sighed. "I hope she does the right thing and hands herself in. I don't think she'll be so lucky if she tries to resist arrest again."

Alex disappeared for a second into the kitchen to turn the kettle on. "Did you get a chance to talk to Melissa again?" She asked when she returned.

"What about?" Bob replied.

"If she wanted to meet up with everybody later on today remember? Stephen asked if we all wanted to go bowling together before your date. I needed to arrange things with him."

"Oh, not yet sorry," Bob grimaced. "I'd meant to ask her last night while I was talking to her on the internet. I'll give her a ring now. It won't take long."

"OK thanks. It doesn't matter if she decides not to go," Alex added. "It's more important that you two enjoy yourselves. I can't keep you company for ever can I?" She chuckled. "I'll still arrange to meet Stephen, don't worry about it too much."

Bob stood up, picked up his phone and wandered off into his bedroom, the door closed behind him.

Alex took the chance to check a few things on the internet while he was gone. The gym didn't as yet have a website set up but she was sure Bob could work something out for her if she asked him nicely enough. If she was ever going to turn around the lagging takings at the gym she needed to find a way to increase its exposure. People first needed to know it was there before they'd come to visit. The gym couldn't just rely on word of mouth and passing trade any longer. A website was as good a place as any to start she supposed.

It wasn't until she started browsing through the local council's website that something caught her eye. A scheme was already set up where certain people could get a discount or even free entry to the council's leisure facilities. An idea was starting to form in her mind. The council was busy closing many of its facilities in an effort to save money. Maybe if she agreed to let similar people use her gym it'd save them more money and hopefully they'd help to promote it in the process. It was worth a try at any rate.

Another thought occurred to her. She could offer to let people from the Foodbank use it at a discounted price. Even if only a small percentage of the people took up her offer, just on the shear amount of people passing through there on a daily basis, it'd boost takings significantly.

Almost ten minutes later, the door to Bob's bedroom opened. Alex watched as he walked out with a huge grin on his bright red face.

"Things went OK then?" She shouted.

"Yes fine," he grinned. "She's agreed to go bowling with everyone. She's going to ring Jennifer and Gary in a second."

"Ah, good," Alex smiled.

"She didn't think there'd be any problem," Bob continued. "They normally hang around together at the weekends anyway. She suggested going after five," he added with a shrug. "Said she needed time to get ready apparently."

Alex chuckled to herself while Bob carried on talking.

"So if you want to give Stephen a call to tell him the good news?"

"Yes, I'd better," Alex replied searching for her phone. "He'll be wondering why I haven't called yet."

Stephen sounded pleasantly surprised to hear Alex's news and arranged to pick them both up later that afternoon.

When her phone rang to announce his arrival, the pair made their way downstairs to meet him.

Alex took the hint of the open passenger door and sat up front in the dark blue M5, leaving Bob to shuffle into the back.

"Are you ready to go meet your girlfriend?" Stephen said much louder than was really necessary.

"It's only a date," Bob cringed.

Stephen laughed as he watched Bob squirm in his rear view mirror. "OK then. Everybody buckled up?"

Alex just about managed to get the seat belt to click into place as the car's engine fired into life. The journey didn't take as long as she'd expected, partly due to Stephens driving. It'd been such a long time since she'd been allowed in a fast car. She'd actually found herself enjoying the ride.

"So why don't either of you drive?" Stephen asked as he pulled up into a parking space in front of the bowling alley.

Alex thought about the question. She had to admit it to herself. Even she found it strange she was still avoiding using a car. Her own license had been clean for a couple of years now and she could definitely afford it. "I haven't needed one for such a long time," she said with a sigh. "I guess I just haven't got round to getting one again yet."

Stephen turned to Bob.

"Oh, don't look at me," he said waving his hands in front of him. "I don't trust myself behind a wheel, not any more anyway."

Alex gave Bob a look she hoped only he caught.

They met the other three inside, Melissa insisting it was easier that way. She'd told Bob they all lived close to each other in the university's halls of residence. Apparently there was always an empty taxi hanging around outside so they wouldn't have to wait.

Bob greeted his date with a little trepidation at first, but she'd clung to him and dragged him over to the arcade machines before he'd had a chance to feel awkward. Gary started chatting away with Stephen about what'd happened at the Foodbank recently, leaving Alex free to catch up with Jennifer. She was happy they'd decided to meet up again. It wasn't easy making friends with new people at the best of times, but with everything that had been going on Alex had understandably been neglecting that side of things.

"I wanted to ask if you'd join us next week?" Jennifer said. "It's the last meeting of the book club before we break up for the Christmas holidays. We're going to have a little party."

"Sure, I'd love to," Alex replied with a smile. "Is there a reading list?"

"We normally make a new one this month so people get the chance to pick books to read over Christmas," Jennifer added, "so it's a good time to join. You won't need to catch up in the New Year."

Alex smiled. She was starting to wonder why she'd never thought of giving a book club a go, since she still spent most of her spare time reading anyway. The only difference now was she could afford to buy the books herself instead of borrowing the old copies from the library.

"Do you want me to meet you there or shall we meet up beforehand?" She asked.

"Oh, it's up to you," Jennifer replied. "You could come over to mine, I'll show you around my flat if you'd like?"

"OK, sounds like a plan," Alex smiled. "I'll give you a ring in the week to confirm things."

Stephen suggested they split themselves into two groups. "Who hasn't been before?" He asked trying to organise everyone.

Only Jennifer raised her hand.

"Oh, that's all right," he added. "Alex and me will have you on our team. Show you how things work."

Stephen walked over to the machine, entered some improvised names into the computer and got the game moving with two easy strikes in a row.

"I come here a lot," he confessed.

The atmosphere was soon relaxed and the friends began to enjoy themselves. It was somewhat helped by the bottles of beer that Bob kept bringing back from the bar. Stephen was however starting to regret the decision he'd made to drive as he looked down at his less than interesting glass of diet cola.

A little while later Alex and Stephen's scores were well ahead of the other team. It didn't matter much to Alex that she spent most of the time trying to coach Jennifer. Her poor scores at the start did little to alter the overall outcome of the game, and even Stephen had to admit that by the end Jennifer was almost bowling respectably.

"So Bob, Melissa, have you decided where you're going to go for a meal?" Stephen asked as they emerged into the open air.

"Bob says he knows a nice new Latin place that's just opened up," Melissa said as she linked him. "It's not too far from here."

"Do you want to jump in the taxi with us?" Gary asked. "There'll be plenty of room."

"It's only just around the corner," Bob replied with a smile. "Ten minutes walk at most."

"Ah OK," Gary replied turning to Stephen. "How about you two? Are you sure you want to go down to the pier. It's going to be freezing?"

"It's somewhere quiet," Alex said turning to

her brother. "Us two have a lot to catch up on."

"Yeah, About twenty five years," Stephen added with a laugh.

"Oh well," Gary huffed. "I suppose we'll see everyone at the Foodbank next week then?"

"Yeah, see you all next week," Jennifer added. "Have a good time," she said turning to Melissa. "Give me a call when you get back, OK?"

Melissa smiled her agreement.

"Come on," Jennifer said turning back to Gary. "I'm getting cold standing here. Let's go find a taxi shall we?"

"Well I suppose we should make a move too," Bob said eager for Melissa and himself to get some time alone. "I'm getting hungry. Let's leave these two to catch up."

"I'm getting hungry too," Melissa said smiling back at him. "You can tell me more about that quest on the way."

"No wonder they get on so well," Stephen said chuckling to himself as they left.

Alex did up all the remaining buttons on her coat and pulled her hat and scarf out of her pocket, she'd come prepared for the cold weather. She was looking forward to getting a chance to talk to her brother in private and had known there was a good chance they'd end up where they were heading.

Alex could see the solitary bench they were

heading towards, waiting in the distance at the very far end of the pier, it was quiet there, private. The pair continued passed the quaint wooden shacks and their colourful signs promising treats and games of all sorts sitting exposed to the open air on their elevated platform above the sea. The tourist attractions were silent now, all the hustle and bustle having long since been closed down for the winter season.

Nevertheless Alex was at least expecting to see a few other people hanging around, maybe a skateboard or two, but tonight the pier was deserted. She shivered as an icy gust of wind reminded her that few other people were brave or stupid enough to be walking around on such a cold night. She chuckled. You'd have to be pretty crazy to think it was a good idea to walk out onto the exposed pier as her and her brother were doing just now. Alex smiled to herself contented.

"Tell me about my mother," Stephen said his voice quiet as they sat down.

"She was an amazing woman, you'd have loved her very much," Alex replied, smiling a mixture of happiness and regret. "She treated me like I was the only thing that mattered to her in the whole world." She took a long deep breath, trying to steady herself. "I miss her every day. It's still just as hard as the first day when I knew I'd lost her." Alex felt her eyes begin to well up.

"Go on," Stephen said, "tell me about her, please? What was she like? At least you had the chance to get to know her," his voice was breaking up. "Now I know I never will."

"She was a quiet woman, she liked to draw, to paint," Alex continued. "She was very artistic, used to run a small gallery when I was young," Alex sighed. "It wasn't until recently when her disease started to take hold that I began to lose her, piece by piece. She was still very caring towards the end, never said a bad word to me, not even when she was in pain."

Stephen sniffled but tried to hide his tears from Alex. "I'd have liked to have met her," he sighed, "but hey, at least I've found out that I've got a sister," he put his arm around her and gave her a hug.

Alex lifted her head, a strange noise had caught her attention, it was there again but it was hard to make out over the howling wind. It sounded like shuffling, it was getting closer. Someone was struggling to walk towards them, limping even. She turned to confront the annoyance only to see a familiar face once more.

"Cat," she yelled in surprise. "What the hell are you doing here? You need to get away, find somewhere to hide before they catch you."

Cat made half a smile to her. "So is this

your boyfriend then?" She said in a numb tone.

Alex coughed surprised again. "No, he's my brother actually."

"Ah," Cat replied still despondent.

"They said you killed a cop," Alex added. "You've got to get yourself away from here."

"It wasn't me and anyway, I'm fed up of running," Cat huffed. "I'm tired. They are going to catch me where ever I go."

"But it's serious, don't you understand?" Alex pleaded. "They're going to try and stop you, take you down."

Cat let out a heavy sigh. "I'm ready for them," she said as she pulled a large silver revolver out from behind her back.

Stephen gripped Alex's arm as she recoiled, feeling nervous himself for the first time.

"Freeze..." The shouted order came from out of the darkness. "Put the weapon down, slowly."

Cat spun around.

"Slowly, so I can see you. I won't warn you again."

Alex could just make out the shape of a policeman inching towards them, his weapon drawn and aimed directly at Cat. All of a sudden the quiet night sky lit up with bright flashing lights and a deafening cacophony of police sirens. Alex watched from afar as multiple armed response vehicles converged on the area, screeching to a halt near the start of the pier.

"Please put the gun down," Alex begged. "Do as he says. I don't want to see you get hurt."

"Place the weapon down on the ground and walk towards me, with your hands in the air," the policeman growled. "You won't get away this time, there's nowhere for you to run."

For a moment Alex saw Cat look at her out the corner of her eye. "I'm sorry," was the last thing she heard her say. Cat's knees buckled as two loud bangs and flashes from the officer's gun silenced her.

It all happened so fast, Alex watched in horror as Cat started to raise her gun. She saw Cat's body twitch with each impact, saw the bright red blood soak through her clothes. Alex tried to stand, to get to her, but Stephen's vice like grip held her back. Cat was too close to the edge when her legs gave way. Without a sound she disappeared from sight.

It felt like an eternity in Alex's stupefied state for the noise of Cat's body hitting the waves below to reach them. She hardly noticed as the policeman ran passed them towards the hole in the railings where Cat had disappeared. Alex stared in a daze as he pulled out his small torch and started to search the sea for signs of movement. The noise of clattering boots jogged Alex back to reality as the rest of the policeman's colleges joined him.

It was gone midnight by the time Stephen had got around to dropping Alex off back at Bob's apartment. Stephen said his goodbyes and shot straight off, said he needed to be up early in the morning. Bob was already there of course, typing away on his keyboard as usual. Entranced by the beautifully rendered imaginary creatures in front of him.

"How did it go then?" The slightly dishevelled Alex asked.

The characters on Bob's computer screen froze as he turned to see where the distraction was coming from.

"Oh hi, I didn't hear you come in," Bob frowned. "What on earth happened to you, you look like you've seen a ghost?"

Alex removed her heavy coat, grateful to be back in the warm apartment at last. "I'm all right, don't worry," she said walking to the closet to hang it up. "Your turn first."

"It went well, at least I think it did," Bob said with a smile. "We're just getting to know each other, taking things slow. You know just seeing how things go for now."

"Good," Alex replied. "How was the meal? I've not been there before."

"Yeah, really nice," Bob replied. "We got a quiet table out of the way. The food was lovely."

Alex smiled at him before flopping down exhausted onto the couch. "I'm glad you had a good time."

"Thanks," Bob chuckled. "She's so easy to talk to. I've never met a girl that was easy to talk to."

Alex gave him a stare.

"Apart from you I mean," Bob laughed. "I didn't mean it like that, you're my best friend."

Alex sighed as she tried to make herself more comfortable. "You mean she plays children's games as well?"

"How many times do I have to tell you?" Bob smirked. "They're made for adults. Look it says for over sixteen's on the box."

Alex chuckled to herself. She still knew how to get a rise out of him.

"If you're just going to make fun of me, I'm going to get back to my childish game," Bob sulked.

"I'm sorry, I was only teasing," Alex laughed again. "I don't mind if you still like playing with toys."

Bob turned back to face her glowering.

"I'm sorry," she continued to giggle, "I'll stop now, I promise."

"Well go on then," Bob frowned, "what happened to you? Why were you so late getting back?"

Alex took a few deep breaths before replying.

"Oh, we bumped into Cat on the pier, the police arrived." She fell silent.

"So what happened?" Bob asked. "Did they catch her?"

"Well no, not really," Alex said turning her face away from him. "They shot her, right in front of us. It was horrible. She didn't have a chance."

"Oh, oh dear," Bob said unsure of what to say. "Is she going to be all right?"

Alex, still not looking at him, simply shook her head from side to side.

"They killed her?" Bob spoke up.

"She fell over the side into the sea," Alex replied. "The splash was so loud. She must have hit the water with such force." Alex's eyes were starting to tear up again. "No one saw her resurface, they searched for ages."

"That doesn't sound good," Bob grimaced.

"I feel so sorry for her," Alex said wiping her face. "She didn't deserve it to end like that."

"She killed a cop," Bob reminded her.

"She said she didn't do it," Alex snapped.

"Oh, stop being so naïve," Bob said with a frown.

Alex turned back to face him. "The Police made us both give a statement before they let us go. Even though it wasn't anything to do with us." She shook her head and sighed. "They seemed happy enough in the end though, we were just in the wrong place."

"Oh I knew I had something to tell you," Bob blurted out. "That Dr Ferrelli replied to my email again."

Alex felt herself perk up.

"He said he'd like to meet you, tomorrow afternoon. He'll be waiting in the coffee shop, where I told you, at four thirty. He'll have a Christmas hat in front of him on the table."

"I think I can do that," Alex said nodding. "I'll ring Stephen in the morning, I'm sure he'll be able to make excuses for me."

"Oh, I already took the liberty of ordering you a return train ticket," Bob added. "I didn't think you'd have time in the morning."

"Thanks, that was thoughtful," Alex replied smiling at her friend. Either this was all going to end badly or she'd find out why those men killed her mother.

Early the next morning Alex switched on the news and waited for the announcement. The report said Police frog men had gone on to spend much of the night searching for Cat in the sea and around the pier. Apparently at first they were hopeful they could recover her alive, by sunrise however, the operation was no longer a rescue mission.

Alex listened as the police officer gave his statement.

'They were now almost certainly looking to recover Cat's body. It was exceedingly unlikely anyone could have survived out there, especially on such a cold night. Even without her injuries she would have almost certainly perished from the hypothermia alone.'

CHAPTER 19

Alex had made a point of not telling Stephen where she was going. She didn't want him to get his hopes up or to worry unnecessarily. It was only now as she faced the long lonely journey that she was starting to wish she'd told him. Maybe it would have been better to invite him along. After all she was his mother too.

Alex arrived at the station with a few minutes to spare, not that it mattered, the trains were always late. She glanced up and down the platform, it was still, quiet. Not many people wanted to head towards the big city at this time of day. She pulled out the ticket from her pocket and checked it a couple of times. Satisfied she let out a sigh.

Alex started to chuckle to herself. She couldn't believe the trains that had been the bane of her life for so many years were actually going to help her find the truth out about her mother. As she mulled the thought over in her mind, the rumbling in the background suddenly didn't appear so bothersome any more.

The journey was quite pleasant really. Alex stared out of the windows transfixed by the beautiful colours of the passing countryside. Her mother would have really enjoyed painting them. Her thoughts were still so stubbornly full of questions about the coming day that she was still sitting there absent minded when she heard the final call for her stop. As a surge of adrenaline kicked in she jumped up and ran to the closing door. The train departed mere moments after she'd leaped down onto the waiting platform. She needed to concentrate, she told herself, if she was going to make it through the rest of the day.

It didn't take long for Alex to find the coffee shop. Bob's instructions had been straightforward enough. The hardest part was trying to make her way through the busy streets and avoid the maniac drivers who didn't appear to care when pedestrians tried to cross the road. Still she'd made it to her destination in one piece and on time too.

    Alex decided to hang back a few minutes, maybe she could get a look at him from the outside. She glanced around and picked out a clothes shop across the street, people would probably just think she was waiting for someone. Leaning against the wall she stared through the coffee shop window. Unfortunately the layout of its interior only allowed her to see a small portion of the main room. The part she could see did however look very inviting, incorporating a well balanced mix of restored original and ultra modern fittings.

    Alex sighed, it was no use, and he could be anywhere inside. She made her move, crossed the road and stepped in through the open door. As she entered Alex took the opportunity to glance around the room. She could see clearer now. There were a few people dotted around but not enough to call it busy. She tried to pick out the likely candidates. He'd be sitting on his own, at least middle aged. Most of the tables were taken up by couples or families. She looked again, there were only a few single men but none had the tell tale hat on display. Alex was starting to worry, she'd made sure to only be a few minutes late, so he'd already be there waiting. She wanted to get a good look at him before introducing herself. Maybe she was too late, maybe he'd already left.

Alex was starting to feel out of place. She could feel people watching her as she stood helpless near the door. She shook herself, forced herself to scan the menus above the counter. Where was he, she thought as she joined the sparse queue?

"I'll just have a black coffee please," Alex said to the waitress when it was her turn. She hoped her voice didn't sound too jumpy. "Do you have any more tables, only I couldn't see a free one?"

"Yes, I'm sure there'll be plenty free upstairs," the waitress replied. "There usually are at this time of day."

Alex looked over to where she was pointing. She'd been too nervous to notice the staircase in the corner before.

"Ah OK, thank you," she smiled.

Alex stood there, anxious, waiting for the few minutes it took for her drink to be made. He must be waiting upstairs. Of course it'd be more private. Then the thought hit her, less people meant a greater chance she could get into trouble if things turned bad. Alex tried to steady herself, tried to control her breathing, but how could she, she didn't know what to expect. She was feeling so anxious that at one point the thought crossed her mind to simply walk back out of the door and head home.

Alex took a deep breath, held it for a second and let it out with a slow controlled sigh. She was going to force herself to stay. She had to go through with it. She had to find out why they killed her mother, why they tried to kill her? Would they try to come after her again? Would they try to harm her new found family? Finding out the answers to those questions was the only thing that mattered to her now.

It took her several attempts before her hand stopped shaking enough to pick up the mug of hot coffee. It was time she told herself. She could hear the whooshing sound of her heartbeat in her ears as she headed over to the staircase and began the lonesome climb. She was sure it was taking her longer to reach the top up than it should have, but she kept going, she willed herself forward.

The room opened up in front of her as she reached the top, she looked around pretending to search for a free table. The walls were lined floor to ceiling with book shelves. A few people were scattered about sitting in the comfy chairs flicking through books they'd picked up, and then, there it was, she saw what she was looking for. In the corner, a bright red Christmas hat sat on a table in front of a lone man looking out of the window.

Alex took a few more deep breaths while she

studied him from her vantage point. He didn't appear too threatening. In fact he reminded her of one of her old high school professors. He looked quite friendly really sitting back in his seat with his hands resting on his slightly rotund middle. His scruffy greyish white hair line was obviously receding but he hadn't made any attempt to hide it. She took a moment to pluck up her courage then began to walk over.

Just before she could reach him, he seemed to notice the movement and turned to look at her. It didn't take him long to work out she was the person he'd come here to meet. She was wearing the strange purple hat that she'd mentioned after all.

"So you must be Alex? The scruffy haired man said as he stood up to greet her.

Alex nodded. "I take it you're...?"

"Yes," he cut her off. "Kevin Ferrelli."

He motioned to the empty seat across from him. "I believe you have some rather interesting questions for me?"

Alex nodded again and smiled as she took her seat.

"I must admit," the Dr. began, "I was quite surprised to receive an invitation from my old university and even more surprised when I realised what it was really about." His voice still sounded hesitant.

"Yeah, sorry about that," Alex replied. "I didn't know how else to get your attention. I thought you'd at least open the email that way," she tried to smile again.

"I thought I'd managed to leave that part of my life behind." The Dr. sighed. "It was a bit of a shock to have it unexpectedly confront me again."

"So you know what happened to Linda, Linda Harding?" Alex replied sitting up and leaning across the table.

The Dr. seemed to give the room another look around.

"Yes, but I'm curious as to why she's of interest to you?" He gave Alex another look. "You don't strike me as the normal science type. I'd like to know why you've come here asking questions that many others would rather remain unanswered?"

"She was my mother," Alex blurted out. "I need to know what happened to her."

The Dr. pushed himself back into his chair. "No, it can't be," his eyes looked wild.

Alex couldn't make out his reaction. Was he scared or excited or maybe both?

"Give me your arm a second please."

Alex sat there looking at him as if he'd suddenly gone mad.

"Reach out your arm please I need to check

something," he added beckoning her.

Alex inched her right hand towards him unsure of what he was going to do. The Dr. reached forward gripping her wrist with one hand and pushing her sleeve up to reveal the skin of her forearm with the other.

"This won't hurt for long, I promise," the Dr. grimaced, "but I need to see if it's true."

Alex felt the pressure on her wrist increase as the Dr. reached into his jacket pocket with his other hand. She started to struggle when she recognised what it was he'd pulled out. The silver edge of a small pen knife glistened in the sun light.

"What are you doing?" Alex shouted.

"Relax," the Dr. said through gritted teeth, "if what you say is true, then this is the fastest way to find out."

Alex tried to wriggle free but felt the man's grip on her wrist tighten again. She felt the pain as the cold sharp metal dug into her skin. She looked down at her arm. A small crimson slither of blood formed where he'd scratched her with the tip of the blade. He kept her wrist held firm with one hand and reached across the table to pull a clean napkin out from the holder. Alex knew what was going to happen. Her eyes darted back and forth between her arm and the Dr.'s face. She watched, almost in a trance, as he cleared away the dried blood from her arm. She knew the wound would be gone. She'd known since she was a child that she healed much faster than other kids, it was ingrained, inherent to her. What she didn't know was how this man she'd never met seemed to know about it too?

The Dr. stared up at her. "I don't believe it, it actually worked."

Alex felt the pressure release on her wrist and snatched her arm back out from the man's cold hand and covered it again.

"You must be Eve," the Dr. said in a quiet voice.

"What worked? What are you talking about?" Alex frowned.

"Your mothers work..." the Dr. added. "You were to be the first."

"You're still not making much sense I'm afraid," Alex said shaking her head.

"There is a reason why you heal so fast," the Dr.'s voice was slow, controlled.

"Really and what is that?" Alex snapped.

"Your mother was a brilliant scientist, but she paid dearly for it in the end," the Dr. sighed. "At first the company we worked for were overjoyed at the progress of the project."

"Wait, you worked with her?" Alex cut in.

"Yes, I was part of her team," the Dr. replied. "It was your mother's project, she was in charge. There were six of us in total. We each worked on different pieces of the puzzle. It was my responsibility to find a suitable delivery method," he smiled. "Only your mother knew the whole story. I suppose that's why they left the rest of us alone."

Alex's breathing was getting erratic, she felt herself getting excited. She was going to find out what happened.

"They didn't know that I knew. They suspected of course, because I was closest to her, but they had no proof. I suppose that's why I was lucky when the time came."

"Please tell me what happened?" Alex said. "I need to know."

The Dr. chuckled. He obviously felt a lot easier after satisfying himself Alex wasn't a threat. "I'm getting there, but you need to first understand the what, before I get to the why."

Alex settled back down into her chair.

"As you might be aware, whilst we were in University together your mother came up with a very interesting idea," the Dr. continued. "One that drew the attention of many powerful people, one that was not to be made public."

Alex nodded along.

"She postulated the benefits of what a new branch of gene therapy could offer to the human race. During her studies she'd seen firsthand the effects that genetic diseases could have on ordinary people. How those diseases could affect families generation after generation. She was determined to find a way to help them."

"Well, that's good isn't it?" Alex said with a frown.

"Yes her intentions were good and I believe that given time the general public would have come around to the idea of genetic manipulation," the Dr. replied with a smile. "At first she was only interested in finding new ways to cure those genetic illnesses but over time she started to see the possibility not only to cure them but to improve upon them. She was starting to see the potential of altering everyone's genetic makeup. She thought she could help the whole of the human race, she thought she had a way to improve mankind, improve upon nature."

"So she started to meddle in things that the company didn't want her to?" Alex asked eager to know the truth. "That's why they got rid of her?"

"Yes, that was partly the reason," the strained voice replied. "In the end though, it was her success that became the problem for them. The company were happy with the minor successes. As long as they could make money from her discoveries, that was all that mattered to them. When she found a new way to combat a certain disease the company could develop new drugs. They made billions from those sales alone."

"So when did the problems start?" Alex asked.

"It was partly my fault I'm afraid," the Dr. sighed. "I engineered a new virus vector that could accurately insert new genes into certain cells. Your mother found out she could use it to more effectively deliver the improved genes to people." "Oh," Alex said frowning again.

"Initially the animal trials were promising," the Dr. continued. "As long as we maintained healthy nutrition levels the ailments of the infected animals disappeared. They also appeared healthier, they got stronger. They didn't seem to age at the same rate as other non infected members of the same species," the Dr. smiled. "Their bodies fought off any new infections they were given. They healed faster than the others, much faster."

Alex looked down at her arm and back up at the man sitting in front of her, he nodded.

"A few months later was when we noticed," the Dr. sighed, "the virus remained active in the infected animal's bloodstream throughout the remainder of their lives. The infected animals could transmit the virus to others if their blood managed to get into another animals body. We soon realised if that if we released it on the public it would have the ability to spread indefinitely. Anyone who came into intimate contact with the blood of an infected person could contract the virus. They could then pass the infection on to others and so on and so on."

Alex looked at him still confused.

"We worked for one of the world's largest pharmaceutical manufacturers," he said staring at her waiting for a response.

Alex just stared back silent.

"How much vested interest throughout the world is there in health care?" The Dr. said watching her. "How much money exchanges hands simply to manage people's illnesses worldwide? Could you imagine what would have happened if that virus was to get out into the world?" he said with a shake of his head. "Relatively speaking, human evolution would have made a massive leap forward almost overnight.

"I think I'm following," Alex said.

"People would no longer get sick. There'd be no more long term illnesses to treat. Think of how many people's lives it could have helped. How many lives it would have improved. But then think what it meant for big business, the price to cure peoples suffering for good was too high. In a world where disease no longer existed there'd be little need for health care. Countries wouldn't need to pour trillions into health. The whole industry would have collapsed."

"Oh, now I'm starting to understand," Alex

added. Her chest was beginning to feel tense.

"Are you starting to realise what your mother was up against?" The Dr. asked. "They had to shut her down, get rid of her work, get rid of her... They needed to be sure the knowledge was completely destroyed. One woman's life for the sake of almost unlimited investment. Think about it, while she was alive, they were all still vulnerable."

Alex gasped.

"I knew where things were heading when I saw it on the news," the Dr. added shaking his head. "There had been an accident in the lab. The report said a major gas leak had led to a large explosion. The entire building was gutted by fire, it had to be demolished."

"They blew it up?" Alex blurted out.

"I knew all of our work was gone, there was nothing left. Getting rid of it was so important to them. The destruction of the whole complex was worth it, if it made sure that no scrap of evidence remained. All they had left to do after was to get rid of your mother."

Alex shifted in her seat and sipped the last of her coffee. She wasn't expecting the news to be so troubling.

"Your mother called me that night and arranged to meet," the Dr. continued. "She told me she'd kept a small vial of serum containing the virus in a briefcase in the boot of her car. Probably enough for one injection, maybe two. I had to help her get it away from there."

"Really? Are you saying some survived?" Alex asked.

"Well, I agreed to meet her at a service station we knew well," the Dr. replied. "She took the briefcase out of the boot and swapped cars with me. She drove off in my private car. Said she was going to move it someplace safe, somewhere they wouldn't find it."

"Weren't you worried they'd come after you?" Alex asked.

"Yes, but I soon found out they weren't interested in me," the Dr. replied. "I was on my way home in the company car when it was shunted from behind. Before I knew it I was surrounded by unmarked vehicles, boxed in. I couldn't see who they were. All the windows were completely blacked out. Someone came up to my window and shone a bright light into my face. They soon drove off afterwards so I guessed I wasn't who they were looking for.

"So you helped my mother get to safety?" Alex said with a smile.

"Yes but not for long," he continued. "We realised she'd never be safe unless they thought she was dead. She decided there was only one way out. She had to die."

Alex gasped again.

"We arranged an incident with an oil tanker," the Dr. continued. "The car she was in was found burnt out. When the ashes were later analysed they showed traces of her DNA. It wasn't much but there was a good chance she'd been in the car when the accident happened."

"Ah... So that's when..." Alex's voice trailed off.

"She had to disappear completely," The Dr. said. "She couldn't go back to her old life. Everyone who knew her had to think she had actually died or they might have been put in danger too. Thankfully your mother had always kept that side of her life completely separate from work. I was the only person she'd told about her family, but that meant it fell to me to inform your father."

"So it was you that my dad spoke to all those years ago?" Alex spoke up.

The Dr. smiled at her. "Yes, I'm afraid I was the one who gave him the bad news."

"So what happened to the virus? Where did she hide it?" Alex asked.

"She was gone for a few days before we staged the accident," the Dr. said smiling back at her." I'd believed she'd gone back home, maybe given the injection to her husband or son. But I must have been wrong. She was heavily pregnant at the time maybe she went through with her original plans." The Dr. sat up in his chair and took a deep breath. "If I'm right and I'm pretty sure that I am, then the virus still exists and I'm looking directly at it."

Alex frowned. "You honestly think I have that same virus inside of me?" She said after mulling things over.

"Can you think of another explanation as to why your skin just healed so fast?" the Dr. asked.

Alex shook her head. "Is that why they tried to kill me too?"

"Pardon?" the Dr. scowled. "What did you just say?"

"My mother and I were attacked a few weeks ago," Alex replied. "They shot me in the back," she shrugged, "but my body healed itself didn't it? I'm afraid they managed to kill her."

"Why didn't you tell me this at the start?" The Dr. said his voice tense. "This is bad... so bad." His eyes kept scanning the room. "I wouldn't have agreed to meet you if I'd known they'd found you. If they've somehow found out you carry the virus we could all be in deep trouble again."

"I don't see how they could," Alex cut in. "My mother wouldn't have told them, she had dementia, she couldn't remember anything."

"Did they drug her?" His eyes locked onto her. "They have ways of making people remember forgotten things."

Alex took a deep breath and nodded.

"Do they know where you are now?" The Dr.'s asked. "Do they know where you live?"

"No... I... I've moved," Alex stuttered. "I've only been back to the apartment a couple of times. I've tried to keep a low profile since the incident."

"Well that's some good news at least," the Dr. sighed. "Keep it up for as long as you can."

"Do you think they'll harm my family?" Alex asked.

"What do you mean?"

"They stole the only photograph I had of my father."

The Dr. looked at her, his eyes wide. "Yes, there's a possibility they'll go after him. If they find out who he is. They'll want to try and keep the infection from spreading before it gets out of control. They'll want to trace anyone who has had close contact with you. If even a small drop of your blood has got into their system you'll have passed on the virus."

Alex sat back in her chair and closed her eyes. She ran the events over in her mind. Then took a large breath to steady herself before she spoke again. "That explains it then."

"Explains what?" the Dr. replied.

"I need to get back and warn them. Would you mind if we kept in contact? You're the only person I've met that knows what's actually going on."

"We would need to keep our association private. It wouldn't be safe talking on the phone. Maybe if we both set up new anonymous email addresses. We would have to keep the messages encrypted, but if you wanted more information, that seems to be the safest way, for now."

Alex pulled another clean napkin out from the holder and ripped it in two. "Here, write a safe word down so we know how to recognise each other's emails."

The Dr. took it, scribbled a note down and handed it back to her just as his phone rang. Alex saw his face drop as he answered it.

"You've got to get out of here, quickly," the Dr. snapped. "I think they've found us."

"Thanks for telling me all this," Alex said standing up. "I had my suspicions, but I never would have been able to find out without your help."

"Keep yourself safe," the Dr. replied. "It's important we keep that virus alive."

Alex rushed back down the stairs and out into the street. She hadn't seen them yet. Her eyes locked onto the blacked out cars a little higher up the road, she froze when the door of the closest one opened. She almost collapsed with relief when a policeman stepped out. She needed to find somewhere alone, to gather her thoughts. What was she going to tell Bob, to tell her brother and father? She'd potentially put all of their lives in danger.

Alex decided to call Bob and let him know she was all right. He'd be worrying about her after all. Her hands were still a bit shaky as she pushed the buttons on her mobile. She held it to her ear and waited for the familiar sound of Bob's voice to reply. The phone clicked straight on to voice mail. She hung up and tried again. She heard the same annoying tone as the voice mail clicked in once more. Alex started to panic, what if they'd already got to him while she'd been here? Her confused mind tried to think what could have happened, tried to think of a solution. She felt a bit silly when she realised he was probably just still at work. If he was busy he'd have turned his phone off. She decided to leave him a simple message. Just so he knew she was safely on her way back, she'd tell him all about it later.

Alex still had half an hour or so to kill before the train arrived. She decided to nip into the small newsagents at the station and pick up a magazine. There wouldn't be much in it she'd enjoy reading but at least it would pass the time. She found an empty bench and made herself comfortable. The journey home wouldn't nearly be as daunting as the one she'd taken to get here.

CHAPTER 20

It had grown late by the time Alex stepped off the train. She took a long look around the familiar surroundings and felt herself relax. It didn't matter how disturbing the information she'd been told, nor the prospects it held for the future. She was just glad she'd found out the truth.

    Even though she now knew the reason for the peculiar things that had happened in her life, the reason why she seemed so different inside, she still felt the same as she always had. She promised herself she wouldn't let the knowledge change her, well, perhaps she'd take a few more risks now she knew why she wasn't as fragile as other people, but that was all. Apart from that she had to carry on. She couldn't let the fear of what could happen interfere with her life.

If bad things were going to happen in the future, there wasn't a lot she could do to stop them. Her mother had cut herself off from everyone she'd known to try and protect her family. She'd lived the rest of her life not knowing what had happened to them, just to try and get away from the fear those people caused. Alex was determined not to let them ruin her life as well.

Alex had a difficult decision to make. What was she going to tell her brother and father? On the one hand she felt it would be wrong to keep the truth from them, they were family after all. But on the other, if she told them everything, she was worried they too would spend the rest of their lives living in fear, just as her mother had done. She didn't want that future for them.

Bob greeted Alex at the door to his apartment. Then promptly kept her talking until late into the evening. Alex knew she couldn't keep the truth from him for long anyway and so spent the next few hours divulging the secrets she'd discovered. Bob only relented when he was satisfied he couldn't extract any more information from her and got up to make them both a warm drink.

"You know, this could be one of the last times I stay here with you," Alex said as she made herself comfortable on the couch. "Eric will be moving out soon. I'll be able to take the rest of my things. You'll have your apartment back to yourself," she chuckled. "Who knows, maybe Melissa will come over more when I'm not around. You guys might even be able to have some fun together."

"It won't be the same without you," Bob smiled as he passed her a hot cup of tea. "I've got quite used to having you around to keep me company."

"It was really nice of you letting me stay," Alex replied smiling back at him. "You know how much I appreciate it don't you? But you need your own space again."

"Yeah, I suppose you're right," he shrugged.

"We'll still see each other though," Alex smiled. "You'd better still come over and cook for me now and again."

"Of course," Bob laughed.

Alex's head tilted to the side. "How are you going to manage to get out of going to the gym now?" She chuckled. "Don't worry," Bob replied with a smile. "I'm sure I can find a way."

"You hadn't better," Alex said sticking out her tongue at him. "I'll be watching you."

"There's still a bit of the meat left on the stove I cooked earlier," Bob said. "Help yourself if you're hungry. There's plenty of bread that needs eating too if you want to make yourself a sandwich."

"Thanks, I might grab one later, after I've had a rest," she replied.

"OK, well I've got an early start in the morning. I'd better get myself off to bed," Bob smiled. "Night."

"Yeah, good night," Alex replied.

"Hey, don't stay up too late again watching telly," Bob added laughing as he disappeared.

He didn't look back at the evil look Alex was giving him but he heard the sound of a thrown pillow hitting his bedroom door.

Alex remembered switching the TV on but not what she was watching. The annoying sound of static woke her up with a jolt. She was still holding the empty cup in her hand, obviously the excitement of the day had caught up with her. She eased herself forwards, placed the cup on the table and turned the noisy TV off. In a sleepy daze she made her way to her bedroom, she still hadn't decided what or whether to tell her brother and father. Hopefully in the morning things would be different.

"Hi there," Stephen said with a big smile on his face as Alex walked through the front door of the Foodbank.

Alex smiled and waved back. "Not that busy today?" She said looking around the empty room.

"No not yet," he smiled. "We'll be quiet now until the week before Christmas."

"Really, I thought you'd be busier this time of year?" Alex spoke up.

"December's a bit different from all the rest," Stephen said with a sigh. "A lot of the unfortunate people, those we try to help, try and hold onto their vouchers until the last minute. It's usually one massive rush in the end."

"But surely people donate more food at Christmas time?" Alex asked.

"Yes, we're lucky," Stephen nodded. "The public seems a bit more generous over the festive period. But like I told you the people who need help can only use the service so many times. They want to make sure they've got food in for the big day. They don't want their families, their children, to go hungry on Christmas Day."

"Yeah, I suppose it must be a tough time of year for them," Alex sighed. "I've never thought about it before."

"So," Stephen said smiling again. "There are still a few boxes that need packing in the back if you feel like it, or did you just come in to have a chat with your big brother?"

Alex's grin faded. "Actually, is there

someone who could cover the front desk for a few minutes? I need to have a chat with you. I can't risk being overheard."

"Oh," Stephen replied taken aback "I'm sure I saw James earlier. I think he's still around. Give me a minute."

Alex took the seat behind the desk as Stephen disappeared through the door. She hoped he'd been right about it being quiet at this time of year. She'd never had to cover the front desk before. Stephen had only been gone a few seconds when the door swung open, just her luck she thought. Alex tried to calm her breathing, but it was hard, she hadn't been told what to say. Her fingers hovered, shaking above the bell to call for assistance. If she hadn't looked up at that precise moment she'd have definitely started to panic.

Alex's gaze met the eyes of the familiar man edging towards her, his head lowered. She tried to place him in her mind but the image she held in her head didn't match the dishevelled one she saw before her. It was him nevertheless, it had to be, she was sure of it. The beard was new but it was those eyes, she knew those eyes, she'd seen them many times before. He was the last person she'd expected to see walk into a place like this.

"Is everything all right Stan?" Alex spoke.

"What happened?"

Her old store manager lifted his troubled head and tried to smile. "More cut backs I'm afraid. I got the same treatment as you in the end. The owner decided he wouldn't need a manager around if he took a more active role and... Well, here I am."

"But you were doing all right, you were making good money?" Alex added.

Stan took a deep breath and sighed. "I suppose you could say I've got a bit of a gambling problem. It's my own fault, the money's all gone."

The door opening behind them interrupted the conversation.

"Oh, I didn't realise we had another visitor," James spoke up. "Don't worry. I'll take over from here. Stephen said he wanted a word with you in the staff room."

Alex turned back to Stan. "If you don't mind, it looks like the boss is calling. James will be able to point you in the right direction though. I hope you manage to sort things out."

"Thank you," she said, smiling at James, before heading out through the open door where he'd just appeared from.

As soon as the door shut behind her she stopped and mentally shook herself. She wasn't prepared for what had just happened. She needed a moment to compose herself.

Stephen was sat waiting in the corner of the room when Alex pushed the door open.

"Sorry, I just had a visit from my past. I couldn't get away," she smiled, still feeling a bit jumpy inside.

"Don't worry about it," Stephen replied. "Come in and close the door. Turn the latch above the handle to the right. That'll lock it."

Alex followed his instructions. She definitely didn't want to be disturbed.

"So what was it you had to talk about that was so private?" Stephen asked in his calm deep voice.

Alex sat down across from him. She was still unsure about how much information to give him but it needed to be done, sooner rather than later.

"I found out some things about our mother's past," she began. "Some things I think you should know."

"Go on..." Stephen replied, "You've got my attention."

"Yesterday," Alex continued, "I had a meeting with one of mother's ex-colleague's. He had some interesting things to tell me.

"Yes, I'm listening," Stephen said sitting up.

"Have you ever wondered," Alex added, "why you're so much stronger than normal people? Ever wondered why your body heals so much faster?"

"Good genetics," Stephen laughed.

Alex stood up and walked over to the sink. "We're the same, you and I."

"What do you expect, we're family?" Stephen chuckled.

Alex strutted back to her chair and sat down. "I'm afraid it's more complicated than that."

Stephen's eyes opened wide as he saw the large sharp metal blade of a kitchen knife in her hand.

"What do you think you're doing?" He blurted out as Alex ran the blade across her palm.

Alex held her hand out over the white table, watching as a few droplets of blood splashed onto its surface.

Stephen, still wide eyed, was staring at her.

"Watch," she said turning her palm upwards to face him.

Stephen reached out for her hand. "But... I thought I was the only one."

"There's a reason we're different," Alex said wiping away the blood. "Just after you we born our mother developed a revolutionary new cure for a number of life threatening diseases," she took a deep breath. "In the process she found a way to alter people's genetic coding. To make them healthier, stronger. To make their bodies heal faster, to make people live longer."

"I don't like where this is going," Stephen replied.

"It involved infecting them with a virus, one they would carry with them for the rest of their lives," she paused and stared at him. "Our mother gave it to us, she altered our DNA."

"She can't have," Stephen replied frowning. "I'd have heard about it. If someone made such a discovery, it would have been all over the news. She'd have been a contender for a 'Nobel Prize'."

"This is where things start turning ugly I'm afraid," Alex continued. "You see the company she worked for found out the true scope of her project. If the virus was to get out into the public, it would have put nearly every health related industry in the world out of business, almost overnight. The shear amount of money they'd have lost would have been staggering."

"But it would have been a good thing surely?" Stephen added.

"Imagine a world where there were no diseases, no illnesses left to treat, no long term health problems that required repeat prescriptions," she continued. "A world, in which people lived to a ripe old age in perfect health. It would have been a utopia for the human race."

"You see, a good thing," Stephen said frowning again.

"Not from the point of the big businesses

that were fighting for their lives. They had to stop our mother at any cost. That's why she disappeared, that's why she had to abandon you and dad. They destroyed her work, tried to kill her."

"So why did they come after her after all those years," Stephen cringed. "Why did they kill her now if they'd already destroyed everything?"

Alex paused for a second. She was about to say aloud the secret she'd originally wanted to keep from him. She had to decide if it was the right thing to do. She stared deep into his eyes and took a big breath. "We are the remaining pieces to the puzzle. Our mother only had enough serum left for us. All the work was gone, she couldn't make any more. The entire fruits or her discovery are still inside us. We still carry the only remaining evidence of her discovery to this day."

Stephen leaned forwards and opened his mouth.

"They must have been able to track her down," Alex cut him off with a shake of her head. "I didn't know bringing her back to this place would put her, put us, in danger. I did it to look after her."

Stephen reached over and put his hand on her shoulder.

"After they found out where my mother was hiding they must have managed to get the truth out of her. That's why they killed her, tried to kill me. That's why they'll try again and again, until they succeed. They can't allow the virus to spread."

Stephen's eyes narrowed. "Do they know about me? About our father? Can they trace us?"

"I'm not sure, it depends what information they got out of her before they killed her," Alex replied. "I don't think any of us are safe any longer."

"What are we going to do?" Stephen said banging his fist on the table.

"I don't think there's much we can do," Alex sighed. "I'm sure they'll find us eventually. I think for now though we need to tell Eric, he deserves to know the truth after all these years.

"Right, I'll give him a call," Stephen said pulling his mobile out of his pocket.

Alex watched as he held it to his ear.

"Hi dad," Stephen began, "listen, Alex has found some information out, something you need to know, something about mother."

"That's great," came the reply, "but can she tell me later. I'm a bit busy at the moment. A couple of gentlemen have arrived. They seem interested in the new owner."

Stephen gasped. "Dad, listen this is important. Stall them do whatever you can but don't tell them anything. I'm coming right over."

"What's up?" Alex said panicked by the expression on Stephen's face.

"We need to get over there now, I think he's in trouble," Stephen replied.

"But who's going to..?"

Stephen cut her off. "James will have to do his best, I'm sure he can cope without us for the rest of the day. Come on we need to go."

Eric was standing at the door as Stephen's car slid sideways into the car park.

"Dad, you're all right!" Stephen shouted.

"Yes, why shouldn't I be?" He replied.

"I thought you were in trouble," Stephen said with a frown.

"Why, it was just a couple of guys from the licensing body," Eric replied. "I was arranging to get it changed over into Alex's name that's all. Why do you look so worried?"

Stephen breathed a sigh of relief and turned to Alex. "Don't worry I'll tell him," he said shaking his head. "You go put the kettle on. I'll need something to calm my nerves."

Five minutes later Alex walked back into the office carrying a tray and three cups of tea.

"So..." Eric sighed, "Stephen's been telling me all about your conversation. I must say, when I found out she hadn't died, I knew she must have had a very good reason to disappear. I never guessed things were so bad for her."

Alex smiled and nodded. "Yeah, it must have been horrible for her, to have been forced into making such an awful decision."

"Would you do me a favour?" Eric smiled. "We missed out on so much of her life and you knew her so well. Would you mind showing us around some of the places she used to like going to. All this talk about her has brought back so many memories. I just want to feel near to her again."

Alex smiled and stood up.

A few minutes later Eric attached a notice to the front door of the gym that read 'Maintenance in progress will re-open again at 5pm'.

"I use it when I need to get away for a few hours," he chuckled, turning back to Alex. "Don't worry. The regulars know I won't be long."

As they began walking out through the car park Alex felt her mobile phone vibrate in her pocket. Bob's name appeared on the screen as she checked the number.

"Hi trouble," Bob said, his voice sounded breathless, "are you still at the gym?"

"We're just about to leave," Alex replied. "Why what's up?"

Bob tried to catch his breath. "Oh... I was on my way over... I finished early again today."

"Well Eric's just closed up for a couple of hours," Alex replied. "I was going to show them where my mother used to like doing her art work.

You know, around the park and then maybe show them around flats where we used to live."

"Can you hang on for a second..? I'm almost there..." Bob said between breaths.

"We're just about to walk out of the..." Alex got distracted by the sound of running footsteps.

"Nearly there..." The phone went dead as Bob appeared from around the corner.

"Oh, hi there," Alex laughed.

Bob was doubled over panting, his hands trembling on his shaky knees. "I'm OK," he managed to say. "I just... need to... catch my breath."

Stephen walked over to him and patted him on his back. "Nice of you to join us."

"Come on Bob," Eric shouted as he walked out of the car park. "Keep up."

The park looked beautiful, backlit by a glorious golden red sunset, but the darkness was beginning to draw in. At first Alex hadn't noticed how few people were in there that evening, but now as the light was beginning to fail, the quietness started to feel almost isolating. Even the wind blowing through the trees was silent now that they'd shed their leaves for winter.

Alex took a moment to break away from the group while they were talking. She just needed a minute or so to herself. To gather her thoughts.

If someone had asked her a month or so ago how she thought her life would change, never in a million years would she have replied like this. She had to admit she'd only pictured darkness for herself in her future. She missed her mother terribly, but in her place now stood a new brother and father. She felt part of a family again. She no longer had to worry about money either. All her debts had been paid off and she could afford to fill her belly whenever she felt like it. Life was being good to her for a change, but it still felt wrong somehow, she didn't deserve it. She felt like a fraud, like someone was going to find out and take it all away from her. The noise and the bright headlights of a passing car awoke her from the daydream and with a sigh she walked back to rejoin the group.

"I'd better show you the apartment block while we can still see," Alex said, hoping the quickening of her voice would encourage the others to move a bit faster.

"OK, lead the way," Eric smiled.

Only the narrow pedestrian access was still open by the time the slow moving group approached the iron gates.

"Are you sure you still want me to show you?" Alex spoke up. "It's getting too dark. You won't be able to see much. We could come back another day?"

"We aren't far are we?" Eric said. "It's fine you carry on, we'll follow."

Eric turned his attention back towards Bob. "Alex is still staying with you at the moment isn't she? He asked. "Your apartment's somewhere around here isn't it?"

"Yes," Bob replied, "why?"

"I just find it odd that's all. Didn't it bother you when you moved here?" Eric continued.

"What bother me? I'm not following," Bob replied.

"It must have been difficult adjusting to life here, especially in, for want of a better word, let's just say such a white area."

Bob laughed. "I don't notice it much anymore to tell you the truth."

Bob joined Alex up front leaving Eric and Stephen lagging a few paces behind.

"Hurry up you two, it's just around the next corner," Alex said beckoning them closer.

Bob noticed it first. He stopped dead in his tracks as the others overtook still chatting away.

Alex turned to check why he'd stopped. His face looked white, panicked. She watched as he lifted his hand and pointed unable to speak. Alex froze, holding her arms out, causing Stephen and Eric to stumble into her. She swung her head back around, her eyes desperately trying to pick out what Bob had seen. Alex watched in horror as the barrel of an assault rifle appeared from the open window of the blacked out van. Inside her tight chest she felt her heart begin to pound as her body released a massive surge of adrenaline into her blood stream.

In the few short moments it took for the bullets to hit Alex, time for her seemed to slow down. She became aware of the pressure building on her arm. Her father was trying to push her out of the way. She tried to tell him, tried to make him understand. She heard herself saying it over and over in her mind, but her lips weren't moving fast enough. The first bullet hit her with a glancing blow to her shoulder as she was spun around by her father's impact. She couldn't tell where the other one hit her. She was in too much pain. In the background she heard the screeching noise of tyres complaining under heavy acceleration and then the black van was gone.

Alex's blurred vision cleared soon after as she heard Bob shouting her name. The floor didn't feel as cold as she'd expected, it was softer too, something was definitely strange. She felt her body moving, it was being lifted up and down. What was going on? She tilted her head, it was her father. She must have landed on him. Her left arm was throbbing. She reached across and held it with her right hand, then rolled off onto the cold concrete.

Her body was still in shock, she felt numb. She couldn't work out where the other bullet had hit her. Stephen's voice was in the background, he was on his phone. Bob was leaning over her, his lips were moving, talking. Why couldn't she hear her father? She forced herself to stand.

That's when she saw him. He was lying on the floor unconscious. Alex's legs buckled with the dawning realisation of where the other bullet had gone. Blood was soaking through the top of her father's jumper. She couldn't tell where he'd been hit. It looked like his neck. He was still alive but she wondered for how long, would he hold on long enough for the ambulance crew to arrive? She had to help him.

Alex stooped down, totally blocking out the pain in her arm she used all of her strength to rip her father's jumper away from the wound. She could at least see better now. The bullet thankfully hadn't hit the delicate blood vessels of his neck, but it had come close. Instead it'd passed through the huge hump of his overly developed trapezius muscle just to the side.

"Is he going to be all right?" She heard Bob's worried voice say.

Eric started to cough but didn't open his eyes. Alex looked down at her father's face, it's expression full of pain. "Don't worry dad," she said in a quiet controlled voice. "I know I can help you now."

"What are you going to do?" Bob asked kneeling down beside her.

"Something I should have done before," Alex sighed. "They're never going to stop, not unless I can even the odds," she clenched her fists. "It's the only way I can fight back."

Alex reached up to her shoulder and pressed on it, hard. A fresh stream of warm crimson blood ran down her fingers.

"What are you doing?" Bob shouted.

"It needs to spread!" Alex yelled whilst removing her hand and holding it a couple of inches from her father's wound.

She watched almost intrigued as the red fluid trickled down her fingers and dropped from their tips onto the damaged skin below.

"I hope this works," she said turning to face Bob.

Alex had to be sure. She moved her hand towards her father's mouth. It'd worked before hadn't it? She let a few more drops of blood drip from her fingers into her father's slightly open mouth.

His eyes began to open.

"You'll be all right dad, you'll see," she said, her voice quivering as she allowed the remaining blood to drain.

Eric coughed to clear his throat. His eyes were wild. He reached up to grab her hand.

"Oh My God, Alex. What have you done?"

The End

Printed in Poland
by Amazon Fulfillment
Poland Sp. z o.o., Wrocław